PRAISE FOR
LABYRINTH LOST

A Bustle Best Book

An NPR Top YA Book

A *Paste* magazine Best Book

A *School Library Journal* Popular Pick

A Barnes & Noble Teen Best Queer YA Fantasy Selection

A Tor.com Best YA SFF Selection

A New York Public Library Best Book for Teens

A Chicago Public Library Best of the Best Book

A Los Angeles Public Library Best Teen Book

An International Latino Book Award Winner

"A richly Latin American, giddily exciting novel."

—*New York Times*

"The best new series of the year."

—*Paste* magazine

★ "This work is a magical journey from start to finish…"

—*School Library Journal*, Starred Review

"Zoraida Córdova's stunning storytelling and wondrous world-building make this one to remember, and bonus: there's a multicultural, bisexual love triangle to give you the swoons."

—Bustle

"A magical story of love, family, and finding yourself. Enchanting from start to finish."

—Amy Tintera, *New York Times* bestselling author of *Ruined*

"Córdova's prose enchants. *Labyrinth Lost* is pure magic."

—Melissa Grey, author of *The Girl at Midnight*

"Magical and empowering, *Labyrinth Lost* is an incredible heroine's journey filled with mythos come to life, but at its heart, honors the importance of love and family."

—Cindy Pon, author of *Serpentine* and *Silver Phoenix*

"A thrilling, imaginative journey through a bittersweet bruja wonderland. I can't wait for the next Brooklyn Brujas adventure."

—Jessica Spotswood, author of *Wild Swans* and the Cahill Witch Chronicles

"An inspired tale of family, magic, and one powerful girl's quest to save them both."

—Gretchen McNeil, author of *Ten* and the Don't Get Mad series

"Córdova's world will leave you breathless, and her magic will ignite an envy so green you'll wish you were born a bruja. An unputdownable book."

—Dhonielle Clayton, author of *The Belles* and *Shiny Broken Pieces*

Also by Zoraida Córdova

The Brooklyn Brujas series
Labyrinth Lost
Bruja Born

The Vicious Deep series
The Vicious Deep
The Savage Blue
The Vast and Brutal Sea

BRUJA BORN

ZORAIDA CÓRDOVA

sourcebooks
fire

Published by Sourcebooks Fire, an imprint of Sourcebooks
P.O. Box 4410, Naperville, Illinois 60567-4410
(630) 961-3900
sourcebooks.com

The Library of Congress has cataloged the hardcover edition as follows:

Names: Córdova, Zoraida, author.
Title: Bruja born / Zoraida Córdova.
Description: Naperville, Illinois : Sourcebooks Fire, [2018] I Series: The
    Brooklyn Brujas ; 2 I Summary: Still feeling broken after her family's
    battle in Los Lagos, Lula invokes a dark spell to bring her boyfriend and
    others back after a fatal bus crash, but unwittingly raises an army of
    hungry, half-dead casimuertos, instead.
Identifiers: LCCN 2017043008
Subjects: I CYAC: Magic--Fiction. I Witches--Fiction. I Dead--Fiction. I
    Supernatural--Fiction. I Families--Fiction. I Hispanic Americans--Fiction.
Classification: LCC PZ7.C8153573 Cir 2018 I DDC [Fic]--dc23
LC record available at https://lccn.loc.gov/2017043008

Printed and bound in the United States of America.
VP 10 9 8 7 6 5 4 3 2 1

For my brother, Danny.
About damn time, right?

Manhattan

El Brooklyn
de las Brujas

PART I

THE HEART

1

They say El Corazón has two hearts:
the black thing in his chest
and the one he wears on his sleeve.

—TALES OF THE DEOS,
FELIPE THOMÁS SAN JUSTINIO

This is a love story.

At least, it was, before my sister sent me to hell. Though technically, Los Lagos isn't hell or the underworld. It's another realm inhabited by creatures, spirits, and wonders I'd only read about in my family's Book of Cantos. The place where I was kept—where my whole family was imprisoned by a power-hungry witch—*that* was as close to hell as I hope I'll ever get.

But that's another story.

"Lula, you ready?" my sister Alex asks.

I stare at my open closet and can't find the socks that go with my step team uniform. I riffle through bins of underwear and mismatched socks and costume jewelry.

"Lula?" Alex repeats, softly this time.

For the past seven or so months, Alex has been extra everything—extra patient, extra loving, extra willing to do my chores. She means well, but she doesn't understand how suffocating her attention is, how the quiet in her eyes drives a sick feeling in my gut because I'm trying to be okay for her, for our family and friends. I think I've gotten pretty good at faking it. But sometimes, like now, I snap.

"Give me a minute!"

I don't mean to snap. Honestly. But everything that's come out of my mouth lately has been hard and angry, and I don't know how to make it stop. That's not who I am. That's not who I was before—

Rose, our younger sister, walks into my room wearing long sleeves and jeans even though there's a heat wave and it's mid-June. Rose has the Gift of the Veil. She can see and speak to the dead. Spirt magic runs on a different wavelength than the rest of our powers, and being so tuned-in to that realm means she's always cold. Rose takes a seat on my bed and picks at a tear in the blanket.

"Can I go to the pregame with you and Maks?" she asks me. "I've never been to one before."

"No," I say.

"Why not?" When she frowns, her round face gets flushed. Sometimes I forget that underneath all her power, she's just a fourteen-year-old kid trying to fit in.

"Because," I say, digging through my dirty laundry. "It's just for the team. You can drive to the game with Ma and Alex."

"And Dad." Rose's voice is a quiet addendum.

Right. Dad. After seven years of being missing and presumed dead, he's in our lives again. It's an odd feeling having him back, one we all share but haven't talked about. He has no memory of

4

where he's been, and even if we can't say it out loud, maybe we've moved on without him. Alex was always the one who said he was gone for good, and perhaps deep down inside, I thought that too. But I always corrected her. I was the one who *believed* he'd return, because sometimes false hope is better than being completely hopeless. I believed in lots of things once.

"And Dad," I say.

The three of us exchange a look of unease. There are too many things that are unsaid between us. I wish we could go back to being loud and rowdy and something like happy. But it's taking longer than I thought.

So here are the things we leave unsaid:

One, we're brujas. Witches. Magical BAMFs with powers gifted by the Deos, our gods. A house full of magic is bound to cause some friction, and after what Alex did, there is plenty of friction.

Two, my sister Alex cast a canto that banished our entire family to a realm called Los Lagos. She got to traipse across its magical hills and meadows with Nova, the hot brujo we never talk about, and her now-girlfriend, Rishi.

Meanwhile, I was trapped in a freaking tree. A big, evil tree. I was surrounded by all-consuming darkness, and even though we're home and safe, I still feel that pull, like something is suckling at my soul and my light, and this house is too small and crowded, and I don't know how to make this fear stop. I don't know how to get over it.

Three, I can't stand looking at my own reflection anymore.

I took all the mirrors in my bedroom down, even the one that was on my altar to keep away malicious spirits. They don't need it. One look at my face, and they'll be scared off.

5

"Ready when you are," Alex says again, her guilt radioactive.

Technically, *technically*, the attack that left my face hideously disfigured with scars was Alex's fault. I'm a terrible sister for thinking it. Forgive and forget and all that. But the maloscuros that came looking for her attacked *me*. Their vicious claws raked across my face. Sometimes, when I'm alone, I can smell the rot of their skin, see the glow of their yellow eyes, feel their presence even though they're long gone and banished.

To be fair, Alex has scars from the maloscuros too. Right across her heart. But she can cover them up. I can't.

Not naturally, anyway.

Having a sister who is an all-powerful encantrix has its benefits. There are a million problems going on in the world, and here I am, worrying about scars. But deep down, I know it's more than the scars. I've been called beautiful my whole life. I've been aware of the way men's eyes trailed my legs since I was far too young. The way boys in school stuttered when they spoke to me. The way they offered me gifts—bodega-bought candies and stolen flowers and handwritten notes with *yes/no* scribbled in pencil. My aunt Maria Azul told me beauty was power. My mother told me beauty was a gift. If they're right, then what am I now? All I know is I left fragments of myself in Los Lagos and I don't know how to get them back.

So I turn to my sister, because she owes me one. But before we can get started, my mother knocks on my open door, Dad trailing behind her like a wraith.

"Good, you're all together. Can I borrow you guys for a minute?" Ma asks. She rests a white laundry basket against one hip and waves a sage bundle like a white flag. "I want to try the memory canto on your father before we leave. The sun's in the right—"

"We're busy," I say, too angry again. I don't like talking to my mother like this. Hell, any other time I'd catch hands for speaking to her like that. But we're all a mess—guilt, anger, love, plus a lot of magic is a potent mix. Something's got to give, and I don't know if I want to be here when it does.

Mom throws the sage stick on top of the clean laundry, scratches her head with a long, red nail. Her black-lined eyes look skyward, as if begging the Deos for patience. She makes to speak, but Dad places his hand on her arm. She tenses at his touch, and he withdraws the hand.

"We all have to pull our weight around here," Ma tells me, a challenge in her deep, coffee-brown eyes that I don't dare look away from.

"Dad doesn't," I say, and feel Rose and Alex retreat two paces away from me. Traitors.

"He's trying. You haven't healed so much as a paper cut since—"

I widen my eyes, waiting for the her to *say* it. *Since Los Lagos. Since the attack.* But she can't.

"You have Alex," I say, turning my thumb toward my sister. "She's an encantrix. Healing comes with the package."

"Lula…" Ma pinches the bridge of her nose, then trails off as my father tries to be the voice of reason.

"Carmen," he whispers, "let them be. It's okay."

But my mother doesn't fully let up. "How much longer will you keep having your sister glamour you?"

Alex looks at her toes. All that power in her veins and she can't escape being shamed by our mother. I might be *just* a healer, but I match my mom's gaze. We share more than our light-brown skin and wild, black curls. We share the same fire in our hearts.

"Until it stops hurting," I say, and I don't let my voice waver.

We share a sadness too. I see it in her, woven into the wrinkles around her eyes. So she just hands me a black bundle—my uniform socks—and says, "We'll see you at the game."

"Close the door," I tell Rose after our parents head downstairs.

I sit cross-legged on my faded flower-pattern rug as Alex prepares for the canto. Since she embraced her power, her brown eyes have tiny gold flecks, and her hair falls in thick, lustrous waves. She even wears it loose around her shoulders, and I think it's because Rishi likes to twirl it around her finger when they think we're not looking. There's a light inside of her. The light of an encantrix and a girl in love. I hate to say *I told you so*, but I did tell her so. Magic transforms you. Magic changes you. Magic saves you.

I want to still believe in all those things.

Rose cleans up my altar, sneezing when she breathes in layers of dust. She lights a candle for El Amor, Deo of Love and Fervor. Beside it, she lights a candle for La Mama, Ruler of the Sun and Mother of all the Deos.

"*Gross*, Lula. When was the last time you cleaned your altar?" Rose asks, wiping her fingers on the front of her jeans.

I only shrug and lie back on the floor. She sits at my feet and holds my ankles. This isn't for magic. I think she's just trying to comfort me in the only way she knows how. Alex kneels right over my head. A year ago, Alex kept her power bottled up. Now, she calls on it easily. She pulls the smoke from the candles, elongating it between her fingertips like a cat's cradle until it encircles the three of us like a dome.

Next, Alex rips the head off a long-stemmed, white rose and sets the petals in a bowl. Our magic, our brujeria, isn't only about putting herbs together and chanting rhymes. Anyone could do that. This canto has no words, just the sweet hum my sister makes as she sifts through the rose petals. The rise of her magic fills the room, settles along my skin like silk.

One by one, she places each petal on my face. She hums until she's covered every inch of pearlescent scar tissue and I'm wearing a mask made of roses. She pushes her power into the rose mask, and slowly, it takes on her magic. The petals heat up and soften, melting into my scars like second skin.

I'm never ready for the next part, but I grab the carpet and brace myself. Glamour magic requires pain. I hiss when it stings like hot needles jabbing into my flesh.

"Maybe we should stop," Rose tells Alex.

I shake my head once. "I'm okay. I swear."

Alex keeps going, holding her hands over my face, waves of heat emanating from her palms. I breathe and grind my teeth through the discomfort.

"There," Alex says.

The earthy sweetness of roses in bloom fills my bedroom.

Nothing coats the senses quite like roses do. Alex and I lock eyes, and there is so much I want to say. *Thank you. I'm sorry. Are you okay?* Her face, right where my scars should be, darkens with red splotches. I recognize the recoil of glamour magic— bruises and redness that match the person being worked on. All magic comes with a cost. The cyclical give-and-take of the universe to keep us balanced.

She never complains though. She smiles. Stands. Busies herself with her phone.

I go to my dresser and I pull out a round hand mirror that I got at a garage sale for a dollar. It's a dull metal but makes me feel like the Evil Queen from Snow White. When I was little, I used to root for Snow, but lately, I feel the queen was way misunderstood. Women with power always get a bad rep.

My mood changes instantly when I look at myself in the mirror. I feel like I'm bound to this bit of magic that gives me back a part of myself, even if it's superficial. The scars are gone. The Bellaza Canto is a stronger form of glamour. When I touch the area where the four claw marks are supposed to be, there is nothing there but flawless, sun-kissed skin.

"Mirror, mirror," I whisper to my reflection, tilting my face from side to side.

I grab my favorite pink lipstick and apply it. It's a coral shade that brings out the honey brown of my skin and make my gray eyes stormier. I fluff my mane of black curls and rub my lips together to make sure my lipstick is even. I wish I could make this feeling last. For now, I'm going to enjoy it until the next time.

"Thank you," I tell Alex, and press a sticky kiss on her cheek.

"Gross," she mutters, wiping it off. Then she picks up the decapitated rose stem and bowl of unused petals. "Let's go, Rosie."

My phone chimes and my heart flutters when I see Maks's name on the screen. I'm outside.

I analyze the message as I put on my socks. His texts get shorter and shorter every day. Part of it is my fault for being so distant. Ever since Los Lagos, shadows seem to leap around every corner and crowds make me feel as if I'm sinking, my head barely above water. Nothing puts a big, fat hex on a social life like the fear of monsters only I can see.

"Today will be better," I tell my reflection, slipping into Maks's letterman jacket before I run down the stairs.

"See you at the game!" my mom shouts.

I wave as I zoom out the door and into Maks's car parked out front. The minute I'm outside the house, I can breathe again. When I'm around Maks, I don't have to think about magic, and I'm ready to sink into the comfort of his humanity.

"Hey," Maks says, not looking up.

He fiddles with the radio stations, but they're all staticky. He ends up plugging in his phone. His personal coach doesn't believe in kissing, or anything else exciting, on game day. I want to believe that's why his voice is distant and that's why he isn't reaching for my hand. But seeing him fills me with a sense of need—the need to be my old self. The need to be happy. So I press my lips on his cheek and leave the pink imprint of my mouth.

"You're in a good mood," he says, thick, black brows knitting in confusion, and I'm bothered that he sounds so surprised. His knee shakes a little, and I place my hand on it to try to comfort him.

11

He always gets nervous before games. But he's the best goalie the school has seen in years. Nothing gets past him.

"Last game of the year. It's a big deal." I smile when he looks at me before putting the car in drive. Relief washes over me when he takes my hand in his and kisses my knuckles, then speeds down the empty Brooklyn street.

"We've beaten Van Buren like six hundred times, but they're still a solid team." He squeezes my hand once, then lets it go.

"You okay?" I ask. As a healer, I can sense the tension knotting his aura. He's always nervous before a game, but today it's worse than usual. Maybe I'm feeling the residual magic from Alex's canto. My magic *has* been way off.

At the red light, he turns to me. His hair is combed back at the top and his edges are freshly buzzed. I brush my fingers at his nape, where the barber didn't brush off all the stray hairs.

"Lula," he says my name like a sigh.

He turns to me again. I can't tell what he's searching for, but when I look at him, really look at him, I remember why I fell for him. The sweet, caring boy whose smile made me dizzy. I always keep a sprig of hydrangeas on my altar because they remind me of his eyes.

We both start when someone honks behind us, and he faces the road again.

"I was thinking," I say, trying to make my voice low and playful, but I end up feeling silly, "we could do something after the game. Just the two of us."

"I already told the team they could party at my house. My parents are on a business trip, and my sister's already at Uki camp for the summer."

I shouldn't be annoyed, but I am. I tell myself he's just tired. He's been practicing extra hard. He's going to Boston College on a soccer scholarship and wants to be at the top of his game.

"We haven't really been alone in a while," I say.

"That's not my fault."

"It's not my fault either. Look, I don't want to fight."

Another red light. He shakes his head, like he's dispersing the thought he just had.

"What?"

"I'm just saying"—he sighs and flicks on his turn signal—"we haven't been *alone* because you never feel like being alone. You've been so off, and I don't know what to do anymore."

"I told you about my dad coming back. And the break-in."

I watch the red light, the people at the crosswalk. We're a few blocks away from school. I recognize a couple of girls from my team by their black-and-red uniforms. A woman dressed in all black trails behind them. She holds a cane that glints in the sunlight, and with every step, her jewelry swings from side to side. She wears dozens of necklaces made of glittering gems and wooden beads. She glances at us in the car, and I swear I've seen her before. For a flash, the dark stare takes me to a place of my nightmares. My skin is hot, and when I close my eyes, I picture the shadows reaching for me with their claws. I grip the car seat so my hands will stop shaking.

"I know you have family stuff," Maks says, thankfully unaware of my tiny freak-out. "I just—I'm not sure how to say it. You're not the same person you were two years ago."

Two years.

Maks and I have been dating for two years. That's two years of dates. Two years of *I love yous* and *I want you forevers*. Two years of going to sleep reading his messages, of hearing his voice just before I drifted off and dreaming about us together. Maks wasn't the first boy to tell me I was beautiful. But when he said it, when he kissed the inside of my wrist and wrote it over and over again, *You're beautiful. I love you*, I believed him.

I roll down the window. My scars burn and I flip down the sun visor and double check that Alex's canto is holding up. There I am. I look like the old me even if I don't feel like her.

Maks pulls into the school parking lot behind the gym and puts the car in park. He taught me how to parallel park even though I don't have my license. It's a weird memory, but it pops into my head as he unbuckles his seat belt and holds the steering wheel with a white-knuckle grip.

"Maks." My voice is small because I know what comes next.

He breathes in long and deep, as if to steady himself. "I think we should break up."

2

El Corazón falls in love over and over,

trying to make his two hearts whole.

—TALES OF THE DEOS,

FELIPE THOMÁS SAN JUSTINIO

P lease, don't make a scene," Maks says softly.

The school band recognizes Maks's car and cheer as they board the big, yellow-cheese buses. The parking lot is full of students, faculty, and parents dressed in Thorne Hill Knights colors, ready to caravan all the way to Queens Village. My body flashes hot at the thought of getting out of the car to join them.

I take a deep breath, anger burning a clear path to my lips. "You *think* we should break up?"

"Baby, don't—" He stops whatever he's going to say next, catching himself on the familiarity, and it's like a fist to my gut.

"*Don't* call me baby."

"Lula. I've tried." He squeezes the steering wheel. "I've tried so hard, but it's been months. I know the robbery was hard on you. You have no idea how much I wish I'd been there to protect you."

"And your answer is this?" I look out my window at my faint reflection. Moments ago, I was so sure today was the day everything would be better. "You can't stand the idea of spending *one more* second with me that you're doing this now?"

He turns to me, daring to look hurt. "That's not true. You should know me better than that. I wanted to wait until after graduation, but my sister said it wasn't fair to you. One minute you're fine, and then the next, you're not."

"I'm trying, Maks."

"What about last weekend? Remember Pierre's party? You just walked out to the middle of the street and stood there, staring into space. If I hadn't come outside, you would've gotten clipped by that car."

I do remember. There were too many people in that house and it was too dark, so I walked outside and stared at the light of the moon. It was the only moment of peace I'd found in so long that I didn't notice the car until Maks screamed my name and pushed me out of the way. He was white with fear, holding my face in his hands until he was sure I wasn't hurt. He drove me home right away. "You have to talk to someone," he told me. And I said, "I'm fine. I promise."

"I'm sorry," he says. "I really am. You're not the same person I fell in love with. You don't want to be around your own friends. You haven't applied to college. It's like your fire is gone."

The unfairness of his words stings worse than this morning's canto. If he knew the truth, he'd surely understand. But how do you

16

tell your *sinmago* boyfriend that the "robbery" all over the New York news was actually an attack by a power-hungry demon witch?

I flip between wanting to slash his tires and begging him to stay with me. *I'll try harder*, I want to say. But I can't, so I just watch as the team loads their gear on the bus.

"Maks," I plead. Doesn't he understand that he's been the only constant thing in my life? "Don't do this."

He finally turns to me. His gaze travels across my face, and I wonder if he's trying to remember why he fell in love with me in the first place. "I never wanted to hurt you. But I have to do the right thing."

"The right thing?" I echo his words. "For yourself, you mean. You can't put up with me so you're bailing. Just say it how it is. Don't pretend you're making a sacrifice."

"You're twisting my words. I've thought a lot about this. I don't know how to help you and I don't think I'm good for you. So I have to make a choice. Even if it hurts us both."

"If it hurts that much, then don't do it." I hate the weakness in my voice. "We can forget about this. Just pretend it never happened."

"I care about you, Lula." He turns to me, and in this moment, I have never loved and hated someone so much all at once. "But I can't give you what you need. Deep inside, you know that. We—"

A dozen hands smack the windows of the car. I jump in my seat, and Maks curses loudly when he sees his teammates using his car like a set of congas.

"Let's go, Horbachevsky," they shout, all wound-up energy and excitement. "We got a game to win, son!"

"I need a minute," I say, pulling down the visor.

"Lula…" But when he looks at me, he falls silent.

He hands me the key fob and gets out.

And that's when I flip back to wanting to smash his car. I watch him lift his duffel bag onto his shoulder. He glances back at me twice before he makes it to the bus, where his boys greet him with fist bumps and cheers that he doesn't return. He looks down at his feet, his lip tugging up into a crooked smile. I've always loved that smile.

I reach for my phone, my hands longing for something to crush. But the spike of anger dissolves into sadness, and I reach out to the first person that comes to mind. I text Alex: Maks broke up with me.

Just then, my chest tightens, and despite the warm early summer breeze, I shiver. My breath comes out in a tiny cloud. My arms are covered in goose bumps beneath my jacket—Maks's jacket. Out of habit, I check the parking lot for shadows that shouldn't be there. But there is only the school mascot, a knight waving a plastic sword, running back and forth in front of the bus. My intuition must be messed up. Maybe my body is just physically rejecting this breakup.

Maks's words play in my head on a loop. *I've tried. I don't know how to help you. It's like your fire is gone.*

I think about my mother and how long it took her to piece herself together after my father disappeared. I used to watch her get ready for the day, painting her eyes and lips in vibrant colors to hide her gray sorrow. She'd stare into her mirror and say, "Don't let them see you cry."

Now, I repeat her words to my reflection. I press my finger

against the tight frown on my forehead. I pull a satin, red ribbon from my bag, the last piece of our cheer uniform. I wrap it around the top of my head and tie the ends into a bow. I fluff out my curls and try not to think about how Maks used to like coiling strands around the length of his fingers. I uncap my shimmering, coral gloss and softly, slowly drag it across my bottom lip, imagining I'm using it to smooth the edges of my heart. This morning I said things would be different. Maybe I can still channel the girl I was before my family's world turned upside down, before I had to hide behind a mask of borrowed magic and rose petals.

My phone buzzes with a message from Alex.

Alex: Come home. We haven't left yet.

Alex: I'm sorry. You deserve better.

Alex: I'll go get pizza and sea salt caramel?

Part of me wants to listen to Alex. A long shower and an evening of eating my weight in cheese and ice cream sounds amazing. But the old Lula wouldn't shrink away and hide. I text Alex back, I'm fine.

Maks might be right about some things. I have changed. But my fire isn't gone. Not completely. I can still fix this. I can make him see that we need each other.

I search deep inside for some of the fire Maks says I've lost and try to remember that even if I feel broken I am still made of magic.

I get out of the car, lock it, and pocket the key fob. The two buses are lined up and ready to go. Those staying behind wave good-bye, whistling between fingertips and shouting calls of good luck.

"Lula, come on!" My friend Kassandra waves from an open bus

door. Her black skin shimmers with the dusted glitter she likes to wear to the games.

I sling my bag over my shoulder and run toward the bus. The door sighs closed behind me, and Manny, the bus driver, nods in my direction as I make my way up the aisle. The air is thick with excitement and a mix of perfumes and perspiration from two dozen bodies that makes my nose itch.

Because I'm the last one on the bus, all the seats are taken except for one. I stand still for too long, and people look at me. Kassandra gives me an *everything okay?* face. Number twelve, Ramirez, looks me up and down, then smiles as if he hasn't been checking me out. Number twenty-three, Samori, waves from his designated seat in the back as unofficial DJ. A couple of girls from my step team whisper behind freshly manicured hands, their eyes sliding between Maks and me. Do they already know? How am I supposed to sit next to him for an hour?

Heat burns my cheeks, works down my neck and across my chest. I have the urgent need to turn back, to steal Maks's car and drive it back home. But Manny closes the doors and starts the engine.

"Lula," Maks says, gesturing to the empty spot beside him. "It's the last game. This is still your seat."

I take a steadying breath and take the seat next to Maks, the same one I've had for nearly two years—the captains of our squads, side by side. Have the seats always been this cramped, or am I now noticing because I'm doing everything possible to keep my body from touching his? I take off the jacket I'm wearing and quietly place it on his lap. From the corner of my eye, I can see him clutch it and turn to me.

"I was going to let you keep it," he says softly, maybe even hurt.

I turn my knees away from him so they're in the aisle. It's hard to look at him and know he doesn't want me. A cry forms in my throat, but I push it back and say, "You wanted this. I'm giving you what you want."

My phone buzzes again, cutting off whatever Maks is about to tell me.

Alex: On our way. I feel his bad vibes from here.

Alex: There's still time to come home.

Me: No, I have to get through today.

I wait for her to answer, but Coach starts his pregame speech.

"All right, boys and girls," he says in his thick Brooklyn accent. "It's easy to tell you that this game's in the bag. We're undefeated, but so are they. We've still got something they don't—the best damn team I've seen in years, and I'm freaking old as dirt."

Everyone laughs except the two of us. Maks leans forward and his arm brushes against mine, warm and familiar and unbearable.

"It's been a pleasure being your coach," he says. "I want you to know how proud I am, no matter what happens."

"You're not going to cry on us, are you, Coach?" Samori asks playfully.

"Shut it, Sam," Coach barks. "All right, Manny. Let's get this show on the road!"

There's a volley of hoots and whistles. No one stays in their seats like they're supposed to. A couple of the guys brought confetti poppers for the end of the game but are starting to set them off as Manny turns onto the highway, and Samori holds his handheld speaker up so music fills the entire bus.

"Asses in seats," Coach warns, staring at his phone. He's so clueless when he's going over plays, he wouldn't even notice if the whole soccer team started stripping down to their underwear.

The chill from earlier returns to my skin, and I reach across Maks to shut the window. As I sit back down, Maks holds the jacket out to me.

"You're cold," he whispers, leaning into my ear because it's so loud around us. "Just wear it. Don't get sick just because of me."

I shake my head. I remember the first time he gave me his jacket. We were in the middle of the hallway and he held it out for me. It was too big, but it smelled like fresh grass and his earthy soap and definitely like boy.

"Lula!" Ramirez turns around in his seat, his big, brown eyes only looking at me. "You dropped this."

He holds a red ribbon with fingers folded against his palm. I touch my hair and realize mine must've slipped off.

"Thank you," I say, and will myself to return his smile.

"You guys going to the prom after-party in the city?" Ramirez asks.

My heart squeezes painfully. I play with the red ribbon in my hands. Thinking about prom makes the last pieces of my old-Lula facade deflate. I spent weeks combing through thrift stores for the perfect blue dress. I picked it because the wildflower-blue color matched Maks's eyes. My tongue is so dry I fear my next words will turn into sand. I should've listened to Alex and gone home. My phone rings half a dozen times, but I just let it buzz in my purse.

"Yeah, man," Maks says overenthusiastically. "See you there."

I watch Maks.

Maks watches me.

"Please stop staring at me," I whisper.

He leans back and lets go of a long sigh. I can't read his furrowed stare or the way he runs his fingers through his hair to give his nervous hands something to do. Is that regret?

He reaches for my hand, then hesitates and pulls back when he realizes what he's doing. "I'm sorry. I don't like the way he looks at you."

My pulse quickens at his words. What is he saying?

Around us, the other boys are dancing in their seats like we're in the middle of a parade. My team stomps their feet, clapping their hands to the chant, "Let's! Go! Thorne! Hill!"

The team's chant gets stronger, the excitement in the air is thick with the desire to win, and I can't help but think it's familiar, like being at a Deathday ceremony. Except instead of summoning spirits, we're summoning luck and courage and victory. Maybe that's the key. My power might not be physical like Alex's, and I might not be able to talk to the dead like Rose, but I can heal. I've healed bones and bruises and cuts, so why not us? Maybe I can summon love, fix the rift I've created between me and Maks.

I know him. I know he didn't mean it, that a part of him still loves me. The pressure of our lives got to us, in between us. Now I know how to make it better.

I wind my ribbon around my wrist, red as love, red as blood, red as want. Let my magic bubble to the surface of my skin. I gasp when my power surges through me, like the slap of cold water, and I shudder from head to toe. Healing magic should be warm, but I can't reel it back now. I breathe faster and faster, think of every kiss and touch and secret we've shared.

"Lula?" Maks inches closer, our thighs pressed side by side, and throws his jacket around my shoulders.

It's working. It has to be because when I look up, Maks's eyes are trained on me. I don't dare look away from his face. There's a nick on his chin I didn't notice before. He must've cut himself shaving, but when I push my magic into his skin, the red cut disappears. His lips part, and we're so close I can feel his intake of breath, the race of his heartbeat.

When he closes his hand around mine, I shut my eyes and memorize the feel of us, skin on skin.

When I kiss Maks, the world falls out of focus, everything around us pixilated except for him. The bus speeds down the highway, dozens of horns blaring, and we slide against the window. I rest a hand on his jawline, freshly shaven and smooth. I push away all other thoughts and focus on us. Whatever broke between us, I can fix.

The kiss feels like a thousand years, but it's been seconds. I pull back to catch my breath, and he leans forward, like he can't be apart from me. He kisses my cheek. My forehead. The tip of my nose.

"I said sit!" Coach shouts at a group of guys dancing in the aisles.

Maks starts to wrap his arms around my waist, but every part of me turns cold. Maks looks down at me, worry riddling his features. Our breath comes out in icy clouds.

There's the crackle of static as the music cuts out. I stand to look

24

around at what's going on. Then the bus swerves, and my feet are no longer on the ground. I don't have time to scream as I struggle to find something to hold on to. Maks's hands grip me hard and pull me back.

"Are you—"

The screech of tires is followed by the warped crush of metal. Then, down is up. Windows shatter. Something hard breaks inside me, at first a dull, pulsing ache. The pain shoots from my belly button right to my heart, and I scream and scream as the bus spins in a fury of broken glass and bodies.

I shut my eyes, and warm liquid splatters across my face. When I open them, blood blurs my vision. I hear my name, distant as a memory, called out until there is nothing but piercing static.

There's a final slam. My body so numb I can't move. Can't stay awake. But I know I'm alive because of my thundering heart. Maks and I lie face-to-face on our sides. I can't feel a thing but see his hand resting on my arm, giving me a tiny shake.

"Stay awake," he tells me, choking on the blood that bubbles from his mouth.

"Maks." Pain slams into me all at once, concentrating on my abdomen, where a metal pole stabs straight through my torso and into his chest.

3

La Mama was lonely up in the sky,
chasing after El Papa, night into day.
Her light so great it left him in shadow.
—THE CREATION OF THE DEOS,
ANTONIETTA MORTIZ DE LA PAZ

ook at me," Maks tells me. His mouth is full of blood.
"Lula."

Maks's ragged voice falls away amid the screams
for help and the crackle of fire nearby. I try to reach for him, but
a sharp pain stabs at my rotator cuff. Every part of me fights to
hurt more than the rest, so I stay as still as possible. There is
one thing I can do. I search for my power, burrowed within me
protectively, and picture my sister's face. *Alex.* I shout her name
in the dark corners of my mind and hope that, wherever she is,
she can sense me. She has to know I'm alive. She has to know
I'm still here.

I move my arm again, screaming through the ache that follows.
If I can't heal myself, then I can at least heal Maks. But my arm
won't go any farther, and the edges of my vision darken with

shadow. My throat burns, liquid choking my windpipe, the taste of a thousand coins in my mouth.

"*Look* at me," Maks repeats.

When I do, it isn't his face I see. It's my own.

Voices. Familiar and strange. Angry and hopeful. Near and far.

"We can't save them both."

"I've never seen anything like this before. How are they both still alive?"

"He won't be for much longer."

"If we remove the boy, she might have a chance."

"Get them on the gurney. Clear it out!"

"God dammit! I'm losing her."

"What's the count?"

"Forty-five dead."

"Forty-six now."

"Get me a crash cart!"

"Come on, Lula."

"Lula, baby? It's Mom. We're all here."

"Can you hear me? It's Alex. I felt you. I felt you right here."

"I'm here with you too."

"You have to live, you hear me? You have to fight—I swear to gods, I will summon your spirit and kill you myself."

"Miss, please, you need to leave."

"Nurse, get them out of here."

"I can't. Let go of me! She's my baby girl—"

"Maksim! Where is he? Where is my son?"

"Get them all out of here!"

"Stay alive."

"Scalpel."

"It's not time yet, nena. I'm watching over you. I'll always watch over you girls. You have a great destiny. All three of you."

"She's tachycardic."

"Lula Mortiz. The Deos blessed you. The Deos will always bless you. Do not betray us."

"She's crashing."

"Baby, it's cold here."

"Pressure's rising! She's back."

"Stay with us, Lula. You're stronger than this."

"Would you like to do the honors and close?"

"Her eyelids are fluttering. She shouldn't be awake yet."

"Pushing one milligram of Midazolam."

"Lula Mortiz. Do not betray the Deos."

4

Sana sana, the body endures.
Sana sana, the body endures.
Sana sana, the body endures.
Sana sana, the body endures.

—HEALING CANTO,
BOOK OF CANTOS

When I dream, I relive every moment of the crash. Maks is throwing himself around me like a shield as shattered glass rains down around us. The bus keeps spinning until there is silence. But when I stand over my own body lying on the bus ceiling, I know this is a more than a dream.

Two dozen broken bodies lie in heaps inside the overturned bus. Some are still alive and crying out. Others lie still. I recognize Kassandra, eyes shut but her fingers twitch with life. I move to hold her, heal her, but I'm an apparition and I pass right through her. I spin around at the sound of Maks's voice.

Maks tries to lift his hand to touch mine but he's broken. He tells my body to look at him. Begs me to open my eyes. He's still holding me, even after everything that happened.

I move on, walking through the bus and onto the scene outside. A dozen cars are rammed into each other. The second bus is turned on its side, and a lucky few are being removed from the wreck by civilians and paramedics. Red, blue, and white lights swirl all across the highway as more emergency vehicles try to make their way through. Cars try to move out of their way as best as they can, driving into ditches off the sides of the road. People leave their stalled cars and rush out to help, taking off clothes to staunch open wounds and wrap around bone jutting through skin.

That's when I notice her.

She was always there, I suppose, lingering in the edges of the dark. An omen at the crossroads.

She stands at the center of the highway, dressed all in black. Her face is pale as the moon and her eyes are black as the longest night. She's completely bald, wearing a crown of twisted, gold thorns that dig into her skull but don't draw blood. Her dress blows in the breeze and she walks with a spear, the sharp end of it a metallic spike that sparks when she slams it on the ground.

She walks right through the bus and I follow after her.

"You," I say as she approaches Maks and me.

Her inhuman black eyes lock on me. "You know my face."

The woman at the crossroads. She looks different now, but I know her the way I know the comfort of a sunrise and the power in my blood that allows me to heal. Lady de la Muerte. Goddess of Death and the Mortal Earth's Dawn.

She moves in slow, careful steps, like she's on delay. She motions outward with her arm. The sleeves of her dress fall back to her elbows, exposing translucent, white skin. Names appear up and down her arms. His name makes my breath catch in my throat. Maksim Horbachevsky. The names keep scrolling, and there are many I recognize: Ramirez James. Samori Jones. Kassandra Toussaint. Noveno—they scroll too fast for my eyes to keep track of them all.

"Why did you do this?" I demand.

"I do nothing," she says. "I collect."

"You can't take him!"

"That is not for you to decide. That is for the Deos to decide."

"You ask too much. You have always asked for too much!"

"Watch yourself, Lula Mortiz. The Deos have also blessed you. Do not betray us."

Lady de la Muerte takes her eyes off me and turns to a boy face down on top of two other bodies. The number twelve is on his letterman jacket.

"Do not betray us," she repeats as she lifts her spear straight in the air and slams it into the boy's back. A great light crackles and winds around the spear, absorbing into the metal.

She's collected his soul.

"She's awake," Rose says.

Her eyes are puffy and her round cheeks are flushed. She's sitting at my bedside, carefully avoiding all the wires I'm hooked up to. Behind her, my dad and Alex snap awake from their sleep.

"Don't try to sit up," Alex tells me. There's a limp in her step and violet bruises dot her neck. They've been healing me.

"I heard you," I say.

"I felt you. When it happened, I mean." Alex presses her hand on mine and looks over her shoulder nervously.

"Maks," I say. "Is he okay?"

"Baby," my mom says, rushing through the open hospital room door. Her skin is covered in angry cuts and fresh bruises. Dad too. I try to think of the healing cantos they'd have had to go through to fix everything wrong with me. "How are you feeling?"

"Alive, thanks to you," I manage. My tongue is thick and my head throbs at the back of my skull.

"We've been healing you slowly since you got out of surgery," Ma says, gently brushing my arm. "We still have the smaller cuts, but the police want a statement."

"Let her rest awhile longer," Dad says softly.

I shut my eyes, tears flooding at the corners.

"What hurts?" Rose asks, looking over my body to see how she can make me comfortable. "I can push the morphine button."

I shake my head. I don't want to keep replaying the accident. I don't want to see Lady de la Muerte's ghoulish face.

"What about Maks?" I ask again. I didn't see Lady de la Muerte take him, but I saw his name on her arm and I remember the voices around me when I was being brought in. *He won't live for much longer.*

"He's in a coma," Dad tells me. He looks older than ever. His gray eyes are heavy with sorrow and the wrinkles on his forehead are like cracks in the sidewalk.

"But he's alive," I say, my voice breaking. "Can we heal him?"

There's a knock at the door followed by a man in brown leather jacket. His cigarette-stained teeth and suspicious eyes mark him as a detective.

"My sister just woke up," Alex says. With the spine-crushing black boots she's wearing, she's almost as tall as the detective. "She needs more time to rest."

The detective gives my sister a side-eye look, and it's that gesture which jogs my memory. He's the same detective that ran the investigation on our "home robbery." When we returned nearly dead from Los Lagos, no time had passed on this realm. Windows were shattered, feathers burned into the walls, floorboards ripped right out. Yeah, a robbery. There was no other explanation that wouldn't reveal us or our magical community. But the cops bought it, and the case was closed. Now, Detective Hill is back and his muddy-brown eyes settle on each and every one of us.

"We're old friends now, aren't we?" Detective Hill asks, trying for charming but ending at patronizing. He looks my dad up and down, then my mother and sisters. "You're all pretty banged up, there."

"We were in one of the accidents on the BQE," Alex lies.

"It's a mess out there," Detective Hill says, running his hands over his thick salt-and-pepper hair as he turns to me. "That's where you come in, Miss Mortiz."

"Yes, Detective," I say, sounding like I swallowed a cheese grater. But the sooner he leaves, the sooner I can check on Maks.

"First of all, I'm glad you're feeling better. It's been a *hectic* couple of days."

"Days?" I try to sit up but a shooting pain keeps me pinned to the bed. "How long have I been asleep?"

"Four days."

"*Four days?*"

"I don't mean to upset you, Ms. Mortiz," Detective Hill says. "But there were a number of casualties and we'd like to get to the bottom of what happened. You're the only survivor who's awake."

"The only one?"

Detective Hill nods gravely. "Do you remember anything?"

"How many—" I'm not sure what to ask. How many dead? Alive? But Detective Hill understands what I want to know.

"Five players and three cheerleaders are in comas. Others are out of surgery, but it doesn't look good. The victims of the pileup behind the bus are still unconscious and the ones who walked away with broken bones say they didn't see anything. No one has been able to give any statements, and you're the only soul who can string a sentence together. So you can see my frustration. This accident added fifty bodies to the morgue and I've got no answers as to how this happened."

"Fifty," I repeat. Then I remember my vision. "Kassandra?"

He flips open a notepad. "Kassandra Toussaint. She goes back into surgery to remove debris from her stomach. Really rare blood type and not enough to go around."

The machines measuring my heart rate go off like a carnival ride.

"Calm down, nena." My mom pushes past the detective to get to my side.

I open my mouth, but it's like I'm breathing through a straw and the rest of me is buried under cement. My mother's hand is warm, resting behind my neck. At first I think she's going to use her magic, but then she simply brushes my hair away from my face, blowing cool breath against my eyelids. Something about her presence calms me in ways I can't explain. I'm not better, not by a long shot, but at least I can breathe again.

"You all right?" Detective Hill asks.

"I don't care who you are," Alex says suddenly. "But I'm going to call the doctor to kick you out if you don't have any more actual questions."

"Don't threaten me, Ms. Mortiz. I thought I'd seen the last of your family five months ago, but here we are again. It seems bad luck follows you." His tongue pushes against his cheek, like he's digging for food particles stuck in his teeth. Then he mutters, "Curious, isn't it?"

"I don't remember much," I say. "I was sitting with Maks. Everyone was listening to music and dancing, like usual. They were excited for the game."

"Does the driver always let you stand up and party?"

"What? No, that's not what I meant."

"But you said 'like usual.'"

"Yes, but—" My head aches at the temples.

"You're twisting her words," Alex snaps.

"Stay out of this, Miss Mortiz," he shouts.

My vision blurs with tears and I breathe fast because my heart is racing. Dad tries to step in, but Ma puts an arm on his shoulder, because we know it would be worse if he gets involved.

"Will you let me talk?" I shout at Alex and Detective Hill. "Yes, everyone was extra excited. It was the final game and most

35

of the team are seniors. Coach kept telling everyone to sit, but they didn't listen. The next thing I knew, the bus swerved and everything turned upside down."

I shut my eyes but can't stop the images from flooding my mind. *Blood and flesh and glass and bones and a woman dressed in black.* "When I came to, Maks was trying to keep me conscious. Then I woke up here."

"Thank you, Ms. Mortiz. You've been most helpful. I hope you have a speedy recovery." Detective Hill looks at Alex. "See? That wasn't so bad, was it?"

I nod and we wait in silence as he slowly makes his way out the door.

"One last thing." Detective Hill turns around. "The scars on your face. They're older than the accident. How'd that happen?"

"We used to have a dog," I say, touching the claw marks raised with scar tissue. "Rabies."

We're locked in a staring match. I'm afraid that if I look away first, I'll be admitting to the lie. Who we are is cloaked in so much secrecy that when it comes time for sinmagos to believe us, we're too suspect. That's why our kind doesn't go to hospitals. We don't seek the police. We get justice ourselves, save our own, protect our magic.

I win our staring match, and it's a small victory. He looks away, eyes heavy with dark circles and distrust. He starts to leave, shaking his head as he says, "Shame. Such a pretty face."

5

La Mama cried and cried, waiting for El Papa
alone, with no one but El Cielo,
who loved her, who greeted her with arms wide open.
—THE CREATION OF THE DEOS,
ANTONIETTA MORTIZ DE LA PAZ

My grandmother always said that our magic was about belief. It's also about intent. The first time I tried to heal, I had no idea what I was doing. I was six and a bird had fallen out of a nest in our backyard. The power slumbering in my body woke, pure and innocent. I just knew that I wanted the bird to be okay. I reached out with my power, unsure of the primordial magic that cycled between us, until the sparrow stretched its wings against my palms and took off into the sky.

I was always glad to be a healer like my mom. Rose has the Gift of the Veil. Alex is an encantrix, blessed with all the gifts of the Deos. Dad once had the power to conjure storms. Our power is what we make it, but we all have our limits. At least, that's what I was taught.

Now, as my family refuses to heal Maks, I start to wonder if perhaps we set the limits ourselves.

I can barely stand, but one way or another, I'm going to get to Maks. I use the rail attached to my bed for balance.

"Absolutely not." My mother blocks my door. Her black curls are wrapped in a colorful scarf, and her dress is a bright blue—the color of La Mama and eternal hope. My mother holds a white quartz prex in one hand, and the prayer beads rattle when she gesticulates and shouts. "You're not strong enough to heal the broken wing on a cockroach, let alone the kinds of injuries that Maks sustained."

"Maks is not a cockroach!" I yell.

"Fine. Butterfly, take your pick. My point stands." I can see in her eyes that she's wavering between thanking the Deos I'm alive and wanting to throttle me herself. "His body is too weak for even the doctors to try to save his life, and they've tried, Lula."

"We can do it together," I say, foolishly hopeful.

"You didn't have enough fun almost dying?" Alex asks. She leans against the wall in front of me, and Dad stays close to the foot of my bed, boxing me in. "You ready to try harder?"

"But you all healed *me*," I point out.

"You're family," Alex says plainly. "Maks broke up with you."

"So, if he hadn't, you'd try?" I rake my fingers through my hair, my scalp throbbing painfully. "You literally gave up your power to save Rishi from dying in Los Lagos. Do you remember that? You did it even though it could've cost you *your entire family*. Maks was there for me when I couldn't talk to any of you. But I'm not surprised you don't get it, Alex. Everything bad that's ever happened to me has been because of you!"

Alex presses her hand to her stomach and gasps like I've struck her.

"Don't talk to your sister like that," Dad says.

"You haven't been part of this family for seven years," I tell him, regret twisting into my heart the moment the words leave my lips, but I can't seem to stop. "You don't get to tell me how to talk to my sister."

"Lula!" Alex's brown eyes follow a path to where Rose sits by the window, playing with the arms of the stuffed animal on her lap. She bought it in the gift shop downstairs, a bright "Get well soon" stitched into a silk heart. Looking at her sitting there, caught in the middle of this fight, my fight, makes tears sting my eyes.

"I'm sorry," I say. The ache in my legs wins, and I get back into bed.

"Maks is in a coma," Mom says, trying her best to remain calm. "The kind of canto we'd have to perform would be dangerous to more than our family. We might as well turn ourselves over to the Thorne Hill Alliance or walk up to a pack of hunters."

"Your mother's right," Dad tells me, his eyes mirrors to mine. "The hunters are out there and have little love for our kind. I wish I could take away your pain. But I can't."

When I was little, Dad used to tell us stories about being young and outwitting hunters. He said they fought with silver swords and sprung from the shadows. To me they were just stories. I would face the Alliance and the hunters if it meant making Maks better.

"But we would be saving a life," I say. "I've read the Book of Cantos dozens of times, and I know there has to be something in there that can help without upsetting the balance of things."

"We have laws too," Mom says, pacing the length of my bed and rubbing the quartz beads in her hands so hard I fear she'll have nothing but pebbles soon. "This far gone, I don't know who you'd get back, but it might not be Maks."

"Brujas who break the order of things always pay a price," my father says.

I can't—won't—listen to this. "Then I call a meeting of the High Circle of Brooklyn."

"No," Mom says, a deep ache in her voice. "I can already tell you they're not going to help."

"How do you know?"

"Because we asked them to heal you," Rose says. "They wouldn't. That's why the recoil is so bad for us. We channeled our power through Alex, and then into Ma, because she's the healer. Even with Alex's magic you're not a hundred percent."

"But the High Circle is family," I say. Maybe not all of them, but our aunt Lady is the Alta Bruja. Valeria is Rose's godmother. The rest grew up with my parents, fought alongside them in their youth.

"They're afraid," Alex says. "There's too much heat. Between the regular cops and the Thorne Hill Alliance sniffing around—"

"Why would they be sniffing around?" I ask. "Brujas aren't part of the Alliance."

Alex shakes her head. "One of the boys who died was related to one of their members. They want to make sure there was no foul play."

"I want to see the High Circle," I say, my thoughts racing to form a plan. "I want them to look into my eyes and tell me there is nothing we can do."

I'm afraid my mother is going to yell at me again. I'm afraid Dad is going to walk out that door and never come back. I'm afraid I won't be able to get through the rest of the day.

Instead, my mom places her hand on my face, tracing her thumb along the scars on my cheek. "If that's what you need to hear, then I'll make the call."

After our parents leave to get coffee, my sisters stay. Rose is wheeling herself around in the chair a nurse brought in case I wanted fresh air. Alex flips through a stack of newspapers, searching for signs of anything strange in even the smallest headlines. She hasn't spoken a word since our parents left, and I feel a tinge of guilt after the mean things I said to her.

I clear my throat and look toward the door to make sure the coast is clear. "I have a plan."

She squints in my direction. "I don't like that face."

"I don't like your face either, but I still have to look at it," I say. She rolls her eyes, and I'm relieved we can still tease each other like always.

Rose perks up and quirks an eyebrow. "What kind of plan?"

"It doesn't matter what kind of plan," Alex says. "Once you get shut down by the Circle, they're going to be watching you."

"No, they won't," I say. "But I need your help. You too, Rosie."

"Me?" Rose gets up from the chair and comes closer.

Alex shakes her head. "We leave Rose out of this."

"No way," Rose says, and it's disconcerting to recognize the

Mortiz-stubbornness in her features. "Don't forget, *my* power's been awake since I was born. Any kind of spirit magic needs me there."

"Fine," Alex groans. "Let's hear this plan."

"I remember a canto," I say. "It's in the Book. It's old. Way old."

"Mom old or Great-Great Grandpa Philomeno old?" Rose asks.

"Older," I say, and her eyes light up with curiosity. "It's a blood healing canto. The ingredients are easy to get. The most important part is—"

"Blood?" Alex asks sarcastically.

"Aside from that, herbs and mirrors blessed by an Alta Bruja."

"Lady blesses all her jewelry," Rose says, smirking despite Alex's disapproving glares.

Alex paces back and forth. Tiny sparks shower over her head like it's the Fourth of July just for us. Her magic still has a wildness to it. Wild magic can't be tamed. I'm surprised she kept it together when Detective Hill was here.

"I'm no one to tell you not to do this." She wrings her hands. "You know I'm not. But maybe I should be. Don't make the same mistake I made."

"Mistake?" I ask her. "The mistake was hiding your secret. The mistake was trying to get rid of your magic and nearly getting us all killed."

"I know what my mistake was," she says, stopping suddenly. "That's why I don't want you to repeat it."

"But if you hadn't done all that, you wouldn't have Rishi. You wouldn't have met Nova and we wouldn't have Dad back."

"Don't." She holds her hand up, as if that'll deflect my words.

There's a crack in her voice. "Don't throw that in my face. Rishi and I would've found each other eventually. What I did was selfish—I hurt you. You were trapped in that awful place and I wish I could take that pain back. Why do I glamour you every morning to hide your scars? Why do you think I do your chores, Lula? Do you think I like being your personal maid? No, but I'm sorry. I'm so sorry for everything I did to hurt you. Every single day you've been distant and sad, and I know it's my fault. *That's* why I take care of you."

"You're right," I say, solidifying the plans in my mind. I know I'm doing the right thing. "You did hurt me. You owe me, Alex. You *owe* me. All I want is to try and heal him. That's it. He's still in there somewhere. What good is our power if we can't help the people we love?"

I can see the war playing out in my sister's mind, but I know she'll give in to me. She always has because she loves me.

"Once," she says, holding up a single finger. "We're trying this once. If Mom and the High Circle figure out what we're doing, it's over. If it doesn't work, you have to let him go."

"I will," I say, kissing her hand, knowing a part of me is lying when I say, "I promise."

6

The Deos, too, learned their limits.

El Fuego extinguished into ash.

La Ola crumbled into salt.

El Terroz clove the earth in pieces.

El Viento fell and kept on falling.

But from their limits, Lady de la Muerte was born.

—THE CREATION OF THE DEOS,
ANTONIETTA MORTIZ DE LA PAZ

To a sinmago, the High Circle of Brooklyn looks like a nice group of middle-aged friends and family who bring me gifts.

But for brujas, it's bad luck to visit the sickly empty-handed. Valeria brings me her famous apple pie. The spice and buttery smell of it reminds me I still have an appetite. Gustavo brings me a new prex made of onyx beads, customary for when someone is ill. Lady and the other three women bring flowers and candles that my mother arranges into a makeshift altar in the corner.

"We prayed to La Estrella to guide you back with her light,"

Maria tells me, her hands cold and clammy around my cheeks, her puckered smile bleeding burgundy lipstick at the edges.

"I'm better thanks to my family," I say, sitting up to get down to business.

Her lips uncurl from a smile into a taut line. The High Circle exchanges awkward glances, but I don't care that I've made them uncomfortable because they would've let me die. My family isn't in the *best* standing anymore either. After what Alex did and after my father's sudden reappearance, the High Circle has been wary of us. Even Valeria, who was my mother's midwife for Rose and who survived the Trujillo reign in the Dominican Republic, thinks we're cursed. They fear the curse of the Mortiz family might cling to them. We've even stopped going to our brujeria classes at Lady's shop.

But despite Alex's canto gone wrong, I think they fear my father the most. When they walk past, they give him a wide birth. He's the inexplicable ghost in all our lives, and no one has yet to make sense of him. Dad and Alex, linked by their otherness, linger against the wall as the High Circle sits around my bed.

"Thanks for answering my call, Lady," I say.

Lady Lunes stands at the foot of my bed. She always looks lost in time, better suited for a smoky lounge from the twenties than now. She wears her long, coarse, black hair wrapped in a scarlet scarf that matches her lips and brings out the mahogany of her brown skin. A necklace of a dozen tiny mirrors hangs from her neck, and her dark eyes travel the room, detached and somber. Hospitals scare all of us who have magic. The air is thick with lingering spirits, not all of them good.

But her voice is calm as she says, "We've missed you at classes. It's been boring without you and Alex fighting all day."

"Why did you call us here?" Gustavo asks anxiously. He's about the same age as my dad, with two sons, one who just had his Deathday. We were not invited.

With their eyes on me, my sisters have a chance to move on with our plan. Time to draw their attention as long as I can.

"I know my parents asked you to heal me, and that you declined." I keep my face stern and my head high, even if every moment of it takes all my strength. At least Valeria and Lady have the decency to look sorry. "And I want you to know that I'm not upset, even if some of us are family. But I want to implore the High Circle to heal Maks and save his life. I've never asked anything of you before, and I'm prepared to pay any price."

"Selfish," Gustavo mutters even before I get in my last word.

"Watch your tongue," my father says. He doesn't move an inch, but Gustavo flinches back as if my dad struck him.

"Stop!" Alex gets up, putting up a barrier between them with her magic. The shield lasts a few moments, rippling like the clear-est water. It reminds them of her power, the power none of them have, not even an Alta Bruja like Lady. "If anyone knows what it's like to confront the darkness, it's me. I defeated the Devourer, or have you forgotten?"

"I was there, Alex, of course I haven't," Lady says dryly.

Alex places a hand on Lady's back and smiles apologetically. Then my sister looks at me and takes a deep, shaky breath. "That's why I can't let you do this."

"Alex, if you ruin this," I say, "I swear on the Deos—"

"What's going on?" Ma asks, eyes darting between Alex and me.

"What aren't you telling us?" Lady points in my direction, her voice fills the room like billowing smoke. "Ever since I stepped foot in this room, I can't get a read on you. Not that it's surprising considering the energies surrounding your family."

"I'm sorry, Lula," Alex says. I start to speak, but she holds her hand up, closes it. My throat burns and I wheeze, scratching at the sides of my neck. She's stolen my voice. A pulsing light is trapped under her fingers.

"What are you doing?" Mom asks, trying to reach over Valeria to get to Alex, but the High Circle stops her.

"Let Alejandra speak," Valeria says, motioning her hand toward my sister.

"Lula saw Lady de la Muerte. She spoke to her during the accident."

I open my mouth, but nothing comes out. It's like there's sand in my throat, even though my air passages are clear.

Some of the High Circle members trade serious glances. Others place trembling hands over their chests. Gustavo whispers a prayer to El Papa, Ruler of the Moon and Father to All the Deos.

"Tell me what you have seen," Lady commands me.

I slap my hand on the bed and point to my throat.

"Oh, right," Alex says, opening her hand and releasing my voice. The sensation is like gargling salt. My throat is raw and grainy, and I swear I'll enjoy the recoil she gets from doing that to me.

I cough a few times before saying, "Yes. Lady de la Muerte appeared to me."

Their collective gasp might as well have sucked out the air from the room.

47

Helena holds her hands together. "What did she look like?"

"How can you be sure it was her?" Gustavo asks skeptically.

"We have to let Lula speak," Valeria says, reverent tears in her eyes. She's got the Gift of the Veil, like Rose. Seers are so close to death, but to see a Deo—that's almost as rare as an encantrix these days. "Go on, Lula."

Which is why what I'm doing makes me more nervous than I've ever been before.

"She's not the way we depict her," I tell them. "She defies age. Her skin is almost see-through, with names written all over her arms, and everything around her feels cold. Right before the crash, the temperature dropped. She had a spear made of onyx with a metal tip. She used it to separate the souls from the dead bodies."

"Incredible. No bruja or brujo has ever seen Lady de la Muerte and lived," Gustavo says, his features twisting to scrutinize me. "Unless they're marked."

"Gustavo, calm down," Valeria says.

He gets up from his chair, as if the floor has turned into flames and he can't get out of here quickly enough.

"No!" Gustavo says. "Don't you see? She was marked by La Muerte. We're not touching her sinmago. If I could banish your family from the tristate area, it still wouldn't be enough to get your Mal Ojo from us."

Everyone is stunned into silence. The Mal Ojo, the evil eye, is the worst curse you can carry with you.

"Tell us how you really feel," Alex grumbles finally. She looks at me and says, "We have enough problems without bringing down the wrath of the gods. I'm sorry, Lula, but I'm not going to do that. Not again."

"Right," I say, venom on my tongue. "It's all fine when you want to get rid of your magic, but when I need to save the boy I love, you have objections."

"Your sister is right," Valeria tells me. "We can pray for him. We can light candles for him. But we cannot interfere when the Deos are involved. We can only ask for them to listen."

"They stopped listening a long time ago," I say.

"Watch your tongue, you cursed girl," Gustavo tells me.

"And you watch yours," my father counters.

"What's the point of this power?" I shout. "Why do we *have* powers if, when it matters, you want to sit back and let people die?"

"No, baby." Lady clicks her tongue and wags a finger at me. "You don't get to lecture us on how to use our power. We've earned our right to live peacefully, by our own terms. Maks is unresponsive. He's practically—"

"Lady," Mom stops her.

"Get out," I say, the machines hooked up to me beeping loudly. "All of you."

The sickly sweet smell of Valeria's pie is suddenly making me nauseous.

"I said *get out*." My voice is hoarse and the scream scratches my still-tender throat.

The nurse comes in to kick everyone out.

I turn my face to the side so I don't have to look at any of them. I know most of this was a charade so they wouldn't suspect my *true* plan. But we all meant what we said. Some words you just can't take back.

"There." Nurse Yana adds another pillow under my head and pulls the covers over me. Her hair is disheveled and her eyes tired and puffy, but she tries to smile. "I know it's hard. But you're alive and you're strong. It's a miracle."

But I want to tell her, "It's not a miracle. It's magic."

The door opens again and in comes Alex and Rose.

"No more visitors," Yana says. "You need to rest."

"Please," I say. "They're my sisters."

Nurse Yana purses her lips, but she caves, winking a big, brown eye. "Just for tonight. The staff is already so busy with run-of-the-mill murders."

I must have a bewildered expression on my face because Nurse Yana blanks and scrambles for something to say. "Sorry, it's been a long night. You two, no upsetting the patient."

"Scout's honor," Rose says, and we watch the nurse scuttle out of the room.

"When have you ever been a Girl Scout?" Alex asks, gathering her hair into a high ponytail.

Rose shrugs. "I don't know. That's what people say when they want to be believed in the movies. I could be a Girl Scout."

"Yes, yes," I say, pulling my covers off to stretch my legs, even though I hurt from my finger joints to my toes.

"Did you bring the book?" I ask Rose, my words coming in a rush.

She holds up her backpack and pats it with her hand. "And supplies."

"Did you really have to take my voice?" I turn to Alex, rubbing my throat.

She coughs, already feeling the recoil. "It had to be convincing. They won't suspect a thing."

"How did you get that off Lady?" I ask out of curiosity.

"An encantrix never reveals her secret." She holds up the necklace of a dozen tiny mirrors.

"Transportation canto," Rose says.

"Can you not?" Alex hisses.

I assess everything we have. I hold the prex Gustavo gave me. Onyx for the dead, for the spirits. Always given to the sickly and ill. I take a tiny pleasure in knowing that his gift is helping us complete the canto.

It's all here. *Hold on, Maks. Please hold on.*

Alex helps me out of bed and says, "Let's wake up your sleeping beauty."

7

Follow my voice, my love, my love.

Death cannot tear us apart.

Take my hand, my love, my love.

Follow the light of my heart.

—LULA'S HEALING CANTO,
BOOK OF CANTOS

We go over the plan once again.

After our parents went home for the first time in four days, Alex helped me put on a loose nightgown. Naked, I traced the horrible scar on the lower left side of my belly, where they pulled out the metal pole.

As my sisters pack up everything we need, I wonder if one day I'll be more than a patchwork of scars.

"We have the Book, onyx, and blessed mirrors, candles, matches, Alex's dagger, and a bundle of desert sage for added witchery," Rose says. She's in charge of supplies because she's the most organized.

"We'll do a few laps around the floor so as to not raise suspicion before going to Maks's room," Alex says.

"Then comes the easy part." I chuckle nervously.

"Healing Maks so he comes off life support? Right. Easy." Alex gnaws at her bottom lip like it's second breakfast. "You'll have to cut yourself for this. Cantos like this require blood. Lots of it. Are you ready for that?"

My heartbeat spikes. My power is to heal, not to destroy. And yet, it's the only choice I can see. Alex has her own scar on her wrist from when she closed the portal to Los Lagos. If the gods require blood, I'm prepared to give it to them. "I'll make myself ready."

Alex holds my stare. "Then let me ask you this. Are you absolutely sure you want to do this?"

"Don't," I tell her. "You said you'd give me this one try."

"I know you believe we're doing the right thing," she says. "But you saw how the High Circle reacted. A literal actual goddess revealed herself to you. You said Maks's name was on her creepy death list. We might be going up against Lady de la Muerte. Even if you're not afraid of that, you've *always* feared the Circle."

Part of me wants to tell her about another name I saw on there. Noveno. Nova. I mean, how many Novenos are there in the world? It has to be him. But I need her focused, so I don't.

Rose stays silent and brings my chair around. She's our peaceful middle ground.

"The High Circle is wrong." Words I never thought I'd say.

"Since when have you thought that way?" Alex asks.

"Since they were willing to let me die."

Alex pushes my chair, and we start to make our way to Maks's room on the other end of the floor.

Hospitals give me the creeps. I'm a healer, and places like this make me feel as if my magic is being dampened by the wires and tubes and needles. I hold on to Rose's hand tighter to make the feeling stop.

"I hate it here too," she says. She can't focus right when she's surrounded by so many people who are crossing over. "It's like a bus station for the spirits."

That makes us laugh, but we stop as a nurse rushes past us. She's too busy to look at the way I grip the armrest settle on or how I can't stop my legs from trembling. When we turn the corner, we pass metal racks of supplies and more people rushing back and forth. No one stops to look at us or ask where we're going.

Except one.

A nurse.

He looks up from his chart as we approach. There's something that makes him look out of place. His scrubs are a lighter blue than the others, and his brown hair is tied back at the nape of his neck. His face looks much too young to be working here, but he's got the dark circles of someone who works these graveyard shifts often.

"Can't sleep?" he asks.

"Just tired of staring at the wall," I say. My heart leaps at the thought that he'd make us go back. He's going to ruin everything. I look up at Alex. "Let's go."

But he stands in my way, brown eyes taking in my state from head to toe. "Is your TV not working? I can get someone to fix it for you."

"No." I grab the wheels of my chair. "Thanks, but I'm fine."

"You've gone through a lot," he says, lowering onto one knee. At eye level, I can see the thick, red scar that cuts across his stark black eyebrow. When he frowns, he looks older, maybe twenty, but still not old enough to be a nurse. "You need to rest."

I take a deep breath. I starc at the nurse's scar. It's on the same side as mine.

When his eyes settle on my scar, I feel a flash of anger. I don't want him to look at me. I need him to get out of my way. I need to get to Maks. Everyone here wants me to rest. Be calm. Be glad I'm alive. So I'll do just that.

"Just one more lap," I say and smile. "Please."

His features soften, and when he stands back up, a lock of his hair falls over his eye. He smirks, like an animated prince, and blows it away.

"All right. But if I check on you and you aren't there—"

"We'll make sure she gets rest," Alex promises. She glances at Rose. "*Scout's* honor."

Rose gives Alex a glare that could burn her alive.

He nods and then goes back to his clipboard. His shiny, black shoes echo as he walks back down the hall. But when he turns a corner, the coast is clear.

"Let's go," I say.

And without hesitating, Alex pushes my chair toward Maks's room. The sound of wheels spinning on the tiled floor fills my ears. My heart squeezes like someone's got their hand in my chest and is trying to crush it because all I can think is, *What if I'm too late?*

"Coast is clear." Rose opens the door to his room, and we go in.

Maks is alone in the dark. I turn on the light on the bedside table, casting an amber glow on the sterile white walls. There are tubes in his throat, tabs and wires trailing from his temples, wrists, and heart. His face is stitched up across his forehead and his cheek, which is red and swollen. The hospital gown makes his skin appear even more gray, except where purple bruises the size of fists cover his arms. Despite all of that, his hair is parted neatly to the side, and I know Mrs. Horbachevsky must've only just left because he smells like fresh soap and her rosary is resting on the table beside him.

"Lula?" Alex gently taps my shoulder, a reminder that we have to get moving.

First, we hang lady's necklace over the door. The mirrors are bathed in sacred waters and blessed with her magic. That way, during the canto, any spirit, alive or dead, human or immortal, will walk right past. We're invisible and in plain sight. I'd smile at how clever I feel, but I can't. Not until Maks can breathe on his own.

Next, I hold his still-warm hand as my sisters pull the bed toward the center of the room.

Rose sets up a circle of squat, silver candles and Alex readies the Book of Cantos at the foot of the bed.

I undo the back of his hospital gown and move it down just enough to expose his chest. My breath catches at the sight of scars, red like a nest of snakes settled on his chest. I hold my hand over his heart. I release a pulse of magic. His heartbeat reacts to it, like he recognizes me. I don't care what anyone says. He's still in there.

"Ready?" I ask my sisters.

"Almost," Rose says, lighting the candles with a metal lighter.

Her hand shakes, and she makes a gasping noise, like she's choking. The lighter falls to the floor and its clatter reverberates in the eerie stillness.

"What's wrong?"

"I'm okay now. I felt someone cross over," Rose says, clutching her chest. Her eyes are glossy and she fumbles to finish lighting the candles. "It's not usually this strong. I think—I think she's here."

Alex parts the blinds with her index finger. She motions for me to look. I drag my legs to the window, and every step feels like I'm walking on broken glass.

A shadow inches its way down the hall. It never touches the floor, the black cloak rippling on air. I recognize the white hand gripping the onyx spear. She clicks it on the ground, leaving sparks in her wake.

Lady de la Muerte is here to collect.

"We have to hurry."

Finally, Rose finishes lighting the candles and a bundle of sage. She stands at the foot of Maks's bed and Alex stations herself to the left. I use the metal railing on the side of his bed to balance myself. I press my hand on my stomach where my scar burns like a warning.

"I'm going to save you," I whisper.

Alex draws her dagger from her waistband and hands it to me. It's small, with a handle made of moonstone, and has a small leather sheath.

"Do it," I say and take the dagger from her.

Alex holds her hands out, the air around us shifting instantly.

She conjures a wind stream that flows from her body, through

Rose, and into me. There isn't any power attached to it, and at first, it's like playing with a strong breeze. It's to get the flow of energy correct, cycling through the three of us, and then into Maks.

I extend my arm over Maks's torso. I drag the blade from my palm, up my forearm, and stop at the inside of my elbow. My blood falls in a red river, running across the muscles of his chest like water around mountains.

The gash doesn't hurt right away, but everything else does. My bones, my muscles, my heart. I take a deep breath to steady myself because my vision spins.

"Alex," I say, to remind her that she can't change her mind now.

She claps her hands together, pulling on her power, on the essence of the flames, on the smoke wafting from the sage. The blood magic pulses harder, in a way other cantos can't. Blood magic is the strongest of any kind. We sacrifice it because all gods ask for it. Blood is life. Blood is everything.

"She's getting closer," Rose says, eyes shut. Her arms are outstretched, palms out, like she's stopping two force fields from closing against her.

"Now!" I say.

It's my turn to do my part.

We join hands, forming a triangle over him.

Healing isn't like other cantos. It's not about the words or ingredients. It's about what's in your heart. Maybe Alex and Rose don't love Maks, but they love me, and I can use that.

I clear my mind and think of the power I've held dear for so long. My magic rises when I call upon it, just like it did for Alex when I taught her how to heal in Los Lagos—the very thought of

Los Lagos sends a shudder down my body that I'm sure my sisters can feel. My mind latches on to that pain, flashing to a more recent memory. Maks in his car, trying his hardest not to look at me. *It's like your fire is gone*, he said.

"Lula?" Alex calls out.

"I'm fine. I can do this."

I shut my eyes harder. Search for love in my heart. My whole life, I've tried to love as fiercely as I could. But didn't Alex tell me once that I gave my heart away too easily?

"Lula!" Rose this time.

"I got it," I say, but there's a shadow around my power, and it clings like everlasting night. I know I have to push through. Little by little, I let the light in. I find it in small moments, like Maks's smile and his laugh. The way he never let go of my hand when we were together. The way he looked at me that made me feel as if he'd never get enough. The way he reached for me when the bus was crashing, using his body to protect mine.

My healing energy starts to flood through me, and I let it flow in the current Alex created at the start of the canto. It cycles through her, then to Rose, then back to me. Again and again, catching momentum until it hits the center of my chest.

Alex is so powerful that the touch of her magic makes my entire body sigh as I experience the exquisite relief from pain, as if I'm made of nothing but feathers. I've never felt power like this. But with it comes a darkness too, twisting around the one I already have in my heart, like two energies fighting for dominance.

Next is Rose. Rose's power is like the slip of day into night. You don't notice it until it's completely dark. Rose's power makes the skin on my arms tingle with cold. It's like turning up my face to the sky and letting snowflakes kiss my skin. It's pure, and the brightness of it nearly overpowers Alex's and mine completely.

We are three points of energy linking like chains until we are one force, and I direct that current into Maks.

"Follow my voice, my love, my love," I say, shuddering with the euphoria of this power. "Death cannot tear us apart. Take my hand, my love, my love. Follow the light of my heart."

My head feels like clouds drifting across a clear sky. I don't know if I'm the one swaying or if the floor has turned into soft earth.

"Lula!" Rose snaps me to the present. Here. Now. Maks.

I'm okay, I think, but can't speak it. I finish the canto. I help guide our powers to heal his wounds. I start with his ribs. The crash turned the right side of his rib cage into a mosaic of bones, and I focus on mending the breaks. A warm trickle of blood runs down my belly.

"Lula!" Alex shouts.

I'm falling to my knees. The pain in my ribs is too much to withstand, but still I bite down on the scream.

"We should stop," Rose says.

"If you stop," I say, "I will never forgive you."

Rose gasps, and her eyes get cloudy and faraway, her body lifts a foot into the air. Her voice is strange, like someone is speaking through her, "*Do not betray the Deos, Lula Mortiz.*"

Rose lands back on her feet and starts to pull her hands away from us, but once we break our hold, the bond will be severed and we won't be able to finish healing Maks. I hold on as hard as I can, by the tips of my fingers, because his life depends on it.

Rose's eyes return to their normal color. "La Muerte is not happy."

"Lula." Alex.

"Lula." Rose.

My ears pop, like I'm being plunged deep into the sea. The recoil is hitting me hard, and I can hear my heart beat in every corner of my body. My skin feels tight, pulled from all sides, and I fear I might tear myself into ceasing to exist.

But I have to be strong. The light of our magic moves across Maks's ribs, then travels down to mend his spine and pelvic bone. I move to his organs, his collapsed lung that needs help breathing. I direct our power toward his chest, but it curves away. I try again, pushing the energy to mend his heart, but I hit a wall.

Something is blocking my magic. I push hard against the invisible force, but it's like running straight into a barricade.

"It's not working," I cry out. "Alex, why isn't it working?"

"I don't know!" I can feel her panic, her doubts, and realize it's part of our power being linked.

A red light pulses in the room over Maks's body.

Rose's eyes become black again, the same way Lady de la Muerte's eyes turned when she took the bodies at the bus crash.

"Rosie, what do you see?" Alex asks, her hands vibrating from the strain of trying to hold on.

"I can feel the others," Rose says, her dark gaze traveling all around the room seeing things we cannot. "She's here for all of them."

"We have to let go!" Alex hisses.

"Keep going," I shout, squeezing both of their hands, palms slick with sweat and blood.

"We can't!" Alex says, breathless. "There's a block on his body, Lula. I can't—"

"Then fix it!"

Her hand trembles in mine, but she doesn't let go.

"I can see their spirits," Rose says, her breathing rapid and labored. "Maks is there too. They're wandering in a room with a thousand doors. She circles them. Wait—she's circling us."

We're out of time.

Then I realize—what makes this magic powerful is the desire to want to do good. To value life. To save those who are hurt. Healing is the purest magic there is, and it's part of my life force. When I look at Maks, I see the parts of me that used to be whole, and maybe it's desperate, maybe it's wrong, but I can't let him go.

"It's over," Alex says.

"Did you just read my mind?" I shout at her.

"I can't help it! The channels are open. I'm picking up thoughts from all over the building, and I can tell you that Maks isn't in there anymore. I told you we'd try once. *Once*. Let him go."

I look down at his unmoving body. He has to be in there. The machines are picking up his vitals. His heart is still beating.

The door behind us blasts open.

Lady de la Muerte walks in.

What I thought was a cloak before is a gathering of shadows that trail behind her, like she wears the dead she collects. Her spear clicks on the scuffed hospital tiles. Names race across her powder-white skin and her lips are the blue of corpses.

"Stand aside, Lula Mortiz."

Nothing good can happen when the goddess of death knows your name.

"Please." I look at Alex and beg. "Please, Alex, please."

Because we're connected by our magic I can hear Alex's heart racing. Because we're sisters, I know she's going to come through for me, even if she thinks I'm making a mistake.

Alex's face is pained with indecision, but finally she turns. Her magic ripples around the room. Lady de la Muerte looks up, almost surprised that I'm still standing in her way. She tries to grab to me, to push me out of the way, but Alex has formed a barrier between us.

"I can't hold her for long," Alex says, struggling.

And I realize, Lady de la Muerte can't take Maks if he's tethered to the living.

I let go of my sisters and press my blood-drenched hand on his chest and recite the Binding Canto. I can hardly hear my own voice over the thundering pulse in my ears, but I shout the words. *"These bodies, these spirits, together as one. This union eclipsed like the moon and the sun."*

The air around us crackles and splinters with light. Lady de la Muerte pounds her fists on Alex's barrier, and it sounds like someone is punching on bulletproof glass.

The red light that ties Maks to me is like a harpoon, digging into my chest. When it finds its mark, it pulls hard. I fall forward on my knees, trying to hold on to the side of the bed, but I slip on my own blood.

The floor tilts, and the room spins, forcing me all the way down. The pain in my bones keeps me from moving. I'm swathed in light, but I can see Maks's hand dangling over the side of the bed.

Slowly, his finger twitches. He lifts his hand, reaching, reaching. And I'm not there to hold him. I need to be there.

My sisters are shouting. Lady de la Muerte calls my name. I turn to her. She uses her spear to stab at Alex's shield. The red light fills the room, pulsing to the beat of my heart. Death stares down at her hands. Her spear vanishes in an iron-gray cloud.

Then Death is still.

The shadows that trail at her back disappear. The names that scrolled on her forearms are gone, leaving nothing but translucent white skin.

There's ringing all around, but I realize it's not in my head. The machines Maks is hooked up to are emitting a round of sirens, whistles, and rapid beeps.

Maks's finger twitches again. I try to raise my hand, but it's like I'm magnetized to the floor, like I'm at the eye of a storm and for the first time in so long, my heart is full. The wound on my arm is starting to sting. But I have to let him know that I'm here, that I saved him. I push and push until I'm there.

When I touch Maks's hand, hold it in mine, the sound of sirens disappears. Even La Muerte is gone. No one calls my name anymore either. There is just his hand in mine. He squeezes once. Just once.

Then, his hand goes slack, and I hear one more thing—the endless, unforgiving trill of a flat line.

8

La Tristesa lives alone in a river of salt,

filled by all the world's tears.

—BOOK OF DEOS

W hat have you done to yourself?" a doctor asks
me, her voice full of pity.

I float between waking and unconscious-
ness as my body is rushed down a hallway. Dark faces surround
me, each one is like staring an X-ray, down to the radioactive skeletons beneath their skin.

"You have betrayed me," La Muerte says. Her voice is inside my
head, louder than my own thoughts and memories.

"You betrayed me first!" I shout. "Where did you take him?"

Strong hands pin me down to the bed. Something pricks my
arm, then a numbness travels along my skin. I lift my head to look
at the hands sewing up my cut, but the fingers that holds the needle
are nothing but bone.

"You're all dead," I say, thrashing and kicking. I scream until my voice is hoarse and it takes half a dozen people to strap me down. My body no longer feels like it's mine. The pain is there, like it has become part of me and I'll never be rid of it.

"*I need a psych eval*," one of the skeletons shouts into the darkness, shoving a syringe into my good arm.

And for a long time, I lie still, staring at the lights on the ceiling, like white suns floating over me. I don't realize I've been asleep until I hear the steady beep of the heart monitor.

Maks was pronounced dead at 2:18 a.m. two days ago.

Two days since both my cantos failed, since my magic failed, since I failed. Two days of questions and tests and people walking on eggshells around me.

When I woke up today, I pretended to still be asleep to avoid the shrink they keep sending in. I don't want to see anyone. Not doctors or nurses or my parents or Alex. Rose is the only comfort because when she's with me, she doesn't force me to talk.

Maks is dead, I think.

Lady de la Muerte took him. Then, she just disappeared. One minute she was there, and the next she was gone. Like Maks. One minute he was awake. The next he was gone.

I try to swallow the terrible taste on my tongue. I'm thirsty. I ache in parts of my body I didn't know could ache. Through the open blinds, I can see Alex talking to the police as Rose lingers against the wall by herself. My parents talk to the doctors. Maks's mother is there too, dressed in mourning black. She keeps her head bent into her husband's chest and a fresh swell of tears streams from my eyes.

None of them are aware I'm awake except for one person—the nurse that stopped to speak to me on the way to Maks's room. I wonder if he's mad, if he regrets not making me go back to my room the night of the canto. I want to close my eyes again, but it was so hard to open them that I stare back at him. He makes for my room, and I sink my face deeper into the covers.

The door opens, and I hear him walk across the floor. I can feel him standing beside my bed.

"I'm sorry about your boyfriend," he says, picking up my medical chart.

He's the first person in this hospital to say that to me. I choke on a sob because I don't want sympathy. I want Maks's mother to shout at me. I want Detective Hill to throw me in jail for murder. I want blame, not forgiveness.

"But you're stronger than this," he says softly.

"How would you know something like that?" I ask reflexively.

"I suppose I'm speaking from what I've seen so far." The sound of his pen scratching against paper bothers me, and I pull up the covers over my ears.

"Your family wants to see you. Should I tell them you're awake?"

"I don't want to see anyone."

"Well, you have to. No one has ever seen anything like this."

"Like what?" Not even Rose would tell me what happened after I passed out the first time. I bring down my covers and look at him. His brown hair is still tied back, and the dark circles around otherwise young eyes are deeper than last I saw him. I wonder if he's gone home at all.

"I'll tell you everything I know if you promise to let your family see you."

"Yes, okay. Tell me."

He takes a seat on the chair beside me. He sighs and shakes his head slightly. "One of your sisters went to get a nurse because Maks's vitals were showing he was waking up. You were on the floor. They carried you out and gave you a blood transfusion. Thankfully, you didn't damage anything vital when you slashed open your arm."

That doesn't make sense. I heard him flatline. How could I have heard him flatline if I wasn't in the room? But saying that would send me to the psych wing.

"Are you sure they took me away?" I ask.

He nods. "We took him off life support because he was trying to breathe on his own. For all intents and purposes, Maks was awake. I checked his vitals. He called out for you. Said your name once. He tried to fight the nurses and ripped the stitches in his abdomen. We were able to sedate him. When we sent him for X-rays, they showed that his bones were healed completely. The bleeding stopped in his stomach. He didn't look like he'd just had his spine shattered or had a metal pole driven through his torso. But by all scientific reasoning, he shouldn't have been alive."

I shut my eyes, fighting the ache in my skull. "Where did you learn your bedside manner?"

"I guess that happens when you're around a lot of dead people. You forget how to talk to the living." The corner of his mouth quirks up, not quite a smile. He licks his lips and sits forward, like he caught himself getting too comfortable. He looks over his shoulder at where my family is huddled, gripping coffee cups like lifelines. Maks's parents are gone.

"Keep going," I urge him on. *Maks was alive.* I didn't completely fail. So what went wrong?

"We called his parents and told them that Maks was awake. They'd gone home for the first time in five days. They came in to see him. He even smiled at his mother. Then, he started seizing. Apparently when he was born, he had a hole in his heart. It was repaired, but the doctors say despite the miracle, his heart gave out."

I try to stifle a cry and it comes out as a whimper.

"Sometimes there are signs of recovery, and then—"

"I don't need to hear that." My canto went wrong. My magic failed me. I've never felt so helpless and alone, and I don't know how to start fixing all the things I've said to my family. "Please leave."

He nods once and moves toward the door. "I'll send your family back in. We had a deal."

I sit up, every muscle in my core and arms throbbing angrily.

"What were you thinking?" Mom says. Now that she knows I'm alive, she's gone from worried to angry. No, the look on her face tells me she's more than angry. Scared. Disappointed. "What if we couldn't get to you in time?"

"It worked," I say and look at Alex. "For a moment, it worked."

My dad sits on the chair beside me. Alex and Rose hover around my bed with guilty looks on their faces.

"You of all people should've known better, Alejandra."

Alex shuts her eyes, prepared to take whatever comes. There's a green ring around her eye when she takes off her sunglasses. I can see the bruises on her chest, barely covered by her shirt. "Ma—"

"Don't *Ma* me right now. All three of you have no idea what forces you're dealing with. You've put a target on this family."

"Carmen," my father says. His voice is even and calm. "She just lost him. Let her grieve."

My mother's chest rises and falls quickly. Her brown eyes glisten. My mother doesn't cry. Ever. Now, she blinks the tears back so not a single one falls.

"Don't tell me about loss, Patricio. I lost you for years."

We're silent.

The steady beep of the heart rate monitor reminds us that we're here, that there is nothing being said for minutes that stretch out, long and painful. Rose trembles and cries silently. Alex frowns at the floor. They hold each other's hands, and a distance grows between them and me.

I'm so weary all I say is, "Can we go home?"

Before my mother can answer, a new nurse comes in.

"You're awake," she tells me, holding up her clipboard to write something. "I'll check on you in just a minute."

"The other nurse already checked them," I tell her.

"What nurse?" Her smooth forehead crinkles.

"The guy," I say. I try to think of his name but can't remember if he ever told us. I look to Alex. "We saw him the other night…"

I leave it implied that it was when we were going to Maks's room.

Alex shakes her head. "I don't think he told us his name."

"What did he look like?" the nurse asks, a hand to her hip. Her voice is high-pitched, and I can sense her sudden nervous energy.

70

I can't really remember his face, but I can remember the most striking parts about him. "Young. Long ponytail. Tan. He was wearing blue scrubs and dress shoes."

"Long ponytail?" Now she looks concerned. "I don't know any male nurse or anyone here who looks like that. Give me a minute."

"What's going on?" Mom raises her voice.

The nurse starts to leave. But I have to know. Who was he? Was everything he said to me true?

"Wait!"

"I'm sorry," she says, "but I have to report this right away."

Then she's gone, rushing out the door with her sneakers squeaking against the floor. We sit in silence for a little while longer. Mom keeps pacing and muttering prayers. Dad hesitates before placing his hand on top of mine, like he thinks he won't be welcome. I'm surprised at how foreign it feels, so much so that I almost pull away. Instead, I just lie there and retrace my steps during the canto—the brightness of our magic and the dark that slithered in there. La Muerte breaking through Alex's barrier. *You have betrayed me.*

Then, my nurse runs past my room and points down the hall. A trio of security guards rush in the direction she's pointing. The static of their walkie-talkies alerts others to a potential threat. I pull off my covers, but my mom presses her hand on my shoulder.

The nurse comes back in. Her cheeks are flushed and she places her hands on her heart.

"What happened?" my dad asks.

"Lula," the nurse says, her voice slow and deep. "I need you to

71

tell me everything that man said to you. Try to remember exactly what he looked like and what he said."

You're stronger than this. That's what he said.

"Why?" I ask. I rip off the tabs that measure my heartbeat to make the beeping stop. "What did he do?"

"He doesn't work here." She traces the symbol of the cross over her chest.

"How can he not work here?" Alex asks. "We've seen him for *days.*"

There's a loud commotion outside my bedroom. Alex goes to the window and pulls open the blinds. Detective Hill runs past with the three security guards from before. More police officers join them.

"Are you saying someone's been posing as a nurse?" my mom asks protectively.

The nurse is in a daze, like she can't believe what she's about to say. "We caught him on security camera entering the morgue. That's where the cops are going now."

I feel my heart sink. "What would he want in the morgue?"

Maks.

"The bodies," she says, trembling. "They're all missing."

PART II

THE BODY

Through and through
the passage of time.
Upward and downward,
your love will be mine.
—WITCHSONG #12,
BOOK OF CANTOS

This could've been a love story.

But Maks is dead and I have to come to terms with everything I've done.

I hurt myself. I corrupted my magic. I betrayed my mother's trust. I made my sisters complicit. I have more questions than answers, more regret than hope, and a pain that might never go away. Yet I'm still alive when others aren't. The world is upside down, but there's a twisting, unshakable hurt in my chest that just wants Maks back.

Maybe I shouldn't. Maybe it's wrong. But I do.

"Lula." Rose's voice brings me back to the present. Her eyes glance toward the news. "Do you want me to turn it off?"

I shake my head and try to smile. She hits the mute button anyway.

I should focus on my visitors.

It's mid-June and two days since I've been home. Our summers are usually spent darkening our skin at Coney Island. But I know this summer will be different because I'm different in ways I can't even explain.

Today would've been prom, but it was canceled out of respect for the families of the dead. My dress is hanging in my closet, wrapped in clear plastic from the dry cleaner. I was going to go to Kassandra's house to get ready, and Paul and Maks were going to pick us up.

At least you're alive, a voice hisses at me.

I catch a silent tear from the corner of my eye and try to focus on my guests. I can't climb the stairs every day, so my parents turned the living room into my bedroom. Ma even brought down my altar, but I can't bring myself to light any of the colorful, new candles the girls have brought for me. A tall, black taper with gold flecks—to banish evil. A cherry-red candle mixed with white rose petals—to mend a broken heart. Simple white ones in tall glass cylinders—a new start.

The brujas from my magic lessons are here to cheer me up, despite the High Circle warning them to stay away. Adrian, whose dad would have a stroke if he knew his son was here, is having his tarot cards read by Rose. Paloma, Emma, and Mayi regale me with gossip about local brujas, but they circle back to me and the accident when the news replays their breaking story.

"That's the detective that was here earlier, right?" Paloma points at the screen. She sits crossed-legged on the carpet, her slender fingers toying with her straight, raven-black hair. "Is he still asking you questions?"

Emma sighs, pressing her hand to her chest. She's got her mother's blue eyes and russet hair. Her Argentine accent is musical, and her voice is as sharp as her features. "You're so lucky. Imagine if you'd been caught working real magic. At least they just think you were going to—" She can't say it, so she points at the bandages on my left arm. "Romeo-and-Juliet yourself."

A dark laugh leaves my lips, and it scares them. "Yeah, *at least* I'm that lucky."

"You know you can talk to us," Mayi says, but her voice is drowned out by Emma.

"I'm just saying." Emma lifts a shoulder and drops it dramatically. "The High Circle—"

"Can't touch me," I say, holding her gaze until she looks away first.

"No." She picks at a loose thread on the carpet. "But the Knights of Lavant can. My mom says the hunters will look for any excuse to arrest us. The sinmago police haven't caught that nurse guy, and a bunch of bodies vanished into thin air. How long before they come looking for you?"

"Let's hope they catch him," Mayi says. "Because then you witches are off the hook."

"We're not *on* the hook," Rose says. She never takes her eyes off the card she flips. The ten of daggers, each one driven through a tiny hare.

I swallow the knot sensation in my throat, but it doesn't help. I have a terrible feeling. It's everywhere—my gut, my heart, my bones. Sometimes when I look at people out of the corner of my eyes, I see skeletons instead of bodies. What if La Muerte cursed

77

me? What if the hunters come for us? What if the Alliance locks me up?

"Maybe we should talk about something else," Paloma says, taking a dulce de leche puff from one of the many sugary treats on the coffee table. It's amazing how some people can avoid reality so easily, turning to something like self-preservation and denial mixed together. "My aunt Reina is teaching me how to conjure crystals. But I can only get them the size of a bead right now."

"You look really good on TV," Mayi says, raising a mirror to check her lipstick. The bright pink is a beautiful contrast on her dark brown skin, but when she presses her fingers to her high cheekbone, her glamour magic ripples.

Mayi was the first person to show up with a bouquet of pink carnations, El Amor's favorite flower, and a tray of her famous brownies dotted with huge chunks of caramel. I know Mayi means well, but everything she says makes me want to smash the candles on my altar and scream. I remind myself that she doesn't know what to say to me. None of them do, so they just talk and talk and don't think of their words. Everyone wants me to *be* better, *feel* better, without giving me the time to do so.

"The camera adds ten dark circles," I say, fastening my bathrobe to give my hands something to do.

"Really?" Emma asks, her lips a round and confused *O*.

"She's just playing," Mayi tells Emma. "You look really skinny though, Lu. Your waist is the size of my neck. What diet did they have you on, 'cause I'm about to try it?"

"The Nearly Dead Diet," Rose grumbles. She glares at Mayi and snatches another caramel brownie from the large tray.

"Don't worry, Rosie. Your baby weight will fall right off soon enough." Mayi smiles, and I'm pretty sure she says half the things she does to get under people's skin.

"I wish I could say the same for your personality," Alex tells her, marching from the kitchen and past the living room archway. Stacks of clean towels and bedsheets are balanced in her arms. She winks at Rose and heads back upstairs.

"No one was talking to you!" Mayi shouts.

She's fought with Alex since they were kids. For a long time, Mayi was the one with a strange power. Glamour magic isn't rare, but it isn't common either. It's unique enough that the High Circle always said they'd keep a spot open for her when she grew into her powers. But when Alex came of age as an encantrix, the invitation went away.

Although, after everything that's happened now, I don't think the High Circle wants anything to do with any of the Mortiz girls.

I almost feel sorry for Mayi. From the corner of my eye, I can see her real face, the one she hides behind her glamour, under the illusion. Her nose is crooked from a nasty fall when she was ten, and her dark skin is dotted with angry-red acne that no elixir has been able to cure. Every time she hides her face behind the glamour, new marks appear on her skin, and in turn, she hides it with more magic. But that's the thing—one of our universal laws is that we can't use our power on ourselves. I can't heal myself and Rose can't see her own future. And so, the more Mayi glamours *herself*, the worse it'll be for her in the end.

"I can't believe you're on TV," Paloma says, voice like sticky syrup. "I've always wanted to be on TV."

Mayi slaps her upside the head. "Do you *also* want to go to the hospital?"

Paloma realizes the folly of her wish and gives me an apologetic smile.

"Where's Alex going?" Adrian, a new addition to our class, asks. He's fifteen and one of Gustavo's sons. He cranes his neck toward the creaky wooden stairs that lead to the second floor.

"She's helping my mother," I say. "Does your dad know you're here?"

"He knows I'm with Mayi," he says by way of explanation. His hair is a mop of straight, inky blackness, and his skin is hazelnut brown. "Are they healing? Can I watch? My dad never lets me do anything."

"Yes, they're healing," I say, slumping down on the couch. I am grateful for my friends' visit, but they've been here for hours, and I'm exhausted from their endless questions about what it felt like to be put to sleep or have doctors prod around in my gut. "And no, you can't watch."

He frowns. "I wanted to talk to Alex about what to do—you know, when your powers come."

"Why don't you talk to us?" Paloma asks, and if her voice were a color, it would be an acidic green.

"Because she's an *encantrix*," Adrian says, as if it should be obvious. "She's the only one in our generation."

"And she knows nothing about magic or our history," Mayi says, sounding more like her mother every day.

"None of that matters," I say. "You can be the perfect little bruja, but the Deos won't care, if they ever cared at all."

"How can you say that?" Emma asks.

"Easy, I use my words." I eat another sweet thing they've brought for me, but the sugar takes like dust and I've lost my appetite again.

"There's no need to be snippy with Emma," Mayi says. "We know you're going through a hard time."

"No, you don't." I sit up, my words turning to poison as they slither off my tongue. "You don't know anything about what I've gone through or what I've seen. You guys want to sit around in a circle and summon ghosts and glamour yourselves for fun, but the rest of us have to deal with real life. My sister is an encantrix, but if you want to talk smack about her, *I* will be the one to end you."

Paloma rolls her eyes and scoffs in my direction. "You're no fun anymore, Lula."

You're no fun anymore.

No.

Fun.

Anymore.

Her words ring in my ears. Maks said something like that to me once...

I don't care what Paloma thinks. They don't understand. Not my sinmago friends and not these *witches*. Magic transforms. Magic is also unpredictable and unforgiving. You don't know who you'll become after wielding it.

Suddenly, despite the room full of brujas and a brujo, I feel alone. My heart gives a sharp jolt, like there's something piercing it. I shut my eyes and let the pain subside.

81

"It's hurting again, isn't it?" Mayi says, frowning. "You should tell your mom."

I breathe in and out slowly. I keep getting this pain in my chest. I have so many broken parts that a tiny pinch in my chest should be the least of my worries. But it keeps happening at odd intervals.

"We can try to heal you," Paloma says. The most Paloma has ever used her power for is to change her failing grades into As. "We're not natural healers like you, but maybe there's something in the Book of Cantos."

"And wind up turning into a slug?" I say, trying to sound like the old Lula. The one they expect me to be so quickly. "I'll pass."

"Have a little faith," Mayi tells me. In this light, she's ethereal. Like a fairy queen lounging, taking slow bites of the chocolate-caramel treats.

"I have faith," I say, gruffer than I wanted to.

But Mayi looks at my unkempt altar and Emma purses her lips skeptically.

"Well," Paloma says, "we've failed in cheering you up."

"I'm sorry," I say. "It's too soon."

These same girls I've know my whole life, girls I've shared magic with, stare at me like I'm a stranger. Their eyes are full of worry and something else I couldn't place until just now: fear. They're all afraid of me, with the exception of Adrian. He looks like he wants to move in and fanboy over my sister.

"Thank you for coming over," I tell them, trying to salvage this visit. Rose goes upstairs to help our parents and Alex.

My friends gather their purses, and I walk them out. The girls kiss me on the cheek and give me their blessings. Before they reach the door, they touch the statue of La Mama that we keep in the foyer, as is customary.

Each girl does this—rubs the hand and walks out. I stand on the porch and watch them exit our metal fence and turn down the street. They hold hands and break into a laugh halfway down the block.

Jealousy tugs at me because I can't remember the last time I laughed like that. I can't remember the last time I didn't have a nightmare featuring shadow monsters or skeletons reaching for my throat.

"Hey," Adrian says, standing behind me.

I jump and swear loudly. "Don't sneak up on people. Why didn't you leave with your Circle?"

"I wasn't sneaking," he says. "And I don't want to be part of that circle. I just came because I wanted to meet Alex."

"I'll tell her you stopped by, kid," I tell him, and start to head back inside.

"Does it get easier?" he asks, shoving his hands in his pockets. At first glance, he's a normal kid—fresh kicks, new jeans, a band T-shirt. Now, looking into his big, brown eyes framed by eyelashes most girls would kill to have, I see the power he doesn't know what do with. The power that haunts my own family. "The magic, I mean. Does it get easier?"

How do I give this kid hope when I don't have any for myself? I swallow the hurt that bubbles up in my throat and blink away the new tears that are multiplying like the heads of a hydra.

"Not always," I say honestly. "It's different for everyone. Have you told your dad?"

He shakes his head. "He wants to wait for my Deathday to let me try any cantos. But look." He holds his hand out, palm up, and conjures a tiny tornado that spins at the center, flecks of dirt and tiny leaves are pulled into the breeze. It's only for a second, but it's some of the most beautiful magic I've seen in so long. Magic without death or darkness.

I take his hand in mine, and the baby tornado disappears as I close his fingers into a fist. "That's amazing."

He looks down at his sneakers shyly. "Really?"

"Yes, really. But you have to be careful. Talk to your dad, okay? I'm sure Alex would love to help you out too. But first, start with family." *Take your own advice*, a voice whispers in the back of my thoughts.

He smiles and runs down the porch steps, waving at me. Most of the brujas I know have faint traces of power, and here Adrian can command the wind. I head back in the house to get Alex, but I notice a bundle left on the floor.

Flowers.

They're still wrapped in plastic. They're the darkest plum, nearly black in the shadow of our doorstep. I never knew flowers could be this color or shape, wild and elegant at the same time, like a cross between orchids and roses. There's no note attached.

I can't imagine who would leave me flowers. A sharp ache pulls at my chest again when I think of the impossible. *Maks.*

I bring the flowers in with me and shut the door.

I sit in front of the TV, but only the evening news is on, and we don't have cable. I flip channels, but the same image appears every time I press the button. A breeze finds its way into the living room, bringing the scent of summer barbecue and car exhaust.

The door must be open.

I shake my head. I thought I shut it. I *know* I shut it. But yesterday I also put the remote in the freezer.

My body aches in protest as I get off the couch again. After I close the door, I turn the bottom lock and the dead bolt and do the chain on top.

I settle back on the couch and wrap myself in a blanket. Wailing noises come from upstairs, where it's all hands-on deck as my mom tries to heal five fairy children who picked a fight with a preteen werewolf pack.

I ignore the tugging sensation in my chest. It's not pain. It's like dust that never settles. It's like the rumble before a storm.

Then, I see the words flash red across the screen. TWO BROOKLYN TEENS FOUND DEAD.

I turn up the volume as loud as possible.

The news anchor looks somberly into the camera and speaks. "Reports confirm two teenage boys were found and pronounced dead on the scene in Concy Island, Brooklyn. Adam Silvera is on-site with the person who discovered the bodies. Adam?"

The camera cuts to a crowded street. The setting sun is red and angry behind the tall reporter as he holds out a microphone to a middle-aged black woman whose eyes look like they're going to pop out of her skull.

"Thanks, Naomi. I'm here with Beatrice Jean. Mrs. Jean, can you tell us what you saw?"

"I just finished my shift at the hospital. I walk home. I've always felt safe. When I tripped over something, I thought I was being attacked. I didn't know what I was seeing. My feet were covered in blood. How did no one *see* them? No one—"

"It sounds like you're in shock."

"Of course I'm shocked. I've lived here for thirty years. I've never in my life seen something like this." She makes the sign of the cross over her torso.

"Thank you for your time." The camera moves away from Mrs. Jean's face, but the haunted look in her eyes lingers in my mind. The mic shakes in Adam's hand. "The police have closed down neighboring streets and are canvasing the areas. There are no suspects. One of the victims has been identified as a student from Thorne Hill High School by his school ID. The other victim carried no identification."

My heart thunders in my chest and I double over as the pain becomes unbearable.

Despite that, I have a driving urge to run. I pull on jeans and a hoodie and head for the door. I don't leave a note. I don't take my phone.

I rub the hand of La Mama's statue as I leave, but when my thumb grazes the porcelain, the hand breaks cleanly off at the wrist.

Words echo in my ears. *You have betrayed the Deos.*

When I unlock the door and step outside, my body sighs. A light, warm as flesh but completely transparent, materializes over my chest. It unfurls into a dozen silver threads that float in front of me like jellyfish tentacles.

One string of silver light is brighter than the rest, and it tugs me forward. I don't know where it leads, but if I want answers about what's happening to me, I know I have to follow it.

10

And they feared
her touch so cold,
her cloak of shadow,
her thorns of gold.

Song of Lady de la Muerte,
Book of Cantos

I race toward the subway. Garbage and dirty water lodged in storm drains cook under the June sun. Nothing smells like New York during the summer. As I pass a mass of strangers, no one bats an eye at me or the silver thread coming from my chest.

I run across the street to make the light. The pain shoots up my hips and settles around my abdomen, and I stumble into an old woman selling mangos from a cart.

"¿Estas bien?" she asks me, raising a gloved hand stained with sticky fruit juice.

I try to smile, but when she looks at the scars on my face, she can't help but jump back a bit.

"I'm fine," I say. "Thank you."

I enter the subway station, swipe my MetroCard, push the turn-stile with my hands, and make a beeline toward the front end of the platform. I tie my hair into a bun and pull up my hood. I'm wearing Maks's hoodie from his first year on the team. It's too big for me, but hopefully it'll help cover up my curves and make me look like a boy. My face has been on the evening news as the only survivor of the crash, and I don't want to be recognized.

The train barrels into the station, stale air pushing against my hot skin when the doors open up. The train car is empty because there's a man passed out across three seats and the air conditioner is broken. It's better this way, less chance I'll be recognized.

I take a seat on the opposite end of the car. I try to breathe through my mouth, but the smell is overwhelming, like stale beer, sea sludge, and urine. It's only a few more stops to Coney Island. I stare at the thin, white scars on the top of my hands from the shat-tered glass that fell around me during the crash. The silver threads from my chest have dimmed except for one, floating in the direc-tion the train is going.

My heart gives another painful tug. I imagine this is what fish feel like when they have a hook driven through their cheeks and then get reeled in. I lean my head back, feeling every bump and jostle the train makes when a whistling noise fills the air.

"Lula Mortiz," something hisses.

The man jerks into a sitting position. His skin is pale and covered in dirt, and his hair is matted into clumps.

His eyes snap open and find me instantly. His irises go from brown to black, then spread like an ink stain across the whites of his eyes. His mouth stretches in an unnatural way, like someone is pulling his jaw open. Tattered shadows slither from the ground and trail inside, rattling his entire body.

My heart races as I dart to the doors. The train is approaching the next stop, but the platform zooms by.

"Oh hell." I rattle off a string of curses and start to run for the red emergency lever you're never supposed to pull. What's more of an emergency than being attacked on the train by someone possessed?

But the train breaks abruptly. The momentum flips me over once, and I hit the sticky floor with a *thud*. I fear I've ripped my stitches as something wet hits my skin. When I touch it and bring it to my nose, it's just ketchup.

The train conductor makes an announcement. We're stuck between stations, the lights flickering inside the car and out in the tunnel.

"Ladies and gentlemen"—*crackle muffle crackle*—"unexpected" —*crackle static*—"shortly."

Great. I'm locked in a train car with a possessed man while my body is being pulled like there's a master puppeteer at work.

I push up on my elbows. My wrist feels sprained, but I rummage through my belongings for something, anything, I can use. My pockets are empty except for a few bucks and my MetroCard and keys!

I crab crawl away from the man, who stands slowly. The last of the shadows enter his mouth, and when he's done shaking, his black eyes snap to where I'm crawling on the dirty floor of the Q train.

I grab my keys and grip them tightly between my fingers. Jumbled thoughts fill my head:

I survived a multivehicle crash and two surgeries, but I'm going

*to be murdered in the subway. Why did I leave my pepper spray
at home? Why didn't I leave a note for my sisters so they'll know
where to look for me? Why did I yell at my dad for the past eight
months he's been home? Why do people throw their garbage here?
Why isn't my power as strong as Alex's? Just—why?*

Then, at that thought, the man reaches for me and I strike my
fist into his gut. He makes a choking sound but keeps advancing.
His breath is hot on my face, and my stomach turns when he grabs
my shoulder. I kick wildly until he stumbles back a few steps, but
I'm positive it hurts me more than him. I scream through the pain
as I roll over. I try to pull myself up, but the train jostles and I
fall again.

"I'm not here to hurt you, Lula Mortiz," the voice hisses. His
face contorts, fighting the thing inside him.

"I don't believe you," I say, despite the fear that makes my legs
tremble. I've heard of possessions but I've never seen one. Its dark
energy ripples beneath pale graying flesh. "What are you?"

The man shakes his head slowly, cracked lips lifting over rotten
teeth. "You know me."

I do. The way my insides twist and my skin puckers with the
sudden temperature drop tell me exactly who this is.

Lady de la Muerte.

Her voice is like a living shadow, slithering and coiling around
my senses.

When I struggle to get to my feet, I drag myself on the floor
until I hit the locked train doors.

"What do you want?" is all I can get out.

"Not want. *Need.*"

Lights spark in the tunnel as the train tries to move but can't. The conductor cranks out another announcement. Something about the breaks. Something about connections. Don't worry. Stay calm. We're moving shortly.

But help isn't coming for me.

"You've betrayed me." She speaks through the man. "You have betrayed the balance of the worlds."

My first reaction is to say, *I know*, but I can't be snarky with Death.

"Then what are you waiting for?" I ask. I hold my arms out to the sides and I drop my keys. I can't fight her. I'm not strong enough to fight her. The train slams to another stop, but the possessed body rises inches off the floor and is suspended in air.

He opens his mouth again, shadows undulating like dark water. "I need you."

"What could I possibly give you? You're a god."

"I am trapped between—" she says, the last word cuts out in static. The possessed man's neck turns at an unnatural angle, bones snapping when the head moves too close to the shoulder. "You must free me."

Death isn't here to kill me. My moment of brief relief is instantly replaced with panic.

"Free you? How? Where are you?"

The man starts to shake and cough up black mucus. His head rolls back and his mouth snaps wide open as the living shadow starts to escape. "Retrieve my spear. You do not know what you've created—"

"Trapped between what?" I ask. "Where is the spear?"

The shadows purge from the man's mouth and leave him unconscious on the floor.

The lights above stop flickering, and the train moves again at a snail's pace. I hold on to the metal rung, unable to steady my hand.

Death is trapped. Death wants me to free her.

I'm swallowing the dryness on my tongue when I realize the man on the ground hasn't moved since La Muerte left his body. The train lurches forward and barrels out of the tunnel and into the light of the aboveground platforms.

The train chugs into the next station. I kneel and put my hand on his shoulder to jostle him awake.

He doesn't move.

I press my fingers on his neck to feel for a pulse that isn't there. The train comes to a stop. I have to get out of here. The thread in my chest returns, silver threads tugging in different directions. I pull my hoodie closer to my face.

When the doors open, I run and don't look back. Before I reach the subway exit, I hear someone scream, "Someone call 911! He's dead."

When I get out of the subway, I leave the mayhem behind, blending into the crowds of the Coney Island station. The sweet scents of fried dough and sunscreen mingle with sea breeze. I take deep breaths to stop myself from shaking. I think of the fate of the man in the car. There was nothing I could do for him. The gods can't inhabit human bodies, not without killing the host, destroying all traces of their soul and leaving behind a hollowed shell. I press my shaky fingers to my lips and whisper a prayer for the dead man.

I cross the street, following the thread that's been leading me here. Sweat drips down my back and between my breasts. I pull off my hoodie and tie it around my waist. I don't have to worry about being recognized here. Hundreds of people disperse from the train station and across Surf Avenue.

I head down Stillwell Avenue until I'm on the boardwalk. Each step is like wading through a vat of mud, but the light of the threads grows stronger. The pain in my chest throbs like a fresh wound. I hang on to the metal railings and wait for the pain to subside.

When it doesn't, I know something is wrong. My family healed me, and while their magic can't fix everything that's wrong with me, I shouldn't feel this way. I shouldn't feel like there's broken glass at my feet and fire in my muscles.

Right now I want my sisters, even if it means listening to Alex yell at me for being reckless and leaving the house in this condition. For being marked by Lady de la Muerte. For not saying a word about this sensation that's *pulling* me toward an unknown. Sea breeze caresses my face, and a swell of angry tears spill down my cheeks as I keep pushing forward.

I follow the silver thread across uneven boardwalk planks toward the parachute tower. When I see the carousel, I freeze. My heart runs laps in my chest and I turn around so I won't have to look at it. Instead, I watch the dark blue waves and the seagulls that fight for scraps in the sand. This is where Maks brought me on our first date.

The carousel had just been brought back to Coney Island, original wooden horses and all. I rode a white horse decked out in gold filigree and brilliant pastels, and Maks stood beside me. No one has ever looked at me the way he did. He watched me like I was a marvel that could vanish at any moment, like surf breaking over the shoreline—there and then gone.

We went 'round and 'round on that carousel all night, stopping once to buy cotton candy. I don't even remember what we talked about. But I remember the world spinning around us, the twinkling lights, the bell-chime music. I remember the way he leaned in to kiss me, a kiss like the melting of spun sugar across my tongue.

The thread in my chest tugs again—hard. I turn in its direction and face the carousel. The sea air has made the paint crackle and chip, and though the gold accents have lost their shine, there's still something magical about it.

There are other couples and groups of kids on the ride. They casually glance at the guy with the stark gray skin and the scars on his face. They stare at the stained T-shirt that hugs his bruised arms and the red stains around his mouth that looks like blood. But in his hand is a snow cone, cherry ice dribbling down his hand and onto his worn jeans.

The silver thread pulses brighter, faster, and the other end drives into his chest. He looks down, then follows it back to me. Dull blue eyes stare at me without recognition.

I swallow hard and breathe slowly, trying to quiet the fear in my heart. Because there's nothing in any world that could've prepared me for this.

I stand at the edge of the ride and wait for it to come to a full stop. Words fail me as I watch him stand, watch his chest rise and fall.

"Lula," he says, eyes darting around my face, like he's coming out of a fog.

He skips the bottom steps and flings his arms around me. I swallow the cry that gathers in my throat.

"I got lost," he says, gripping my hair and squeezing me until I'm afraid my stitches will rip.

I hold him tighter out of the fear that my legs will give out beneath me. I don't know how this is possible. His skin is cold and his wounds still look fresh, but he's breathing. He's here. La Muerte's warning flits through my mind. *You have betrayed the balance of the worlds.* But I don't care.

Maks is alive.

And nothing—not even La Muerte—will tear us apart.

11

Las Memorias, sisters two,

one who forgets and

one who thinks of you.

—Twin Sisters of the World's Memories,
Book of Deos

A third body was found today in Brooklyn. An unidentified man was discovered dead on a Coney Island–bound Q train this evening. Witnesses describe a young Hispanic boy running off the train in a hurry before the body was discovered. If anyone has information on the suspect, contact the police."

The news plays on the small screen in the back of the taxi that takes Maks and me back to my house.

He stares out the window the entire time. His eyes focus on the strangest things, the flurry of dust in the air, the play of light and shadows as we drive through an underpass, the peeling stickers on the partition, and the single drop of water that hits the window announcing rain.

Every few minutes, he looks at me, and it's like nothing has changed, even though the stitches on both of our faces and bodies say otherwise.

I reach for his hand. The cold of his skin is jarring, but slowly, he stares at our hands and threads his fingers with mine. Familiar.

"What happened to me?" he asks.

I think of my mother's words at the hospital. *I don't know who you'd get back, but it might not be Maks.*

I don't know what to tell him. *You were dying and I tried to save you? You were gone and now you're here?* I try to form a coherent explanation, but what if it scares him? When I was little, when my dad first disappeared, I remember asking my mom, "Where did Dad go?" And she looked at me with a smile and eyes glistening with tears too stubborn to fall. She talked about everything but. "Do you want to see something cool?" she asked me. "Want to see the Circle make magic?"

And I did, because magic was the best thing in my life. Magic was a living, beautiful force that coursed through my veins.

That's when my mom took me to her High Circle meeting and I watched them dance around an ailing person. They covered her in wet corn leaves and used bushels of branches to slap her skin red. They threw flower petals in the air and lit bundles of sage and prayed to the Deos in the Old Tongue. I watched from a corner, promising not to move, to touch, or to make a sound. Respect the Deos, protect our magic.

Now, when Maks asks me what happened to him, I know why my mother always changed the topic. Maks is different. He defies reason, magic, science. But he's still mine, and I have to help him find answers for the both of us.

"Want to see something cool?" I ask him.

The cab driver stops in front of my house. Our car is gone, which means that my family is probably out looking for me and I have time to hide Maks. I don't have anywhere else to take him, and despite the tension of the past few months, home has always been the safest place I know.

I dig into my jeans and discover I don't have enough cash to cover the ride. The cab driver starts clucking his tongue, demanding his money.

"I got it. Hang on," I say.

Maks stares at the divider. He traces the crack that splinters from the center.

Then I realize, Maks isn't wearing his own clothes. They're too tight and dated. Where did he get them? Who did he take them from? How did I just notice the dark stain on the pant leg? But before I can start to answer all of this, we have to get inside.

I reach into his back pocket and pull out a thin leather wallet. A voice in the back of my head tells me there's something wrong. To put it back and listen to the warnings I've been given. *You've betrayed me. You must free me.*

But instead I open the wallet and pull out the bills I need, plus a big tip to keep the driver's mouth shut. I put the wallet in my hoodie pocket and decline the receipt he offers me. The taxi pulls away the second I shut the door.

Maks walks ahead of me and through the front gate, looking up at my narrow, old house.

"You've never let me in here before," he says, holding his hand out for me to take.

I smile, but it hurts, and I take the arm he offers. Maks always wanted to plan dinners with my parents, but I always came up with an excuse. Relief gives me a moment of clarity. Maybe he's slowly getting his memory back. Maybe everything will work out.

I turn the key and leave my sneakers at the front door. The statue of La Mama with her broken hand stares at me as I shut the door.

"It smells like Christmas," he says, every word slow and thoughtful. Maks always had a calm, relaxed quality about him that I loved. He wasn't as hyper or loud as some of the other boys on the team. But the stillness of the way he's speaking now feels wrong.

"Rose baked," I say. I might be imagining things. I should be happy he's here. He's really here. "Are you hungry?"

He jerks back when he sees my hand reaching for his cheek. His eyes widen, the blue turns pale, his pupils shrink to pinpricks. He rakes his nails across his throat, leaving sharp red lines.

"Oh God…I ate—I ate—"

"What's wrong?" I ask, still reaching. "It's okay. Whatever it is, I'm going to help you."

He keeps walking backward, toward the front door. I want to grab him. I want to help him. I want to hold him in my arms and fix this—whatever this is. But he walks into the statue of La Mama. The statue topples over and I dive to grab it, pressing it against my chest. Blood seeps through the bandage on my arm. I'll have to change it later. I pull myself up and put the statue back in place.

"I should go home." He paces the foyer. "My mom is waiting for me. I was supposed to play and I forgot. I should go home."

"Wait," I say, keeping my distance. He's like a spooked horse and I don't know what set him off. "You can't."

"Why?" He squints and presses his hands against his temples, as if the light in the living room is too bright. I flick it off, leaving only the sunset casting a warm glow through the windows. He turns around, pressing his fists against the wall. He grinds his teeth, then slams his fist over and over until it goes through.

"Stop! You're going to hurt yourself."

"I can't! Everything already hurts. I don't know. I don't know what is wrong with me." He pulls his hand back, bits of Sheetrock crumbling around his bloody fist. He wipes his hands on his jeans. He looks at them. They're still dirty. "I'm sorry."

"Your parents aren't home." It's a lie. But how can I send him home like this? What if he hurts himself? Or worse, what if he hurts someone else? "You have to stay here for a little while. Do you trust me?"

His eyes snap up in my direction. He takes my face in his hands, and for the first time since I've known him, a pang of fear strikes my heart. "How can you ask me that? Of course, I do."

I rush to the closet in our infirmary room, where we keep spare clothes for our patients, and grab a clean white shirt and sweat-pants. Hopefully they'll fit better than what he's wearing now.

As I make my way out of the infirmary and down the hall, my footsteps are heavy. There are too many questions floating around my head, too many things to do. So I focus on what I can handle right now. *Get Maks clean. Make a calming draught. Get him fed.*

In my head, he's old Maks. Playful Maks. Sweet Maks.

"I smell like a Dumpster," he says when I push open the bathroom door. He takes his clothes off and tosses them in a pile on the corner. "How can you be around me?"

"This is nothing compared to the way you stink after you've been practicing for eight hours straight." I get the water running for him because the knobs are old and reversed.

"What the f—" he shouts. I look up to see him stare at his chest. "Where did all these scars come from?"

I'm afraid he's going to punch another hole in the wall. I don't move. I look at him and tell him as much truth as he'll be able to handle. "We had an accident. You keep forgetting."

But he doesn't rage out. He wipes the steam from the mirror and looks at himself. "I can't tell what's a memory and what's a dream. I'm sorry I scared you before."

"It's okay," I say, but my gut tells me it *isn't*. "It'll be okay."

He frowns, dark eyebrows knitting together. His fingers, cold and gentle, skim the scars on my cheek. "Was this from the accident too?"

I nearly jump out of my skin. It's been days since my last Bellaza Canto. I hold my hand over my scars.

"No, Lula," he says, taking my hands in his. He kisses my scarred knuckles. "I swear, I didn't mean to make you feel bad. I've always loved your face. Still do."

When he talks like that, it's easy for me to want to forget everything that happened, to want things to go back to the way they used to be for so long.

But Maks's skin has a dull paleness that worries me. I rest my hand on his shoulder, try not to wince at how cold he is. I can hardly breathe as my hand roams the muscles of his chest, searching, searching.

I've found it—the whisper of his heartbeat, so faint it's hardly there at all.

While Maks gets cleaned up, I work on a sleeping draught in the infirmary. It's strange being in here, putting a potion together after avoiding it for months.

The walls are papered with a green leaf pattern that looks newer than any part of our old house. Ma says it makes patients feel more at home. Alex thinks that the kind of folk who come to us for healing can't get to a hospital anyway, so they won't mind the faded paint in the rest of the house.

The room is filled by an exam table, two twin beds for patients to sleep, and a giant altar dedicated to La Esperanza, Goddess of Sighs and All the World's Goodness. I'll find the ingredients I need against the wall with blackout curtains. The shelves are lined with jars in all shapes and sizes that contain ingredients from every corner of the world: the tears of an infant, the feathers of a blue jay, the eyes of coquis, the hair from a widow's head, all alphabetized by Rose on one of the nights she couldn't sleep.

I turn on the electric kettle and get the jars I need. I scoop dried poppy leaves, chamomile oil, and fresh lavender into a tea pouch. I hold the tea and stand in front of the altar of La Esperanza. Fresh flowers in tall vases of water are set around her feet. Her dress is bright pink, and a crown of silver stars and lilacs rest on her pale-pink hair.

I want to say something, a rezo to make up for all the prayers that have died on my lips, but it's like the words are caught in my throat. So instead, I light one of the tea candles.

La Muerte's shadow voice echoes in my mind. *You do not know what you've created—*

"Lula?" Maks shouts my name and I jump.

I hear the rattle of the fence outside and go to the window. Rose is opening the gate so my mom can pull into the garage.

I hurry out into the hall where Maks is shirtless, his black hair dripping water down his neck. The dirty clothes and towel are in a bundle in his hands. He holds his hand up to shield his eyes from the light in the hallway.

"Come," I say, trying to remain calm, though it's not just for his sake now.

The door downstairs opens, and I hear my sisters call my name. Alex shouts, "Lula! You better be home!"

"I'm fine. I'm in my room!"

I shut the door once Maks and I are inside. I hit the lights, leaving only my reading lamp on.

He stares at every detail. The midnight-blue comforter and white pillows are undisturbed. The flowers at my bedside are long dead in their vase. Maks gave them to me a month ago, when he was trying to cheer me up and I simply couldn't.

I set the tea on the bedside table and close the curtains. I find a match and light some of the dusty candle stubs. My altar has never been this neglected. My first impulse is to clean it. I've offended the gods enough to last me a lifetime, if I even get a whole lifetime after this mess. Right now, all I care about is helping Maks. After all, the Deos abandoned me first.

"Your parents don't know I'm here?" he asks softly.

I shake my head. "It's complicated."

He stands behind me and wraps his hands around my waist. I flinch as his fingers graze the line of stitches on my belly. I breathe through the pain. After all the magic my family spent on me, they should be healed by now.

"I can hide," he whispers against my ear. "I think I could get used to you taking care of me."

I turn around in his arms and reach for the tea. "Start by drinking this. It'll stop your headache and help you sleep."

He takes the mug from my hand but sets it back down on the nightstand. He walks across the length of my room and points to a map of the world pinned to the wall. I had this idea that I'd put a pin in every place I'll travel to one day. But the only pin is in New York, the rest of the world untouched and foreign to me. Maks takes a pin from my desk. He stares at it for a little while.

"Can I?" he asks.

I stand next to him and place my hands on his hips and lean into him. He smells like soap and something I can't quite place— something that shouldn't be there. Smoke? Maybe it's just from the matches I used to light the candles.

He traces his finger from New York to Europe. His finger draws a few circles, like he's searching and can't quite find the place. Then, he lands on Kiev, Ukraine, and pushes the pin.

"My mom took me once," he says. "When my grandmother

passed away. She was one hundred and ten years old. The oldest woman in her village."

He's told me this story before, but I smile and say, "That's amazing."

"I have good genes." He pushes his shoulder against mine and smirks. "I bet I'll live until I'm one hundred and ten, like her."

But you didn't, I think, and a pain tugs at my belly.

"Maks," I start to say. I have to try to explain to him everything that's happened. That way we can get some answers together. I know my family will be upset, but Alex will understand. She has to.

There's a hard knock on the door. I feel Maks tense all over.

Speaking of *El Pain in My Neck*, Alex yells from the other side of my door. "Lula, what the hell is wrong with you?"

Maks twitches, like the thud of her fist is causing him physical pain. I try to soothe him, running my hands along his arms. He shuts his eyes and shoves me away. He loses his own balance in the process and ends up falling against the closet door with a loud thud.

"Lula? Are you okay?" Alex jostles the locked doorknob. "What happened to the wall downstairs?"

"I was working out anger issues," I shout. "Leave me alone."

"My head," Maks says through gritted teeth.

"Close your eyes," I whisper. I brush my lips along his temple, his ear, his jaw. I brush his hair back and murmur soft sounds to try to calm him down. *The calming potion.*

I pick up the cup and bring it to his lips. "It tastes a little weird but it'll help you sleep."

"Lula!"

"This is disgusting." Maks gags and spits on the floor.

"I know, baby." I brush his hair back. I gently tap my finger on his temple. "But it'll help you. I promise."

He nods and drains the cup. He starts to stumble, the draught taking effect instantly. I guide him to my bed to break his fall, then pull back the covers so he can get in. He crawls in, then reaches for me.

"Lula, Lula." His breath is quick and fluttering. He holds my hand and squeezes so hard I'm afraid he'll crush my bones. "Don't go. Leave that light on, please."

"I'm not going anywhere, okay? I'm right here." I rest my head on his chest. His skin is so cold, colder than Rose. When his whistling breath signals he's asleep, I pull off the arm wrapped around my waist. I have to get Alex.

But when I sit up and turn around, she's standing in the doorway, a look of terror on her face.

"Oh, my Lula. What have you done?"

12

La Esperanza hides in the recesses of the soul,

where no one thinks to search.

—REZO FOR LA ESPERANZA,
GODDESS OF SIGHS AND ALL THE WORLD'S
GOODNESS,
BOOK OF DEOS

L et me explain," I say.

I slap my hand over her mouth to muffle her argument, shutting the door behind us. She tries to mumble through my hand but can't, and finally, she bites me.

I swear loudly. Her eyes go wide, flicking behind me. I turn around as Maks stirs in his sleep. He kicks at the comforter and calls out for me again.

"Yeah, explain away, Lula. Because you have no idea what's going through my head right now." Alex holds her hands out as if she's reaching to choke me. The shadows of my room cut across her face. In this moment I am both relieved that I've been caught and terrified of what she'll do.

"I felt this pain right here," I say, pressing my fingers to my chest. "These threads appeared right over my heart. Dozens of them. One of them glowed the brightest."

"Lula, we—"

"You said to explain," I say softly. "So let me. After that you can yell at me some more."

"Don't worry. That's coming." Her hands are at her hips and she makes the same face our mother makes when she's pissed off, all wide eyes and pursed lips.

"At first I thought I was the one who was following the sensation. But when the pain got stronger, I realized that it was reeling me in. I got on the train and then Lady de la Muerte appeared—"

"Stop," Alex says, digging her fingers through her hair. "I said I wouldn't interrupt but I need a second to process this."

I wish she could see what I saw. Then the skepticism that steels her stare might become something like understanding.

"Try actually seeing the Dea of Death possessing a human body. It was awful. It was like she filled his whole being with her essence. His neck just snapped from it. After she spoke to me, I ran and the thread led me to Maks. I didn't know I'd find him there, but, Lula—our canto. It must've worked, right? I felt his pulse. He doesn't remember the accident, but it's him."

Now I'm the one pacing. Every step aches, like there are splinters inside my bones, so I lower myself to the floor and sit. Alex sits down with me, her eyes never leaving Maks, even though he's stopped moving.

"We did it," I tell her. "Somehow, we saved him."

"Then where did he go? Where did the others go?"

A sickness creeps along my skin. I've been so consumed with Maks that I didn't stop to consider the others. "I don't know."

Alex takes a steadying breath. I'd pay anything to be able to read her mind. "What did Lady de la Muerte say when she spoke to you?"

When I think of Lady de la Muerte, a dull ache spreads across my chest. Not because of what I saw her do and not because I'm afraid she's going to do that to me, but because I felt her pain of being stuck in between realms. It was how I felt in Los Lagos, in the Tree of Souls.

"She told me to find her spear. That I betrayed her."

When Alex was little, she bottled up her emotions so tight it caused her to hide her power deep down. Now, her magic glides on her skin. She pushes a pulse of it up my arm, and in that moment, I feel what she's feeling—afraid. Anxious. Helpless.

"*We* betrayed her," Alex says. "You didn't do this alone. But how do we find her spear?"

"I don't know! She slithered out of the body before she could tell me. He died right in front of me."

"We have to tell Ma," she says. "Of all the Deos, Lady de la Muerte is the one we know the least about."

I snatch my hand back. "Telling Ma is not an option."

Alex grabs hold of my shoulders. "Don't you see? We trapped a *goddess* in between worlds. We've broken the balance of life and death. Maks didn't just wake up and walk out of that hospital after our canto. He died. I saw him flatline. Whatever is happening is beyond the reach of two brujas. We need help. La Muerte needs to be freed. What if failing means we lose *you*?"

ZORAIDA CÓRDOVA

"Alex, please. Ma will bring the High Circle into this. What if they want to hurt him?"

"You might not want to hear this," she says quietly, "but he doesn't belong here."

"Well, he *is* here. We have to help him."

"We have to *free* La Muerte." She looks at me so sternly I cower. "I'll do whatever it takes. I'll find something—"

"It has to be me," I whisper.

"I'm the reason this happened."

My laugh is bitter, but I can't stop it. "You wouldn't have done it if I hadn't guilted you."

"I would have," she says, and though her voice is hard, there's a crack at the end. "Because you're my sister. You might be a pain in the ass, but you and Rose are all I've got. I'd do anything for you."

She gives me her cheek and I wonder why everyone in my family does this—tries to act as if nothing hurts us. All that power coursing through my little sister's veins and she still doesn't want me to see her crying.

"We've all made selfish choices. But you can't play with death like this, Lula. Keeping Maks here won't make things go back to how they used to be. Nothing will because we aren't the same girls we were once, and that's my fault. But we can get through this together, just like you and Rose and Ma did for me. Just like we're trying to do for Dad."

My eyes burn and I choke on a sob as she holds me until it passes.

"What do we do? Alex, I don't know what to do."

We watch Maks turn fitfully in sleep for a few moments. Alex

110

stares like she's expecting him to wake up and attack us. I tell her about his outbursts and how sometimes he's *there* and sometimes he's not.

"Are you sure it's a good idea to keep him here?" she asks.

"Where else can I take him?" I try to stand, but my leg muscles cramp. Alex helps me up.

"Okay," Alex says, pacing once more. Candlelight plays with her shadow, making her look taller and longer than she already is. "First, you should make more of the calming draught. Dilute it so that it doesn't give him the sleeping side effect. We can study him."

"He's not a lab rat," I counter.

"I'm not saying he is. But we have to figure out what triggers his violent outbursts. How are you going to explain the hole in the wall to Mom and Dad, by the way?"

I press my hand over my rapid-beating heart. "I—I don't know."

"Forget it. You make the potion. I'll look through mom's books to see what I can find about La Muerte's spear. The last bit will require help."

"What kind of help?"

"Well, we have to figure out *what* he is."

"He's Maks. I'm telling you. You'll see when he wakes up."

"He may have a heartbeat, but normal people don't vanish from one place and appear in another. Whatever he is, we need to know. And the only person we can trust who knows about spirits is—"

There's a quiet knock on the door. Her soft voice filters from the other side. "It's Rose."

"I was just going to get you," Alex says as she opens the door.

Rose walks in. She looks at Maks but doesn't have the same

reaction that Alex did. Her fine, straight hair is loose over her shoulders. Her face is calm, as if it's every day I have my formerly deceased boyfriend sleeping in my bed.

"It's not what you think," I tell her.

One corner of her mouth quirks. "I think I finally found the reason my head feels like it's being hit with a sledgehammer."

"What do you mean?" I ask.

She sighs, as if I'm missing the obvious. "My power isn't like yours or Alex's. It's linked to spirits. When we were in the hospital, it was the worst, which isn't surprising. But when we came home, it still bothered me. I thought it might be residual. I was listening to what you were saying—"

"You were listening?" Alex asks, her voice louder.

"What else is there to do in this house?" Rose rolls her eyes. "I've been eavesdropping on you guys for years. Anyway, when a person and their spirit are aligned, everything is copacetic. One of the reasons that I can *hear* spirits is because the alignment is gone. They're detached from their body. Most spirits move on to the next life. I don't hear from them. The ones that don't move on make the most noise. They're calling out for something that they've lost."

"Like the ones in the River Luxaria in Los Lagos?" Alex asks.

"Those are spirits that *refused* to move on," Rose says, taking off her glasses to rub her eyes. "I can't always hear the spirits in other realms, unless they're looking for me. Being a seer means being a beacon for the undead. My soul glows. If they can see it, they come for me—usually to ask for help I can't give them."

"That's what's making your head hurt now?"

Rose gnaws on the inside of her cheek and nods. "There's a rift in the balance. I should've felt it sooner, but it's hard to separate that with all the magic we've called on this week."

"I'm so sorry, Rosie," I say.

"No, Alex was right. I wanted to help you. I'm responsible for Maks's condition too. *Something* happened during our canto. You said you were going to get me because I can feel his spirit, determine if he's really human."

"And?"

The three of us stand at arm's length. If we reached for each other, we could make a perfect triangle.

Rose licks her lips and glances at her feet before saying, "Maks's soul is detached. It's like it's stuck, halfway in and out. I don't know *what* he is, but he isn't completely there. I thought he might've been to another realm like Dad. But Dad's soul is fine, except a faint red glow, like something inside of him has changed. That's not the biggest problem though."

I take a step closer to my baby sister. I remember holding her as a baby—her fat cheeks always bright red, her tiny hands so cold, it scared my mother.

"I've been feeling this way since we got home. But Maks only got here today. Maks's spirit isn't the only one that's detached." She takes my hand and the chill of it makes my body shiver. "Yours is too."

13

Bathe in the sun.

Sleep with the moon.

Our souls are as one,

our ending too soon.

—WITCHSONG #7,
BOOK OF CANTOS

My soul is detached?" I ask my sister. My hand goes to my chest as if I can feel the part of me that's untethered. But all I find is my racing heart beneath my skin. "Are you sure?"

Rose never fidgets. But now, she bites her thumbnail down to a stump and can't seem to stay in one place.

"It was faint before, but now that Maks is here it seems to be getting worse. When I look at people," she says, "I can see the outline of the soul. When everything is right, it's only the faintest glow. For example, Alex's is in place. I see the usual white light but—"

Alex snaps her attention to Rose. "What do you mean but?"

"*But* there are black and red outlines too. That's your soul being touched by your time in Los Lagos because time works different. And then, because of the curse you cast."

Alex looks down at her hands. A black, eight-pointed star is marked at the center of her palms. Thin lines spread from it like a burst of lightning, the mark she retained from welding such power, for banishing her magic.

"Why didn't you tell me before?" Alex asks.

"You see this all the time?" I ask Rose, and all I want to do is hug her. "How can you stand it?"

Rose lifts her shoulder and tries to brush it off. Turns her face toward where the candles on my altar are nearly extinguished. "No one ever asks. Besides, it doesn't happen all the time. It's mostly when I have my lessons with Valeria."

We watch my altar silently, shadows dancing against the wall. One candle has burned all the way down to the metal strip and goes out, a long smoke line shooting upward.

"I'm sorry," Alex tells Rose.

"Don't be. I don't like to talk about it," she says, leveling her brown eyes back on us. "When it does happen, I can usually ignore it. After having this power for so long, I just do what I can until my Deathday helps me balance it. It's like always being surrounded by noise—eventually it fades into the background. But now I can't ignore it because whatever we did has affected you and Maks."

"We have to fix him," I say, and part of me wonders why it's so much harder to ask for help from the people who love us. "Ma has enough on her hands with trying to be the midwife and healer to every magical being in the tristate area. The High Circle would probably put a stake through my heart without asking questions.

Dad doesn't even remember the last seven years. It has to remain with us."

I place my hands on my sister's shoulders. The next candle blows out.

"I'll get you fresh candles," Rose says.

"I'll get the books."

"I'll make the potion."

I walk up to my altar and blow out the last flame.

I get to work in the infirmary. I have to wade through everything I'm feeling and come out standing still.

My fingers tremble as I comb through our supplies and collect the jars of ingredients. My legs ache for a rest. I catch my reflection in a mirror, wishing I could see what Rose sees. Without her, how would I ever know my soul was detached? I press my finger over my heart, where I first felt the thread that led me to Maks. Was that a symptom? When I heal others, I always ask: When did the pain start? Does it hurt when I press right here? What hurts the most?

If I were to do that to myself now, I would answer, "It started with the maloscuros. It hurts when I come in contact with anything— when I sit, when I stand, when I blink, when I breathe. One pain always tries to overpower the others, so I don't know what hurts the most."

If I right my spirit, if I free Lady de la Muerte, if I help Maks will all of this stop hurting?

"Lula?" Mom's voice makes me jump. I drop the jar of lavender I was holding.

"Sorry—I'm trying to make a calming draught."

"I'll get it," she says, soothing. She must be trying to give me space because she doesn't even ask me where I went. "Sit."

At the word *sit*, my body groans. If I were made of metal, I'd be the creakiest robot ever, all rusted joints and pieces in need of repair.

"Why didn't you ask me to make you one before?"

Because it's not for me, I think. My heart races as she moves around the room. I've never lied to my mother like this. Not ever.

She gets a broom and dustpan from the corner and sweeps up the mess into the trash. The lavender heads are too mingled in with the glass to salvage. She goes to one of the wooden drawers, pulls out a new bundle. The scent reminds me of nights when I was little. A few weeks after Dad disappeared, she started making us all lavender and honey tea. Then we'd climb into her bed and sleep huddled together, a gathering of sorrow.

"I want to try and do things myself."

She nods slowly but finishes the potion for me anyway. Her brown fingers move swiftly, and she barely looks at the jars that she pulls from the crowded shelves. She knows herbs by scent, not sight. She knows bones by their touch and weight. She's the best healer and bruja I've ever known, and I'm certain if I tell her what I've done, it would crush her.

"I know things are hard right now," she tells me. She grinds the mixture a little longer than I would have before putting it in the tea bag. "But the best thing to help you feel like yourself is getting back into a routine."

A heavy thump resounds somewhere in the house. Ma doesn't seem to notice, but I fear Maks might be waking up.

"I can't even think about a routine right now," I say, and that's the most honest thing I've said all day.

She lets the tea steep before handing it to me. Her palms are still warm when she cups my face.

"Why don't you help your father and me with this delivery tomorrow?" she asks. Another thumping sound, like a mallet hitting wood, makes both of us turn toward the door. "What are your sisters doing?"

"Delivery?" I ask, trying to keep her attention on me.

"Remember? We're going to Montauk this weekend. I've delivered human children and mermaid children, but this will be my first half-human half-mermaid. Though I suppose mermaids are already half-human…"

"Ma, I can't."

"I don't want to pressure you." She throws her hands up in the air. She pulls out a heavy leather bag from the closet. "I didn't want to leave you so soon, but I know you girls can take care of each other."

She's right about that at least.

"But it might be good for you." She grabs thin glass vials of blue cohosh, milk thistle, gnarly roots with tiny, green sprouts, powders of all different colors, candles, and shells. She fits everything in her travel bag.

There's a loud creaking sound, and this time, I know it comes from my bedroom. My mouth is dry with lies, but this is the closest truth I can manage: "I'm not ready."

"You'll never be ready if you don't try." She places her hand on her hip. Her head is cocked to the side. It makes me think of the homeless man in the subway, his head turning sideways and crunching.

I pull back when she tries to caress my arm.

"I'm sorry," I say. "I need more time."

I can see the struggle in her eyes. "Okay, baby. I'll save you a plate for dinner."

Then I leave her and hope that Maks is all right as I rush to my room.

Alex and Rose have already made themselves comfortable. They brought up a plate of sandwiches, and Alex thumbs through the Book of Cantos as Rose lights enough candles to illuminate the whole room. A bundle of dried roses and desert sage emits a thin line of smoke.

Alex looks up and shuts the book. "What did Mom say?"

"She wants me to go to the home birth with her tomorrow," I tell them. "You guys could've been quieter I could hear you from the infirmary."

Alex and Rose trade glances.

"We've been reading and your undead boyfriend has been sound asleep," Alex says indignantly. "A sentence I never thought I'd ever utter."

"Then what was the thumping sound I heard?"

"Maybe Dad's fixing the hole in the wall." Rose gives me a side glance.

I ignore her and go to the window. I pull back the curtain. None of the usual front-stoop hangouts. Just shadows and empty streets.

"What is it?" Alex asks.

"Nothing. Just shadows playing tricks on me." I shut the curtains and turn back around. "Did you find anything in the books?"

"There are more claims of seeing La Mama's face in a random brujo's pancake than about Lady de la Muerte."

"There's just one rezo." Alex drums her fingers on a page in a thick hardcover of *Tales of the Deos*.

"Read it," I urge her.

She clears he throat. "'The Deos too learned their limits. El Fuego extinguished into ash. La Ola crumbled into salt. El Terroz clove the earth in pieces. El Viento fell and kept on falling. But from their limits, Lady de la Muerte was born.'"

"That's it? So the limits of the gods?" I say, frustrated. Rose presses her finger to her lips, but I'm not done. How can we have so many books and end up with nothing? "That's a freaking bedtime story!"

"Lula," Ma shouts from down the hall. "You okay?"

"Fine!" the three of us say at the same time.

"Lula." This time it's Maks. He sits straight up. I say his name to get his eyes to focus on me. But when he does, his irises are pale, ice blue, and bloodshot red. Something's changed, and he inhales deeply. His movements are predatory as he catches the whiff of the sage smoke.

No, not the smoke. His head snaps toward my sister.

He lunges at Rose.

14

In 1965, a man in Caracas, Venezuela, lost his wife the same day they were married. The man, son of a brujo but with no powers of his own, used every measure he could to bring her back to life. But the person who awoke was not his beloved.

—EL LIBRO MALDECIDO/THE ACCURSED BOOK,
FAUSTO TOLEDO

Alex blasts a force field that crackles with lightning when Maks slams into it. He tumbles back and hits his head against the window sill. We rush to Rose's side.

"I'm okay," Rose assures Alex, who brushes Rose's hair back over her face. "He didn't touch me."

I walk around the bed to where Maks is slumped on the floor, attempting and failing to get up. I'm afraid to touch him, but when he looks at me, his eyes are back to normal. He presses his wrist to his temple and groans.

"Oh God," he says, his voice is scratchy and deep. "What happened?"

"Are you okay?" I help him back up to my bed. Even through his T-shirt, he's cold.

"Did I fall off the bed?" He starts to stand, then notices Alex and Rose. Rose watches him carefully while Alex balls her fists as if trying to reel her magic back. He lifts a hand and waves at them. "Whoa, hey, guys."

"What's the last thing you remember?" Alex asks him, stepping forward. Her arms still tremble from the blast of magic, but she stuffs them in her pockets to make it stop.

"It's all pretty blurry," he says, a smile quirking at his mouth. He scratches the back of his head and rubs my arm absentmindedly. "I was having some weird-ass dreams. I think it was that tea you gave me. Why are you guys looking at me like that? Did I do something stupid?"

I hold my hand up to stop Alex's next statement.

"Something like that," she says, and narrows her eyes at me. "Think hard, Maks. What about before the tea?"

"Last thing I remember?" His eyes slide out of focus, pupils opening and closing like the aperture of a camera. He stares at a blank spot on my wall so long that I reach out and place my hand on his knee and squeeze gently. He clears his throat and stares at me, like he's trying to remember my face. It was the same look he gave me in the car that morning on the way to the game. Then, his features soften and he smiles at me. "I don't know. It's like flashes. Lula said we were in an accident. Was it after the game? Is everyone okay?"

Rose scoffs and throws up her hands, as if to say, *Are you kidding?*

"Yes, it happened on the way home from the game. How do you feel?" I ask, avoiding his other question.

"Like death." He leans back on the pillows. "What time is it?"

"Ten at night." My heart is beating wildly as I stand between Maks and my sisters.

"Damn. Did my mom call?" he asks. "She hates when I don't show up for dinner."

I want to speak, but a memory of Mrs. Horbachevsky crying for her son strangles me.

"Your parents are out of town and you're staying with us for a bit. You hit your head in the accident, so you're having trouble remembering. There's pizza in the fridge, if you're hungry," Alex says quickly. "Rosie, bring some up?"

"Thanks," Maks says. He picks up a geode from my nightstand and turns it in his hands.

Despite the worry that mars Alex's forehead, there's a flutter of hope in my chest because when he smiles and speaks and laughs, it feels just like it used to, before everything happened.

He asks about the game. He asks where our parents are. And I lie. I lie so well that I bet I can convince myself that the game really happened. That Maks saved two dozen goals and the Thorne Hill Knights were the first undefeated soccer champions we've had in years. That the accident wasn't that bad, and everyone lived, and we were safe.

Alex sits on the floor, flipping through a comic book, hiding the Book of Cantos behind her. She hasn't stopped frowning, but when she met Maks, she was frowning, so this is just her natural state as far as he's concerned.

When Rose returns with half a pie, Maks puts away three slices. I forget what it's like to have an appetite. I nibble on a piece of crust, and in the end, Maks eats the slice I can't.

He's in the middle of telling a joke, something about the offside rule, when he doubles over on his knees.

"Alex," I shout. "Don't hurt him."

"Only if he tries to hurt one of you first," she says coolly, holding her hands up at the ready.

But Maks isn't attacking anyone. He's on his knees, a terrible whimper racking his body as he violently throws up.

"This can't be good," Alex says.

"Shut up and help me!"

Rose finds a towel and wipes at the corners of his mouth; worry cracks her usually calm demeanor when he looks up with blood-shot eyes.

"What's wrong with me?" Maks asks, eyes clearing up again. He shivers, fat beads of sweat running down his forehead. I grab the calming draught and bring the mug to his lips. He sniffs at the empty space between us and growls deep in his throat. He wrenches his face to the side.

Alex grabs hold of Maks while I try again, holding the calming potion up to his lips, but he shakes his head and turns away.

"It will help you sleep," I coax.

He's short of breath and breaks away from my sister. "Lula, something's wrong with me."

"I know," I whisper, pressing my hand to his forehead. He wraps his arms around me, tea sloshing over the brim of the cup. I bite down the pain that shoots across my stomach. "I'll help you. I promise."

He leans into the cup, and I tilt it up until it's drained. The effect is instant. He sways into me, but Alex and Rose grab him by his arms and move him onto the bed. He mutters nonsensically and reaches for me, holding on to the tips of my fingers until he falls asleep.

"What the hell was that?" Alex hisses.

"I *don't* know," I say through gritted teeth. My racing heart won't let me think clearly. I grab a clean cloth and dab it across his sweaty skin. His stitches are already falling out. The scars that poke from his collar are almost completely healed.

"Lula, what's wrong?" Rose asks, eyes wide as a doe.

There's a sharp tug at my chest and my stomach, and a hot, wet warmth. I press my hand to my side and it comes away bloody.

"Alex," I cry.

"What?" she snaps. She's shaking baby powder on the pool of vomit to make it easier to clean up.

"Alex, look." Rose nudges her shoulder.

She finally looks up. A startled gasp parts her lips as she blasts her magic to catch me before I realize I'm falling.

Even as I come to, I recognize the scent of mom's cooking, along with something extra—rose sage for anxiety and peaceful dreams. But I don't remember having any dreams. There was only an endless dark, as if I were dead.

Sunlight breaks through the corners of the closed curtains where they don't quite rest against the wall. Maks is asleep. The incense smoke covers the smell of puke, and a brown stain marks the carpet. Alex sits on the floor reading a leather-bound book.

"Hey," I say, testing my voice. When I swallow, my throat feels raw.

Alex stands at once and comes to my side. She picks up a glass of cloudy water with white chunks in it. "Drink this."

"What is it?" I ask, groggy. My body feels like I've run a marathon but without the runner's high. I pull myself up against the headboard and grimace at the coppery morning breath on my tongue.

"Coconut water," she says irritably. "Electrolytes and potassium."

"Mad brujeria," I say, trying to joke as I drink.

Alex doesn't laugh but sits at the edge of my bed. "He woke once. I made more of the draught. He's in and out of awareness. We need to do something."

"Did you tell Ma?"

She shakes her head. "I said you weren't feeling well and that I'd heal you, which I did. Mom and Dad are getting ready to go to Montauk after dinner."

"I'm not hungry," I say. Then I realize, her hair is pulled back and wet. She's wearing gym clothes. "Wait, I've been asleep for a day?"

"Fifteen hours, actually," she says resolutely. "Lula, you have to eat something. You're weak and you aren't healing right. Rose and I spent all morning trying to figure out what could be happening to you and Maks, but there's nothing—not in the books at least. Please, just let us take care of you."

I don't want to argue. I take the towel and clothes she picked out for me. I shower and wash the dried blood off my skin. In the rising steam, I trace the circular, snakelike scar on my abdomen and the long scar that trails from my wrist to my inner elbow. The ones on my face are minuscule compared to these.

I rinse the suds from my hair and skin as my thoughts race. Maks could've hurt Rose. If Alex hadn't been there—but she was. When Maks wakes up, who will he be? Lady de la Muerte's voice clings to the shadows of my thoughts. *You have betrayed the balance of the worlds.* Maks and I are connected to her in ways I can't understand yet. I don't think I'm strong enough to help us all.

I turn off the water and get dressed as quickly as my stiff muscles will allow.

Alex locks the door to my room, and, leaving Maks as comfortable as we can, we head downstairs. The smell of roasted pork and fried yucca does a better job of waking me up than the shower. I haven't been hungry in days, but suddenly, my belly rumbles.

Rose stands in front of the television in the living room with her finger pressed to her mouth and her eyes set in deep worry.

"What is it?" Alex asks, trotting down the steps two at a time.

"I was flipping through all the news for something *weird*, and I didn't have to wait long." She takes the remote and raises the volume. "Remember those bodies they found? They revealed their names and cause of death."

An anxious knot starts to twist in my gut. The reporter in the studio stares at the camera with red-rimmed eyes. "—we're following the story closely. Something like this has never happened in this city, not in broad daylight, and not that I've ever seen."

Her coanchor takes over. No makeup in the world can fix the sickly green pallor of his skin or the terror in his wide, brown eyes.

"You're right, Gaby. This case has the NYPD out in full force. Commissioner Brentwood is holding a press conference tonight.

He wants to assure the city that those responsible for this heinous crime will be found and held accountable."

"Do the police have anyone in custody?" a third reporter on the split screen asks.

"Not at this time," Adam answers.

"Any news from the crime scene, Adam?" Gaby asks.

"There is unconfirmed speculation of cult activity," Adam says.

Adam looks over his shoulder and wipes his brow with a folded handkerchief. It's nearly five o'clock, but the summer sun is lazy to set, and the bright-yellow glow lights up his face. "All is quiet from the NYPD at the moment. They have yet to release a statement but a source from the medical examiner has confirmed cause of death. The two young men have been identified as Robbie Duran and Gregory Amadeu. Both bodies, which were found at different locations, had their hearts ripped out of their chests. According to the chief medical examiner, their...their hearts have not been recovered.

"The NYPD has issued this hotline for anyone to report tips or *anything* suspicious. Mayor Bloomberg has issued a curfew in the neighborhood of Coney Island tonight. Back to the studio."

"They said earlier one of the boys, Robbie, went to your school," Rose says. "I don't know the other."

"Oh no," I say, because I've seen that name before. My heart is in my throat as I go to the table in the foyer, where I left my keys the day I brought Maks home. I open the drawer and fish between unopened bills and envelopes until I find the wallet.

Alex and Rose gather around me. I can't bring myself to open it, so Alex takes it. Her eyes scan the name on the identification behind the thin plastic cover.

"Read it," I say.

Alex breathes quickly, shuts it. "Robbie Duran."

"Oh gods." I cup my hand over my mouth. I shut my eyes and think back to the ride on the subway. The thread that led me to Maks. His lips stained cherry red from the ice pop in his hand.

Maks.

"We don't know Maks did this," Rose says, more like she's trying to convince herself than us. "Maybe he found the body and took what he could. Maybe—"

"There's nothing we can do right now," Alex says, and I'm surprised at how calm she can be at a time like this. "But our books have turned up nothing on Maks's condition or anything new on Lady de la Muerte's staff. We need to speak to someone who can help us figure this out. What about Mayi and the girls?"

"So you can fight the whole time?"

Alex rolls her eyes. "I'll behave for this."

"Not to be a snob," Rose says, "but if *our* books turned up empty, there's no way they can help. It'd be like me asking you two to help with my calculus homework."

Alex holds up a finger to Rose's face and says, "Rude."

"Maybe Rose is right," I say. Then I remember a name scrolling on Lady de la Muerte's forearm the day of the accident. I meant to tell Alex before, but now it's been so long and I don't know how she'll react. I'm unable to look at her face. "There's another option. Someone who knows about blood magic."

"No," she says, as if I've invited Death herself into the house.

"His family knows the darker side of magic better than we do," I remind her. "He knows brujos who deal in the afterlife.

Angela the Great is his grandmother. She's written the deadliest poisons and—"

"I know *very* well the kinds of poisons Angela has written," Alex says. "But I'm not asking Nova for help. He's the one who helped put you in Los Lagos, or have you forgotten?"

"I will never forget Los Lagos." I want to strangle her for being so stubborn. "He gave up his power to save us."

Alex holds up a finger to her chest and stabs at her solar plexus. "*My* power. That was never his. He stole it from me."

"He brought Dad home," Rose whispers.

"I'm not sure if we can trust him either," I say. "But I'm saying that he knows things that might help. Maks is up there in my room, and right now it's possible he's responsible for two awful murders. We need some sort of help, and it can't come from Mom and Dad."

"Girls?" Dad says, walking toward the foyer where we've been lingering. "Dinner's ready."

The ceiling creaks. We all look up as though expecting a phantom to materialize or the rusty chandelier to rattle. My whole mouth is dry and my heart beats a guilty rhythm against my chest.

But all my father says is, "I keep forgetting to fix that ceiling."

Ever since Nova brought my father back, we've made it a point to have dinners at the kitchen table. Ma thinks it'll restore a sense of normalcy, and the three of us don't have the heart to remind her that we've never been normal.

Normal families don't spend time in other realms. If Alex won't let me ask Nova for help, then I can make Dad try harder to remember. Maybe he can give me a clue as to how to free Lady de la Muerte and help Maks. I know when I dream, I remember Los Lagos, and perhaps that's the key to where he's been.

"Dad," I start, pushing rice around. I'm too nervous to be subtle. "What do you dream about when you sleep?"

He looks up, surprised by my question. For a moment, I can see the man he used to be, holding a sizzling pot full of meat and potatoes, dancing around the kitchen to a song that was all saxophones and congas. Now, his gray eyes appear haunted and lost.

"Shadows mostly. Why?"

"I wonder if maybe the answer to getting your memories back is in your dreams. At this point, everyone in the family has been to another realm. But we can remember. I just don't know why you can't."

Alex gives me a *what the hell are you doing?* look, and Rose picks the red peppers out of her yellow rice.

Ma takes a drink of her seltzer water and sighs. "When things calm down, we'll try again. At least we're together now, thank La Mama."

"Why? The Deos weren't the ones who brought him back," I say, then cover my mouth immediately.

"Yesterday you said you weren't ready to cast magic. What's changed?" Mom asks, her eyebrow quirked high. She has the kind of knowing stare that can draw out the lies from even the best liars.

"It's not magic," I say, picking up my fork and keeping my gaze down. "It's the realms part. I think that might be the answer to all of this."

"Lula, if something's wrong, please talk to me."

For a moment, I want to confess everything to my mother and let her make everything better the way she always has. But she has already suffered so much, and I can't add to her worry.

"I'm fine, Ma," I say, and smile through the pain in my abdomen. "Alex and Rose are taking care of me."

She's about to say something, but a soft knock on the back door makes her jump. Dad gets up to get it. But when he opens the door, there's no one there, just the scent of nearby cookouts. He stares out into the backyard for a long time.

"Patricio." Ma calls out his name like a lifeline.

He shuts the door and takes his seat. Clears his throat. "My dreams are fractures, like my memory is a glass wall and it's been punched right at the center. But what happened to me can wait. First, I want you to concentrate on healing."

I wonder, is that what Maks is feeling now that his memory is gone?

"We'll get through this. The whole world always feels turned upside down," Ma says, a sad smile as she looks around the table. "We're brujas. We've been through worse."

And I don't have the heart to tell her that, perhaps, she's wrong.

Alex, Rose, and I clean up after dinner while Mom and Dad get ready to go out to Montauk for the home birth.

"Easy on the plate," Alex says, taking the wet dish out of my hands to dry it.

"It's not exactly porcelain," I say.

"Who's going to buy new ones to replace the ones you break?" she sasses me.

"Sorry, *Mom*. I have a few things to worry about, like *Maks* possibly murdering strangers and ripping out their *hearts*."

"Did you fix Maks a plate?" Alex asks somberly. "Maybe he'll keep something down this time."

"Dad didn't eat, so I'm going to try to give Maks those left-overs." I don't voice my fears out loud. *I don't think this is what Maks wants to eat.*

"Are you worried about Dad?" Alex whispers. "He's getting thinner and thinner. Pernil and yucca used to be his favorite."

I shake my head and grab the soapy plate like a steering wheel. I watch the water run down, transfixed by the way it washes away the suds. "I can't. This is all too much. Why can't the Deos cut us some slack?"

Then, the plate snaps cleanly in half.

Alex takes each half of the plate from my hands and throws them in the garbage.

"Is there a saying about what message the Deos are trying to send when your dishes break?" Alex asks. "You need to ease up on cursing the gods. Especially when I'm standing right next to you."

I know she's trying to lighten the mood and make me smile, but the muscles of my face feel stiff.

Rose walks in from the backyard shivering and holding something in her hands. "Why is it so cold all of a sudden? It's June."

"You're always cold," Alex tells her.

"Exactly." She shrugs. "If I'm complaining, then maybe we should worry."

"What's that?" I ask.

Rose sets the thick, black box on the table. It's the size of a shoe box but taller. A black satin ribbon is tied in a bow at the top.

"I don't know," Rose says. "It was just at the door. I noticed it when I was walking back in."

"Maybe it's a gift from a patient?" Alex asks, though she doesn't sound convinced.

Sometimes, the people we help in our clinic leave presents behind because we don't charge money to use our power. They send small tithes, like a bag of rice or baskets of fruit or things for the house like potted mint and flowers. *Flowers.* I think of the deep purple flowers that I found on the porch yesterday.

I press my hand on top of the box to send a pulse of magic to sense for organic matter, but either I'm too weak or there's something blocking it.

"Open it," Alex says. She raises her hands and the tips of her fingers crackle with energy.

"What if it's one of those horrible clowns or, oh, the plague?" Rose asks. "I don't think you can contain plague with electric shocks, Alex."

With that seed of doubt, we just stare at it. I pick it up and shake it, and it makes a clinking rattle. It isn't exactly heavy, but there's a heft to it.

I pull the satin, black ribbon. The bow comes undone and I lift the lid.

"That's weird," Rose says.

There's a thick, white note card. Quick, black letters scrawled across it, as if whoever was writing was furious while doing so.

"You have twenty-four hours to destroy the abomination. In the meantime…"

"In the meantime what?" Alex asks.

I pick up the box. "It's still heavy."

Alex leans over my shoulder. "It's a false bottom."

I feel against the surface and find there's a tab that folds up. The false bottom gives way to a metal lining full of ice.

We suck in sharp breaths all at once and scatter back.

"Is that real?" I ask, my knees shaking with the need to give beneath me.

"What *is* it?" Rose grimaces. "That can't be—"

Alex's body is tense, as if she's trying to stop her instinct to run as she says, "It's a human heart."

15

It is by the blood spilled by this alliance, and all who witness, that any

who harms humankind shall meet the penalty of death.

—THE THORNE HILL ALLIANCE,
THE TREATY OF NEW YORK, SECTION 1

I shut the box in my hands and hold it close to my chest.

"It hasn't been twenty-four hours," Rose says, panicked. "Has it?"

"Who sent this?" Alex picks up the card and flips it over.

"How am I supposed to know?" I say, voice climbing octaves. "Lady de la Muerte?"

But she's trapped between realms. It can't be her, which means someone else knows about Maks.

"Whoever knocked on the door during dinner," Alex says, pacing again. "Dammit."

"I knew I heard a weird noise yesterday," I say. "What if they've been watching the house this whole time?"

"Hunt—" Alex is about to say but there's a thundering bang on the front door.

"Girls?" Dad calls out from the living room. Whoever is on the other side alternates between jamming the bell and punching. "Stay in the kitchen!"

My mom races downstairs and meets my dad at the front door, the pounding doesn't cease, this time accompanied by someone screaming bloody murder.

"What are they doing?" I shout.

"You heard what Dad said." Alex grabs my arm and keeps me back.

"Get him upstairs!" Dad shouts. "First door on the right."

"Hide that," Alex warns me.

I panic and put the box in the freezer. We run to the living room, where our parents are helping two bloodied guys climb up our steps.

"Clean this up," Mom orders, looking back at us. She has her game face on. When people come through that door asking for help, she doesn't cringe or hesitate. She looks at the injury and gets to work.

Rose brings the mop and bucket from the kitchen and I go and close the door. Two sets of footprints trail blood from outside.

"I'll clean out here," I tell her.

I limp around the side of the house to grab the hose and spray the cement where the blood leads directly into our house. I can't get enough slack on the hose to go down the block. I curse at the heavens. I can only pray for rain.

My street is too quiet for this time of night, but I'm grateful I don't have to explain the bloody sidewalk to my neighbors.

I wrap the hose around my shoulder and close the fence

behind me. For the first time in my life, I don't feel safe in my own house. I was born here, literally in the living room. When my mom went into labor three weeks early, I sped into this world screaming and eager. Alex took forty-eight hours. Rose was right on time.

After everything I've done, a dark thought tugs at me. *I wonder if I'll die here too.*

Up on the second floor, the light in my room is still off, which is a small relief. I can see shadows moving in the infirmary window. There's a scream, like the call of a banshee trailing in the wind.

"I should help," I say out loud. "Even if I'm not ready, I should help."

Then, I jump as a shadow moves at the side of the house. And I realize, it's not a shadow. It's a man dressed from head to toe in black.

"Who the hell are you?" I shout.

He starts to run. It's so dark I can't see his face. The light at the porch isn't turning on, so I fumble with the hose, point it in his direction, and spray.

I hear him grunt, the blast hitting his side. He's fast and, in two swift movements, jumps over the side of the porch and into the neighbor's yard.

"Stop!" I shout. I start to run, but a pain shreds my sides. I take a knee and wait for it to subside. "Alex!"

She comes running out. "What's wrong?"

"There was someone watching through the window."

She comes over and pulls my shirt up. The look on her face tells me something is wrong.

"Forget that," she says. "I have to heal you again."

I start to shake my head, but the pain is too much, and so I sling my arm around her shoulder. Step by step, we get back inside and sit in the living room.

"Did you see the patient?" I ask her, eyes darting up the steps after our mystery callers.

"Ma said to wait until she needs me. Rose is up there now. Whatever it is, it sounds like it's really bad."

I laugh, a bitter, manic thing.

"What's so funny?" she asks, setting me on the couch.

"Remember when all you wanted was to be a normal girl, and I'd get mad at you?"

"I was an idiot." She smirks, making her face brighten with mischief.

"You were smart."

"Don't tell me you want to trade in your powers. Because I've been down that road and it doesn't work."

We're quiet, the scurry of footsteps on the ceiling and the cry of the injured man is our soundtrack for the evening.

"Everything will be fine," she says. Her ponytail swishes from side to side when she moves. She lifts up my shirt and examines the area. I see her make a face, then try to cover it up.

"What?" But I feel the itch and burn of part of the scar opening up again.

"I healed this last night. It isn't taking. I'll do it again." She walks into the foyer and makes a right toward the supply closet.

"Ma needs you," I say.

She shouts back, "She has Rose and Dad."

"Alex."

"Just lean back." She holds a six-inch quartz crystal with raw edges. She places the cold stone on my warm skin.

Her conjuring magic thickens the air with a velvet mist, cycling around her hands, and I sigh with relief as the pain lightens. Her dark brown eyes focus on the aura around me. As hard as she tries to hide it, I see the worry coiled in her stare, and I fear things might be worse than she's letting on.

When my sister's magic touches me, a tender warmth spreads from the bruised area on my side. My muscles relax, and if I didn't have so much to do, I'd fall asleep right here and now, even though I slept through most of the day.

"There," Alex says. The crystal is pitch black, a sign that the malady is gone. She holds it up for me to see. Crystals can usually be cleansed, but when they're used to suck sickness out of the body, they turn black like this and there's no going back. We usually bury them or throw them out to sea. "Want to keep it in a jar and name it?"

"Thanks," I say, standing. I wiggle my toes and find I've almost forgotten what it's like to feel no pain. "But no."

"Do you hear that?" Alex asks. She sets the crystal on the table and looks up at the ceiling.

"The screaming stopped."

As if reading each other's thoughts, we head upstairs. We stand outside the infirmary door. Mom's and Dad's voices are quick and worried. There's another voice, familiar and strange all at once. I can't place it, but then I see Alex's face darken with anger. The lightbulb in the hallway makes a sound like ice breaking through glass, and then we're cloaked in more darkness, and I wonder, why are we always trailed by shadows?

Alex yanks open the door and I follow her in.

Everyone turns to look at us. Mom, Dad, Rose, and—

"Alex," he says. His brilliant green-blue eyes search her face. He's been crying. His light brown skin is speckled with blood.

"Nova," Alex says sharply. "It's been a while."

16

Why am I torn in two?
My head on earth,
my heart with you.

—SONG OF EL CORAZÓN,
BREAKER OF HEARTS AND
LORD OF ALL THE WORLD'S CONFLICT,
BOOK OF DEOS

What are you doing here?" Alex asks Nova.

"I didn't know where else to go," he says, shame thick in his voice.

Nova Santiago is a complicated guy. I want to hate him. He was the one who set Alex in motion to Los Lagos. He betrayed her. He almost poisoned Rishi. He was a pawn of the Devourer, the demon witch of Los Lagos. But he also feared for his life. He wanted to live. Now, more than ever, I think I can understand his desperation.

Plus, Rose was right. He brought back our father. He didn't say how he found him, but he doesn't exactly seem like the conversational type. Nova always knows more than he lets on. Maybe the tattoos on his chest and the black magic burns on his fingertips scare people away before he can get close. I wonder if he prefers it that way.

Rose sits on the empty table beside the bloody guy Nova brought in.

Nova clears his throat. He scratches the back of his buzz-cut head and can't seem to figure out where to place his hands, so he balls them into fists on his lap. He looks at my parents apologetically. Ma is cleaning her hands on a towel. My dad leans against a wall patiently.

"I was at Prospect Park with my friend Silvino," Nova says. "Vino's like us. Nothing special, but he can conjure shields. Comes in handy when we squat in the park."

"What were you doing?" Alex asks sharply.

"Summoning the god-dammed apocalypse," Nova says, rolling his eyes at my sister.

Rose covers her mouth, too late to hold back a loud barking laugh.

Nova shakes his head and stares at the shelf of jars, like he's making it a point to avoid Alex's eyes. "It's nice out, so we were just chilling, eating dinner. Out of nowhere this guy attacks us. Got the drop on Vino."

"Did you see the attacker's face?" Mom asks, folding another wet cloth and placing it over Vino's forehead.

"Too dark." Nova meets Alex's eyes. It lasts for about three seconds before he picks someone else to look at. Me. "There was something wrong with him. He couldn't speak, like he was chewing on his own tongue. When I blasted him with light, I could see his neck was covered in open wounds. First I thought vamp, but the way it moved... It's like he was a—" Nova hesitates. He looks around the room at my family and then at Vino.

Vino's head inches back and forth and he mutters slightly. Bandages cover the wound my parents healed, but his skin is covered in sweat.

"A what?" Dad asks. His voice is even, encouraging, the way he would talk to us when we were little.

"A zombie," Nova says, then laughs. "It's ridiculous, I know."

Mom and Dad look at each other. I wonder if they can hear the thundering of my heart.

"Raising the dead is nearly impossible," Ma says, stroking her chin. "It violates one of the fundamental laws of magic and life. Besides, the only vudú priestess strong enough to raise the dead is retired in the DR."

"Maybe it isn't magical," Rose suggests. "It could be a virus."

We all turn to Vino, turning fitfully in his sleep—just like Maks has been.

Ma shakes her head and holds out a hand to banish the thought. "His blood was clean when we healed him."

"Raising the dead is rare, but it's been done," Dad says, tracing his short beard methodically. "It never ends well."

"But it *has* happened," I say. Their eyes turn to me. "Where?"

"I heard stories as a child." Ma scoffs and places her hand on her hip. "But we all did. It's the only way they got us to behave."

Nova shrugs, dispelling the talk of zombies with a wave of his hand. "He could've been cracked out. He didn't try to go for Vino's brain. That's the weird part."

"Oh, *that's* the weird part in all of this?" Alex asks.

Nova smirks in Alex's direction but still won't look at her. "Just when I was starting to miss your smartass mouth. No. He went for Vino's chest. Couldn't even use his powers to shield himself. After I scared it away, we tried to run, but Vino was bleeding too much. I didn't know what to do."

"You did the right thing," my mom says. "Maybe this is the person the police are after."

"The police?" Nova asks quietly.

"Someone is ripping hearts out of people," Rose says.

Then I realize my fears about Maks were all wrong. And before I can think better of it, I shout, "Oh, thank gods."

"Thank gods?" Mom asks me, a hand on her hip. "Lula, this young man almost died."

"I just meant—" I start, looking to Alex, who shakes her head. "Thank the Deos it isn't zombies."

"Perhaps not zombies," Dad says, his gray eyes focusing on me, "but it does sound like casimuertos."

"Casi-what?" I try to repeat the word. *Cah-see-mu-erh-toes.*

"What's that?" Rose asks.

Dad strokes the tip of his short beard. His stormy-gray eyes are tiny as he squints, searching for a memory that might not be there.

"I used to know this story by heart," Dad says, a self-deprecating chuckle on his lips. "It's the punishment of the Deos when a bruja violates the laws of life. The corpse kills and consumes its prey, trying to return to life, but it can't."

I stop listening to him. My heart is a bass drum in my ears. *This is Lady de la Muerte's punishment.*

"Lula, are you okay?" I hear my dad's voice, drifting softly in the distance.

The killer can't be Maks. But he had the wallet of one of the

145

victims. Maks couldn't have attacked Vino because he was here with me. Maks is not a casimuerto because he's not a corpse; he's a person. I feel his heartbeat. But there's also the heart in the box. And that note... Destroy the abomination.

Dad's hand presses down on my shoulder. A gentle squeeze that brings me back here, in the infirmary, Nova and my family looking at me.

"Sorry. Headache."

"Are the casimuertos like the maloscuros that attacked us?" Rose asks. "We thought *they* were stories too."

"No, not exactly," Dad says. "The reasons they were created was similar."

"Any violation of the gods results in punishment," Ma says. "Maloscuros were once brujos and brujas who were turned into demons that hunt for power. But casimuertos. Casimuertos can be anyone. My dad once told me a story of a woman who tried to raise an army of them to destroy the villagers who stole her farm."

"Seems reasonable," Rose says dryly.

"My grandmother told me the same story," Nova says, a sad smile tugging at his full mouth. "In her version, it was her cheating husband, not villagers. And they all died in the end."

"Charming," Alex says.

"The thing that attacked Vino can't be a casimuerto," Nova says, leveling his bluish eyes to mine. "Because the bruja wielding the magic would have to be dead or so weak they'd be dying. That kind of power—the power to reanimate the dead—it burns through the body and soul like *that*." He snaps his fingers to demonstrate his point.

146

"Come. Enough ghost stories," Ma says, throwing the dirty towels in the lidded bin. "Vino's stable but he needs rest. Alex, change the bandages in the morning. We'll report the attack to the High Circle on our drive to Montauk."

"Perhaps we should stay," Dad says, and I do my best to remain calm when his stare finds mine. "I don't like the idea of you all staying alone."

Part of me wants them to say. I want my parents to fix my mistakes and make it all better. But I'll be eighteen in weeks, and I have to start taking care of myself.

"We'll be fine," I say. "We won't leave the house. You guys go."

"I'll hold down the fort," Rose promises.

Alex rubs her lips together nervously but nods. Ma picks up the leather pack she stuffed full of supplies and lifts it over her shoulder.

"I'll be back tomorrow," Nova says. He rubs the blood splatter on his cheek. "If Vino wakes up before that, call me."

"Where are you going?" Dad asks.

Nova looks at his sneakers. "I left my stuff in the park."

Dad shakes his head and waves his hands like a crossing guard. "No, you're not going anywhere. Not when there's a killer out there, magical or not."

"I can't," Nova says. His eyes land on Alex, and then he backs away from the door.

"There's a bed right here," Dad tells him, and it's the most animated he's been in a while. "You found me, son. You brought me back. It's not safe tonight. You're staying here."

Rose looks from the injured boy to the empty bed and makes a face. "You want him to sleep next to an almost-dead guy?"

"Rose!" Mom hisses. Then she turns to Nova, all the patience in the world. "Nova. When you said you left your things in the park, what did you mean?"

Nova clenches his jaw but answers. "Nothing, Ms. Carmen. I really gotta go."

Nova starts to push past us, but Alex raises her hand and shuts the door with a blast of her power. Nova is about to hit it with his fist, but then looks down at Vino sleeping and changes his mind.

He turns to Alex and holds up an accusatory finger at her nose. "I *hate* when you do that."

Alex grins but doesn't let up. "Please, just answer my mom."

Nova grunts and holds his hands like he's about to choke the air. "My sleeping bag. My backpack with my food. Is that what you want to hear? All my damn stuff." Then he looks at my mom. "I'm sorry for raising my voice in your home, Ms. Carmen."

Ma takes three steps toward Nova and something tugs in my chest because I can feel his sadness coming off him in waves. She places her hand on his cheek. He won't look at her. He keeps his eyes shut and takes a deep breath, like it costs him everything not to cry in front of us. "Stay here tonight, Nova. It's late. Please."

Nova sighs deeply and whispers, "Thank you."

My parents rush to get things in order before they leave. Dad embraces Nova like a son and I try not to let it bother me. Why is it so easy for Nova to hug my father, but I can't? I push the thought away for now. I have to go check in on Maks, and in this flurry of activity, I can make my exit. Rose gets clean clothes and towels for Nova. Alex heads to her room to call Rishi, but before she does, she gives me a stern look as if to say, *This isn't over.*

I know it isn't. It's just beginning.

"Good night," I say, my body ready to crash.

But I hear my father tell Nova, "I'll bring up some ice for that bruise."

My blood runs cold and I remember the black box. The thing inside it. Dad's heading to the stairs but I shout, "I got it!"

Pain swims across my eyes as I sprint downstairs and wrench open the freezer door. I grab the black box and a couple of ice packs. Cold air blows against my face as I slam the door shut.

"What's gotten into you?" Ma asks, stepping into the foyer with Dad trailing behind her.

"Just trying to be helpful." And every. Single. Step. Hurts.

My mom studies my face. Can she see my lie? If she does, she doesn't say anything. She holds me for a long time, and I kiss her cheek, wishing I could tell her everything.

"I love you," I say, and she says, "I love you more."

Dad kisses my forehead, and they hurry out the door. I lock the door behind them, and when I make it back upstairs, winded and clutching the cramp in my side, Nova opens the door to the infirmary.

"Make yourself at home," I mutter.

He's shirtless, so I can see the full extent of the bruise that covers his right shoulder, like El Papa gripped him and left his mark before letting him go. Nova quirks his eyebrow at me and holds his hand out for the ice packs.

"Thanks," he says, then eyes the thing in my hands. "What's in the box?"

I limp five paces away from him and to my bedroom. "Ice cream."

I shut the door and lock it. I rest my head against it and breathe long and deep. My body longs to fall into my bed, but my mind is still processing today's events. The stranger sneaking around the house, the attack, the black box. I hold it against my belly, the cold delicious against my burning skin.

When I open my eyes, Maks is standing in the center of my room, candlelight bouncing along his features. I swat my hand against the wall to hit the light switch, but he rushes me, closing the distance in the blink of an eye. He rests his hands on either side of me. Blue eyes bright as headlights, he leans in, gently digging his nose into my neck, my hair. Fear and want twist in my belly.

"Baby," he whispers. He pulls back to look at me, lost, confused, and *strange*. Then he presses his hand on the center of my chest and says, "I'm so hungry."

17

Her eyes were clear as milk and stitched with blood.

He wanted to save her but she wanted him gone.

—EL LIBRO MALDECIDO/THE ACCURSED BOOK,
FAUSTO TOLEDO

My boyfriend is eating a human heart.

His hands hold it like a ripe mango, juice dripping down his chin, his wrists. His tongue clicks against the roof of his mouth with every swallow. His fingers press so hard against the organ I fear it's going to pop.

It's a heart, I think to myself. *It can't pop.*

I sit with my back against the door. The house is as still as it'll ever be, but everything feels loud—the creak of old floorboards, the whistles of snoring down the hall, the static buzz of a lightbulb left on, the rusty twinge of a door left ajar, the pop of the candles on my altar.

The loudest sound of all is the slick, wet sound of Maks devouring. He seems both thrilled and terrified. Every few seconds he stops and looks at me. His eyes wide and begging for answers I don't have, his chest heaving as if I should stop him, save him from this.

When Maks is finished, he sits and looks at his red hands. There is nothing like staring at your open palms, blood filling the creases like rivers across a barren land. He rubs his thumb across his fingers, like a reminder that, yes, those are his hands.

"Maks?"

I think about what my dad and Nova said. The note in the box. *Abomination. Casimuerto.* I don't like the way those words sound on my tongue.

I pull at my magic. It's a weak pulse, weaker than it has ever been. I let it flood through him and I search for the one thing to reassure me that he's still Maks—his heartbeat.

I can hear it, *feel* it, beating to the same rhythm as mine.

"Lula," he says, his features contorting into confusion. "What's wrong with me?"

I sit on my knees and brush his hair back. I pull him close to my chest. How can I tell him everything and make sure he doesn't hurt anyone?

"There was an accident."

"I can't remember anything." He wraps his arms around me and holds me tightly, and deep down I recognize the desperation that he clings to because I've felt that too.

I shut my eyes, hot tears rolling down my face. "I know. We'll fix that."

He touches the bloody mess around his mouth. He frowns at the sight. I grab a candle from my altar and take his hand.

"Come," I say.

It's well past midnight but I don't want to wake anyone up. I also can't leave him anywhere by himself. Not after his violent outbursts, not after he lunged for Rose. I take him into the bathroom, leave on the vanity lights because the ceiling ones bother his eyes. I let the water fill the tub with suds.

"Everything aches." He takes his shirt off and groans with the stretch of his muscles. He strips down his pants and steps into the hot water, his legs parting the suds as he lowers himself.

I grab a face towel from a shelf and kneel at his side. He rests his head back on the tiles, so still I press my finger to his shoulder to bring his attention back to me.

"Sorry, I was trying to sort out my memory," he says. "I've never felt this way before. It's strange, like I'm far away from myself. I can see these are my hands, but they don't *feel* like my hands. I can feel my heart but—" He turns to me.

"I know, I don't feel like myself either," I admit. I dip the towel in the soapy water and clean the blood off his face. He shuts his eyes and leans in.

"This feels familiar though," he says, smiling like his old self. "I could get used to you taking care of me."

I try to smile, but I can't. He said that before, like a record that's scratched. What have I turned him into?

He pushes the bubbles in the bath around and frowns when he finds the scars on his torso. "Why did this happen to us?"

Why does anything happen? I think.

Because cars collided and people died. Because no matter how hard we pray or how much we believe, the gods abandon us to ourselves, to the whims of others. Because it was meant to be but we weren't. Because life is a series of inexplicable accidents and we don't get to choose the good or the bad. Because I made a choice.

I wring the towel over the tub. The water turns pink. The blood on his face is all gone. His bone structure sharper.

"It just did," I say.

When I look into his eyes, they're the same blue I fell in love with. Eating the heart seems to have helped him recover the pink in his cheeks and the warmth of his skin, but for how long? Now all I need is a lifetime supply of human hearts until I can figure out how to fix all of this.

He holds his breath and sinks below the water. He stays down there for a few seconds and then comes back up, sucking in a mouthful of air.

"How do you feel?" I brush the wet hair out of his eyes, revealing the long scar across his forehead.

"Stronger than before." He takes my hand, the washcloth falling into the tub, and presses it over his heart. "I don't remember getting this scar. But I remember you, reaching out to me. Like you were the only thing I could hold on to. I know that doesn't make any sense."

"I'm sorry."

"For what?"

For whatever comes next. "For never introducing you to my dad. And for being different the past few months."

"We can get through anything, Lula." His finger traces the length of my jaw, bringing me toward him by my chin.

He kisses me swiftly, and for the briefest moment, it feels like it was before. Before. Before. I've wanted to go backward for so long that I don't know what it's like to move forward.

When I pull away, my body shivers from the coldness of his touch and the metallic taste of his lips.

I give him clothes to change into after he towels off. He runs his hand through his black hair. His cheeks are red from the hot water, and his face is riddled with pearly scars.

I shut the lights off behind us and walk down the hall, back to my room. Maks goes in first, but before I can follow, I hear a footstep warp the floorboards behind me.

I snap around and see Nova standing in the hall, the door to the infirmary open behind him. I assure Maks I'll be right in and turn to Nova.

He runs his hands against the shaved sides of his head, swearing under his breath.

"I should've *known*," he says, a scoff trailing bitterly. "All the questions you were asking. The reason why you were so cagey now. Are you going to tell me what was really in the box, Lula?"

Oddly enough, having Nova talk to me like this feels like I've relieved a great pressure from my chest.

"I think you know," I tell him. "I wanted to contact you. I figured if anyone could give me an answer to what's happening, it might be you. But Alex—"

"Alex didn't want to see me." He rests his hands on his waist and walks closer, the muscles of his chest rippling and tense. "*How* did this happen?"

"Nova, please. There's so much to explain. I know I have no right to ask you this, but I need your help."

"No." He crosses his arms over this chest and shrugs. "I can't get involved."

I place my hand on his arm, so warm compared to Maks. To me, even. "I can't go to my parents or the High Circle. The Alliance would lock me up. The hunters would have my head. Alex and Rose know, but this is beyond us."

In the dim light, I can see him shaking his head, and a soft, frustrated sound escapes from the back of his throat.

"I figured if anyone knew what I was going through, it would be you," I whisper.

"Was he the one who attacked us?" Nova asks.

"No, I swear! He's been here for the past two nights."

Nova's quiet for a while. The sounds of the dark return, louder than before. Something pinches at my side, like nails grabbing hold of my skin and twisting hard. But I've gotten better at hiding my pain, so I stand and wait for Nova's word.

"I don't know much, but I can contact people who might. After that, I'm out. I don't want to be involved with you guys any more than I already am."

A wave of relief crashes over me.

Nova doesn't return my smile and turns his back on me, heading down the hall to use the bathroom. In the dark, he says, "I hope you know what you're doing."

One thought echoes through my head as I return to Maks: *I hope I do too.*

18

Take from my blood.

Take from my soul.

Take all of me

even if I am no more.

—SALVATION CANTO,
BOOK OF CANTOS

I wake to a scream.

I sit up straight, disoriented and drowsy. My eyes are so tired they feel swollen and refuse to open.

"Lula, what's wrong?" Maks's voice, far away even though his hands are on my shoulders.

Then I realize I'm the one screaming.

I'm the one trying to break out of his arms, kicking and flailing because the pain that sears my skin is so strong I just want to crawl out of it.

"Lula?" This time it's Alex. She bangs on the door; then there's the thick blast of magic shaking the room until she's in.

"What should I do?" Maks asks. His voice is nervous, and I can sense—no. I can *feel* his frantic energy like it is part of me. "Help her!"

I turn on my side and bite the pillow to drown my scream. The pain bursts out of my abdomen, skin burning to the touch, swollen and wet with sweat and blood.

More footsteps and voices fill the room. There's not enough air for all of us and I choke. Everyone is talking at the same time, my sisters and Maks and Nova. Their voices like knives at my eardrums.

"What's wrong with her?" Nova.

"I don't know! She just started screaming." Maks.

"When will Ma be back?" Rose.

"I don't know." Alex. "Get me two crystals and the sleeping draught."

"No." Me. "No sleep."

"What's she saying?" Maks.

"Shut up and let her work." Nova.

Footsteps. Stomping. Shouting. Screaming. Fists. Fighting. Crashing.

"Both of you." Alex. "This isn't helping."

"Here." Rose. "Ale, I can't sense her."

"Don't talk like that. I need your help." Alex. "Not you, Nova. My sister."

Alex calls on her magic. Cold stone on my skin. Shut eyes. Darkness. Sleep.

"Lula. Lula, open your eyes!"

I do as Alex says, but when I open my eyes, I'm not in my room. I'm not anywhere I can recognize.

I'm haloed by a tumultuous black sky pinpricked by lightning. The ground is fluid, black water beneath my bare feet.

"Hello?"

Lady de La Muerte appears in front of me in a whirlwind of smoke and shadow.

"I see you're out doing my bidding." La Muerte speaks in that cold way of hers. She tilts her head to the side to examine me. Her skin is the gray of death. The air around us is enshrouded in a bone-chilling cold. I touch the tips of my ears and they're hard as ice. But the pain in my side is fading.

"Am I dead?"

"Not yet."

"Why?"

"You *broke* the balance. You created abominations. You trapped me between realms. Now you must free me."

"I'm not a goddess. I don't know how to start. I don't know *where* to start."

"Find my spear. Kill the casimuertos."

"There has to be another way. A way to heal Maks *and* free you. What about the other Deos? Where are they?"

"The Deos are where they have always been." Lady de la Muerte walks around me like a feline considering its prey. Her black dress hangs off her slender body. She walks right up to me and presses her finger on my chest, her black crystal nail digging into my skin. "We require as much as you ask for."

"The Deos ask too much, then," I say. "I can't be the one to free you."

"Why is it that humans like to say that the Deos ask *too much* when it is you who want the world to change at your whims and desires? We gave you the world. Find a way to live in it."

She floats around me. Her arms are bare, like before, but the markings on her skin are fading, every name diluting like a drop of ink in water.

"What's happening to you?" I ask.

She runs her long, thin fingers along her arm. "These are the names that should be claimed. But can't be. Instead, they float adrift on my skin. Every day the balance remains broken, more souls will be trapped in the in-between."

I get close enough to see the faded names. We stand on the water, the coldness seeping through my socks and freezing my feet.

"Are they all casimuertos?" I ask.

La Muerte looks up at me. Her black eyes hold entire galaxies if you look long enough.

"No. But lost souls share the same kind of darkness." Her movements are twitchy, and for a moment, she shudders. "Do you know what a world without death is?"

"Safe."

"*Stagnant.*"

I shut my eyes, my lashes, coated in frost, rest on the tops of my cheeks. "I don't know what to do."

"*Stupid, wretched witch.* I have told you. Find my spear. Kill the casimuertos. The longer they live, the others will—"

"Others?"

When Lady de la Muerte smiles, it is like looking into your greatest fear and losing to it. She knows it; she feeds on it. "You tethered more than Maksim Horbachevsky. What do you think happened to the other bodies?"

"I didn't—" A knot forms in my throat, blocking anything I could say. I've felt them. The never-ending pain, the silver threads. It wasn't just Maks. I knew but I didn't want to know.

"Selfish, stupid, reckless *human*. Get out of my sight."

I swallow the bile on my tongue. "I don't know how I got here."

"Here? The outside of the world. Cold and brittle. There is no life or death here. It is one of the many in-betweens of the universe. Get to work, Lula Mortiz. Destroy the heart and make the sacrifice. Or the unbalance will remain, and the world you love will fall to the chaos you have unleashed."

I feel myself sinking into the blackness at my feet. She leans into my face, and I can smell the rotting earth on her breath, winter on her skin.

"I don't have the power to fix this," I shout.

La Muerte places a hand on my chest and pushes the air out of my lungs. "Then *find* it."

19

Her pain is exquisite.

Her love is sublime.

La Tortura consumes.

La Tortura divides.

—REZO FOR LA TORTURA,
CHILD OF EL CORAZÓN AND LADY
OF LOVE UNREQUITED

She's awake," someone says.

My hearing is interrupted by a hard ringing sound.

"Thank God," Maks says. He's sitting on my bed, holding my hand.

When I sit up, the pain I felt before is gone. "What happened?"

Nova reclines on a chair near the door. He's scowling, arms crossed over his chest. His blue-green eyes could burn holes through my skin.

Then I see the bruise on his cheek.

I look up at Maks, who has a bruise on the opposite cheek.

"Alex is getting supplies," Nova says roughly.

"Supplies for what?" I pull my hand from Maks's. I pull the

covers off and notice Rose sitting cross-legged on the floor, hands resting on either knee.

"No talking yet," she says. "I need to get her out of my head."

"Her who?" I ask.

"Lady de la Muerte."

"What happened?"

Nova holds the sides of the chair. "Your sister has the Gift of the Veil."

"I *know* that," I say through gritted teeth.

"Then you know she can see *between* worlds. The Realm of the Dead specifically. Now that you've essentially torn up the balance of life and death, it's easier for the other side to try to inhabit your sister."

"No one is inhabiting me," Rose growls.

"Like possession?" Maks asks. "Is that what was happening to you, Rosie?"

I turn sharply to Nova. "Stop."

"You need to tell him. Like ASAP because if not, the shock on his sinmago ass could mess things up more."

"What did you call me?" Maks shouts.

"Wait," I say, standing up. For the first time, I notice the handful of crystals stacked on my nightstand, all cracked in half and completely black. It took four of them to heal me? "What does Rose getting possessed have to do with anything? Why can't my all-powerful *encantrix* sister heal me?"

"What's an encantrix?" Maks asks, frustrated. "What is going on?"

"It has to do with what you've done, Lula." Nova stands,

pushing himself up in a flash. "I swear. You Mortiz girls will burn this world to the ground if you're left unchecked."

"Hey!" Rose screeches. She forgoes her meditation position and points a finger at Nova's chest. It doesn't matter that she's fourteen and half his size. She has to adjust her glasses with her free hand, but her intention is clear. "I haven't done anything. Don't just lump me in with these two."

"Rosie—"

"No. Leave me alone. I can't think with you near me." Rose shakes her head and starts to storm out of the room. "Good luck with your zombie boyfriend."

She slams the door behind her.

"I take it back," Nova says, smirking at me. "She's my favorite of you three."

"If the world ended right now," I say, "it would be a whole lot easier."

Nova goes back to his chair, suddenly amused as hell. "Thanks to you, we're halfway there."

"Wait," Maks says. "What did she mean by zombie boyfriend?"

Nova picks up a book from the stack that's beside his chair. *The Creation of Deos.* Alex used to bother me and say the only studying I did was about magic. Well, clearly, I didn't study enough because I made the same mistakes she did.

Nova opens the worn book, written by one of my ancestors. It chronicles all the gods and myths associated with them. It makes the Greek gods look tame.

"Lula—"

"I guess it takes jocks a little longer to figure things out," Nova mutters.

Maks snaps his fingers. "That's where I know you from. You're from Van Buren, aren't you?"

"No, asshole. You almost *ran me over* eight months ago."

"Clearly I didn't do a very good job."

"Maks!" I shout.

Maks is a lot of things, but he's not hurtful. He turns his face to the side, and it bothers me that the motion is so close to the way La Muerte twitched her head.

"Lula, please tell me what's going on. I can't remember a single thing that happened. The last thing I remember was— waking up and going to the boardwalk. Then there's only black and voices. I'm covered in scars. Last night I—" He drops his voice. "I ate a heart."

Nova's eyes widen in my direction. "Well, it's a good thing I didn't ask you to share that *ice cream*."

"Tell me the truth," Maks says, his voice harder than before. "What did Alex do to you? What is wrong with me?"

I walk around my bed to where he stands looking just as lost as when I found him on the carousel.

"I can explain everything."

"Tell me the *truth*," he repeats.

I hate that Nova is here, watching us. If he had any sense of decency, he'd step out and give us privacy. But nothing, not an empty room or a stadium full of people, will change the words I'm about to say to Maks.

He holds my hands with his, crossing our fingers together the way we've done so many times, and I can feel his heart racing like my own.

"Did I die?" He sounds out every word, and I know the answer he wants me to give him.

I shut my eyes, a well of tears spilling down my cheeks. Maks, his eyes wide and blue and desperate and waiting for an answer I'm afraid to utter myself because it makes this, all of this all true.

"You *are* dead."

He pulls out of my hold.

"Half-dead," I try to correct.

Nova lowers the book so I can see only his eyes. "Technically, *casimuertos* translates to *almost* dead. Not half-dead."

"I'm going to casi-kill you myself if you don't shut up," I say as an empty threat.

It doesn't do much to help Maks calm down either. He paces in a circle from one end of the room to the other. For a long time, I say nothing. The only sound is Maks's feet on the wooden floors, and Nova turning the pages of the book.

"I'm not sure how it happened," I say finally. In a way, the truth undoes some of the knots in my chest. "I was trying to heal you. I told you we were in an accident. All of us. The buses crashed with a semitruck and other cars."

Every time I try to grab his hand, he yanks it away.

"There was a metal pole driven through our bodies." I keep going. It's like opening up an endless well after a drought.

Maks stops in his tracks. He touches the scar on his chest hidden beneath his shirt.

"They tried to save us both, but I had a higher chance of surviving the surgery, so they pulled you off first."

He looks down at the ground for a long time. "I remember screams. No images. Just screams."

"They took us both to surgery, but you fell into a coma. They didn't think you'd come out of it. I tried to heal you."

Maks finally meets my eyes. "The way Alex did with you?"

"Alex and Rose helped. You started to fade, and the goddess of death came for you. I was desperate. I couldn't let go, so I panicked. I tethered you to me—to my life force. I heard you come alive. Then you were dead and *gone*, but a few days later I found you. I found you, Maks."

"My parents," he says, after a long silence. "They think I'm dead?"

"Yes. Your body—all the bodies went missing from the morgue. The police are looking into the body snatchers."

"And the—hearts? In the news. The two guys with hearts torn out of their chest?"

I can't tell him that I found him holding one of the dead boy's wallets. I just can't. I grab on to him and don't let go.

Maks shakes his head. "Don't. Don't touch me. Please. You need to—I need—first you tell me I *died*. Then you brought me back only to have me die again. Then my *body* went missing. Not to mention my sudden desire for human hearts and the guy in the next room who tried to kill your sister. Please, Lula. Give me a minute."

I turn to Nova. "What's he talking about?"

Nova slams the book shut. "You missed the best part. My friend

Vino? You know how I brought him here for help? Because that's what the Mortiz family does, right? *They help.*"

"Stop being an ass," I tell him. "What happened to Vino?"

"He changed," Nova says, eyes raking Maks from head to toe. "Into one of them."

"But Maks didn't go anywhere near him."

"Right." Nova looks like he's mentally walking on a tight rope and anything I say might tip him over. "It was the thing in the park. Which means, we've got a whole mess of casimuertos to find."

"Where's Vino now?" I ask.

"Ran off," Nova says, pressing his full mouth shut to stop from shaking. "I stabbed him. I stabbed him right in his neck. He was trying to hurt Rose, and no matter how hard we hit him, he wouldn't get off."

"And he still ran?"

Nova nods, then hits his fist against the wall. "I shouldn't have come here."

"But you did," I snap. "You're here. You have two choices. Either help us and prove that you've changed, or go squat in the park because all you know how to do is run from your problems."

The door opens and Alex walks in holding a plastic bag full to the brim.

"Glad everyone's getting along," she says darkly.

"To be expected," Nova mutters. "What's that face for?"

"It's the only one I've got," she says. She rolls her eyes and I can see the struggle in her body because I know her better than she knows herself. "Nova. I need—"

"No," he cuts her off.

"You're not even going to hear me out?"

Nova squeezes the bridge of his nose with his black-tipped fingers. "I know what that bag is full of. I know you want to see her."

Alex shakes her head, not ready to give up. "Do you know anyone who might know as much about death and blood magic?"

"It's a bad idea, Alex."

"I wouldn't ask if it wasn't urgent."

"It's always urgent. Don't you get it? That woman kicked me out. She's the only flesh and blood I have in this city because the siblings I got left are either locked up or in a ditch somewhere. I don't want to see her."

Her breath hitches, and I swear she's letting herself feel sorry for him, despite swearing to every Deo in existence she'd never forgive him. Meanwhile, Maks is busy admiring the scars that riddle his body. I want to look away from Nova's pain, but I can't because as much as I hate it, I know what he's feeling.

Alex places her hand on his. "I'm not asking you to come. But I won't go see her without your okay. Not after everything we've been through."

Nova looks at my sister's face, and I see how much he cares about her. He keeps his arms crossed over his chest, his hands tucked into his armpits. Then his glance falls to me. Does he wonder if we're the same? Desperate and willing to do anything? Whatever it is, he nods once, and I suppose that's as good as we're going to get.

"Who are you going to see?" Maks asks me.

"The scariest bruja in all of Brooklyn," I tell him.

Nova's laugh is bitter as he says, "But I call her grandma."

20

Bay Ridge is bright with new shops and an excess of hipsters priced out of Williamsburg. I don't come down this way a lot, but the pizza and bagel shop Dad used to love is still open, sandwiched between a barbershop and a dollar store, where bearded old men bake in the sun on a rickety wooden bench. Kids about our age gather in groups at bodega corners and under the shade of bus stops, cutting school because it's June and the end of school is so near you can taste the sweetness in the summer heat.

Alex and I cross the street and turn a corner that marks the start of the poor side of town. Within a block, the houses are more rundown, more worn. Not even a fresh coat of paint would fix the cracks and lopsided porches or tilting foundations.

A group of guys whistles at us, but we keep walking, linking our arms together. They laugh and shout out obscenities. Alex's hand tightens around mine and the surge of her magic prickles my skin.

Something pops, and I whip around to see a lamppost shattering over the catcallers. Some of them scream. Some cross themselves. None of them bother us anymore.

Alex's smile is feline and I can't help but laugh. But a block later, when we reach the little bakery with frosted windows, we stop.

The awning over the store is ripped, and though it's a dirty brown now, I can see splotches in the fabric where it used to be red. There's a wreath on the door I recognize as a protection spell. Black branches are twisted into a ring, and at the center is a cat's cradle of copper wire with a glass eye at the heart. El Mal Ojo. When I was little, and I saw other brujas place the eye on their doors or walls or wear it as jewelry, I thought the eye could truly see. Even though now I know it doesn't, it still gives me the creeps. I always thought it was strange that a curse and the thing that protects you from the curse are called the same thing.

When we open the door to Angela's Bakery, the bells at the top jingle a pleasant chime. Despite the shabby exterior, the floors are clean, there are two tables where people can sit and eat their pastries, and the cloying sweetness of citrus and lemongrass clings to the air.

"Hello?" I call out.

No one comes to the door, despite the chiming bell.

"Deos help me," Alex says, pressing a hand on her belly and shutting her eyes. "It smells incredible."

We both inhale dreamily. Butter, fresh bread, and burned sugar waft across my senses, and, for the first time in so long, my mouth waters with hunger. I press my hands against the glass separating me from rows of decadent cupcakes topped with sugared rose petals. They almost look too pretty to eat and remind me of the canto Alex used to do for me. I touch the scars on the side of my face.

"Do you think Nova would kill me if I bought some empanadas?" she asks.

"Why do you even care if he gets mad?" I ask her. "You treat him like he killed your pet. Huh. Technically you killed your pet…"

Alex practically growls in my direction. "I'm going to ignore that. Anyway, I thought Nova and I could be friends after he showed up with Dad. I could get over the betrayal. But sometimes, when I sit and think about how lucky I am, how I love Rishi and how she makes me happy, how my family is safe, Nova just breaks into my thoughts and I feel helpless and stupid all over again. I just wish he didn't get under my skin."

I tap my nails on the glass and consider what my sister is feeling because I'm the one who hasn't let her forget what she did. Maybe I'm the one who has to tell her what she doesn't want to hear. "I think there are many different kinds of love. I think you want to love him as a friend because you share a darkness that no one else can understand. You'll never really be friends if you keep blaming him. But for right this second, you just have to be allies."

She acts like she didn't hear me and presses her finger against the counter. Her eyes are set in a frown as if the rows of fried puff pastries oozing caramel did her wrong.

"See something you like?" a raspy voice asks behind us.

I grab Alex's hand and jump.

A tall old woman waits behind us. Brown skin sags along her jawline, and her long neck is ringed with big, colorful, wooden jewelry. Her thick, curly hair is white as salt and decorated with black feathers. The petals in the resin-covered orchids that dangle from her long earlobes bring out the fuchsia accents in her wildflower-printed dress. There's a softness to the curves of her body.

But her eyes—sharp circles the color of raw tourmaline framed by high-arched eyebrows—betray everything else. They belong to someone who has seen more than her share of dark days, and when they settle on me, I feel like she knows all my secrets.

"The Mortiz sisters." She almost sounds amused. She nods her head at Alex and holds out her hands in a display of welcome. "The encantrix herself. What can I do for you?"

Alex's jaw is set, and I pray, *I pray* she doesn't ruin this. Angela is the woman who let her own grandson live on the streets. She's a woman who dreams up poisons the same way others do wishes. My sister frowns, leans forward to speak, but I cut her off.

"We beseech your help and information," I say, squeezing Alex's hand as hard as I can.

"My, my—" Her dark eyes flick from Alex to me, a wicked glee sparks at the center. "Can I offer you something? Pan de bono, right from the oven? Un cafécito?"

And because it would be an insult to turn her hospitality down, we croak out, "Yes."

While Angela busies herself behind the counter, Alex and I sit at an empty table. She does not look amused when I yank her ponytail and hiss, "*Behave.*"

"*I'm not a dog,*" she mutters, and slaps my arm.

It's only the lightest tap, but I can practically feel myself bruise. The ache pulses hot, and when Alex turns her face to watch Angela, I lift the sleeve of my shirt and my heart sinks at the sight of the black and blue. I hide it and tell myself I'll deal with this later.

"I figured you take yours black and bitter," Angela says to Alex. The older bruja sets three steaming cups on the table and takes the empty seat in front of us.

Alex purses her lips and I pinch her thigh under the table. I take my coffee and hold it up to my nose, inhale the frothy milk and a hint of sweetness. Alex stares into her cup as if she can see her future reflected in the rippling, black surface.

"It's coffee, not poison, niña," Angela says, her voice losing its amusement real quick.

Alex fake smiles but sets her cup down without taking a sip. "Well, you *did* write the book on the subject."

"Believe me, if I wanted to hurt you, I'd be more creative."

"Mmm, this smells great. Thank you." In an effort to find a middle ground between them, I drink. The coffee is strong, the milk creamy and sweet with brown sugar and honey.

Angela quirks a brow, and her demeanor softens when she turns to me. "Only the finest coffee from Santo Domingo. Does your mother know you've come to see me? Why not turn to Lady Lunes and the rest of the *High Circle*?"

Alex and I look at each other.

"Because they can't help me," I say, and I can't resist taking another sip. The sweetness coats my tongue and my muscles are more relaxed than they've been in ages. "Our family's books aren't enough. Besides, if it were up to them, I'd be dead. What

I've done—what's happening—is beyond anything they've ever handled. It's beyond us all, really, and I think it's just starting."

She considers this, and her silence stretches too long for my liking. She points a pointed, black nail at the package Alex brought with her. "Is this your payment?"

"This is for your foster kids," Alex says. Then she takes a stone out of her pocket. It's a glittering, purple stone. "*This* is for you."

"Amethyst?" Angela says, then chuckles, as if we've brought her a bit of rock from Coney Island.

"No," my sister says. "It's a stone from Los Lagos. From Las Peñas."

Angela's face falls abruptly. She picks up the stone and weighs it on her palm, then shuts her eyes and inhales. It's like she's sensing the power in the crystal right through her skin.

"Not interested," she says, placing the stone back on the table. Her black eyes gleam and a tiny smile plays at her lips.

Alex sits back so quickly her chair scraps the floor. "Why?"

"Alex," I say, a warning in my voice.

"I'm doing the favor of hearing you out. But you should've told my grandson to come himself." She picks up her coffee—black as her eyes—and drinks deep.

"This has—" I try to say, try to be the voice of reason. *This has nothing to do with Nova.* That's what I want to say, but the words won't come out.

Angela drapes an arm over the back of her chair, the queen of sugar and venom. Her lip curls, and I realize my mistake too late.

"So you two thought you'd just show up here and ask for my help?" she asks. *Black and bitter.* "You think you know all about my family, don't you? Do you know where I come from? We were run out of our island because of who we were, and when we came here with nothing but the clothes on our backs and fists full of seeds tucked into my pockets, we *made* a home out of nothing. You do not know my family, Alejandra Mortiz. So do not come into *my* shop with that scowl on your face like you *know* me. I don't care if you're the only encantrix in your generation. You'll always be the reason my grandson gave up his only chance to have long life."

Alex is at a loss for words. For once.

Angela stands and I know any chance of understanding Maks's condition and freeing La Muerte is slipping.

"I'm sorry," I say, reaching for the sleeve of her dress. "We didn't mean—"

She narrows her eyes. "And you. Don't get me started on *you.*"

I recoil slightly. "What about me?"

She holds her hands inches from my face and I fight the urge to jump back. People say that Angela Santiago dabs her potions on her fingertips. That if she touches you, your skin will grow sores or burn off or decay. They say she killed each and every one of her husbands, some slowly, some quick. They say her elixirs keep her from dying. So here she stands, with black eyes that could cut right through me, with poisoned hands, with a lineage so cursed no one dares to speak ill of them. And yet, her voice softens when she talks to me. "You are the reason the Veil of the worlds is broken."

"I've done a terrible thing," I tell her, and my tongue is loose and my mind fuzzy. I drop the coffee cup, the warm liquid sloshing over my hands. "I brought Maks back from the dead and now people are dead and I want him to be alive but he came back wrong.

176

Lady de La Muerte is trapped between realms and she says I'm the one who has to free her but she's wrong because I'm not strong enough. I'm not even strong enough to help myself and I don't know what to do."

I slap my hands over my mouth to stop the rush of emotions that beg to form into words.

"Lula?" Alex slams her first on the table and turns to Angela, who is watching with fascination. "What did you do? You said—"

"I said I didn't poison you," Angela says. "I never give my help unless I know everything my querent knows. It'll pass in a moment. Now, where does my grandson fit in all this? Did he send you?"

I tell her about Nova and his friend showing up. My breath is hard and labored because I want to fight whatever this truth potion is. I look at Alex and I know she's going to be upset that I kept this from her. But Angela leans toward me, her eyes trained on me, her hand extended like she's got an invisible reel on my voice and is tugging until she has what she's looking for.

"I saw his name," I say, my words a rush of wind. "Nova—his name appeared on La Muerte's arm. It was just one word. Noveno. I didn't know—"

Angela's eyes are glassy and hard, her mouth a snarl when she says, "You didn't *want* to know."

"Why didn't you say anything?" Alex says.

My lips are numb. Perhaps the side effect of the drink. I look down at the spilled coffee and shake my head. There is so much wrong that I don't know what I could possibly do to make it right, even if Angela decides to help us.

"Nova has been on La Muerte's sights since he was born,"

Angela says, more calmly than I expected. "I've tried so hard to help that boy. I hoped—"

It's like she catches herself because she snaps her gaze up and lets her words fade.

Perhaps I look pathetic. Perhaps the scars on my face and the hollowness under my eyes tells her to have pity. Perhaps she's afraid of the rift I've caused in the balance because she sighs and says, "I will tell you what you want to know."

"Thank you," I say, and I can't help but cry.

"But I don't want a silly rock from a banished land. I want you to make me a promise."

"What kind of promise?" Alex asks sharply.

Angela slides her eyes toward Alex, actively ignoring my sister's tone when she returns to look at me. "I want you to promise you'll keep Nova safe."

"You kicked him out," Alex says in a tone that would get her a smack from Ma. "How is that keeping him safe?"

I pinch her and she jumps, making sparks sputter over her head.

"Every family heals in their own time. You should know, what with your father's return and all. But Nova's my flesh and blood. I can't lose him and I can't help him. Promise you will do everything in your power to protect him."

Angela fishes through the tangle of necklaces she wears and finds a silver locket. When she pulls the bottom part off, she reveals a thick needle. From the perfume locket, I can smell something like roots and dirt in oil form.

I hold out my hand nervously.

Angela's whole face wrinkles as she grimaces at my gesture.

"Put your hand away. You think I want to make a deal with some-one marked by Lady de la Muerte? It has to be her."

I wish I could read my sister's thoughts. She's in a staring match with Angela Santiago, and I'm afraid that between them, the whole bakery will combust with their magic. But then, Alex turns to me and I can see her make the choice.

"What happens if she fails?" I ask.

"The poison activates and spreads to her heart."

"No," I say, and when I stand, Alex's eyes notice the fresh bruise on my arm that has somehow spread below the hem of my sleeve.

"Lula," Alex says softly. Her hand guides me back to my seat, and everything about this is wrong because she's my little sister and I should be the one protecting her.

Alex holds her finger out. "I, Alejandra Mortiz, swear by the Deos to do everything in my power to protect Noveno Santiago. From my blood to the Deos."

Angela looks pleased and pricks my sister's finger. A bead of blood bubbles to the surface, and though she remains still, I can see the flash of pain in her eyes.

"Please," I tell Angela. "I need to know everything about the casimuertos and Lady de la Muerte."

Angela stands, her chiffon dress billowing around her ankles. "Follow me."

We walk past the counter and into the back. Baker racks are stacked with pastries, and every surface is finely coated in flour.

Angela stops momentarily with her hand on the next doorknob. "Ah, you might want to hold your breath."

"What? Why?" Alex asks.

I take a gulp of air, like I'm about to dive into the deep end, as Angela opens another door and leads the way.

It's a small greenhouse with bright lights hanging from the ceiling. All kinds of plants sprout from bins and pots. Some snake around bamboo shoots all the way to the ceiling, and crystal beans sprout from bright-green blooms. There are rows and rows of exotic flowers I've never seen before in the lushest hues: reds as bright as love, the blue of sorrow, and black roses whose velvety petals hold beads of condensation.

I can't help but wonder what these flowers smell like. I want to open my mouth and gasp in awe, but my nose already itches terribly, and my lungs burn with the need to breathe.

Finally, we reach the end, go through yet another door and into a narrow hallway.

Alex and I suck in air, and I bend over and sneeze ten times in a row.

"Ay, Deos, qué dramáticas," Angela grumbles.

The light above us flickers, and I can tell Alex is nervous. I hold her hand and give it a gentle squeeze.

Angela unlocks the door with a skeleton key, and the hinges whine as she pushes it open. She reaches into the dark and pulls on a chain. The light takes a few tries to turn on, but when it does, I can't believe what I'm looking at.

There's a life-size statue of Lady de la Muerte against the far wall. I don't want to be the one to tell Angela Santiago that Lady de la Muerte doesn't exactly look like that. The pale skin and the scrawling black ink on her arms is right, but this statue gives the goddess of death a beautiful, young face and a halo of dark hair. She holds a spear, the metal spike splintering a large stone beneath her feet.

Hundreds of small, white flowers and melting candles are lined on the floor. The entire *room* is her altar. That's when I notice something else between the flowers. Skulls. Some human, some animal, all covered in traces of dirt as if fresh from the grave.

I resist the screaming urge in my gut to turn around. Instead, I lick the dryness on my tongue and smile.

"What a lovely room of skulls," I comment.

Angela chuckles in that gravelly voice of hers and turns to a wall of books. They're all old and mostly the cloth hardback kind you only get at used bookstores. None of them have names on the spine, but she thumbs her finger along them like she knows their contents by touch. When she finds the one she's looking for, I'm disappointed. It isn't a giant tome of a book like *The Creation of Brujas* or The Book of Deos. It's a thin, worn thing, barely a pamphlet.

"That's it?" I say.

Angela gives me a *look* and flips the book in her hands. "Fortunately for the human race, we haven't had many recorded cases of casimuertos. Zombies…now that's a different story."

"See? I said he wasn't a zombie," I tell Alex.

"I never said he *was*," she says. "I said 'zombie*like*.'"

"You two done?" Angela raises her eyebrows, jingling keys around her finger.

I reach for the book, but Angela holds it back. "This ain't the library. It's the only copy."

"Like, ever?" Alex asks.

Angela glances darkly at my sister. "Read it, don't touch anything else, and when you're done, come see me."

She walks out without another word and back through her poison garden.

"Charming," Alex says in a huff.

"You're lucky she hasn't killed us by now and added our heads to her altar of death."

She doesn't disagree, and we start flipping through the pages.

"I can't read in Spanish," Alex says, handing the book over to me.

I'm not much better, but the diagrams help. The cover has a faded symbol burned on the center, and it takes me a moment of staring to realize it's an anatomical drawing of a heart. I flip it open. The title page reads *El Libro Maldecido*.

"*The Accursed Book*," I translate for her. I flip the page. There are anatomy drawings of the casimuertos. Arrows point to its heart, eyes, and brain. My fingers tremble when I turn the page. The event is marked by a year and location. *1913. Vinces, Ecuador.*

"It says here that there was a case in Ecuador. A circle of brujas was trying to save the life of one of their own after she was murdered by her husband. The woman was presumed dead, and the canto unsuccessful. But the next day, the dead woman rose and started killing people in her town. They too rose as casimuertos soon after."

My heart sinks like an anchor plummeting to the bottom of the sea. I look around the room for somewhere to sit or some water to satiate my parched throat but find neither. I lower myself onto the floor and Alex follows. My feet throb like my toes have just been smashed.

"What?" Alex asks, staring at the spines of books Angela asked us not to touch. "How did they get rid of them?"

"They didn't," I tell her. "The village was razed to the ground."

"Okay, so not helpful." Alex reaches over me and flips to the next page. There's a diagram of an open chest with several lines extending out of it—just like the spool of silver thread that I saw coming from my chest.

Next page. A crude drawing of a casimuerto, blood dripping from its eyes and mouth, a heart gripped tightly in its fist.

"The casimuertos must feed off human hearts to quell their ravenous desire to live," I read the caption. "It is never sated."

"Endless supply of human hearts," Alex says dryly. "Do you think we'll be able to get that at the supermarket?"

"*Stop it*," I growl. "You're not helping."

"I'm sorry, but I have to laugh in the face of our impending doom by zombies."

I glare at her. She holds her hands up in defeat. "Fine, *casimuertos*."

"Another case recorded in 1683, outside Salamanca, Spain. An encantrix raised an army of casimuertos to do her bidding. Lady de la Muerte cleaved the bruja in two and struck her undead army from existence with her spear."

"Then why the hell hasn't Lady de la Muerte done that to you?" Alex asks. "Not that I want her to."

"Because she's trapped between realms," I say. "Here, this one is recent. Juan Buenavista, a grieving young husband couldn't see his bride go. Maria Azucena was killed leaving the chapel on their wedding day. Juan, son of a brujo but with no magic of his own, took her to the desert and made a deal for his soul with El Corazón to bind her life to his. The longer she lived, the weaker he became, and the stronger her craving for human hearts grew. Caracas, Venezuela, 1965.

"That's why I haven't been healing properly," I say. I want to shut the book and set it on fire. "So basically, everyone dies. That's the moral of the story."

"No," Alex says, pointing to a thin arrow at the corner of the page. "There's more."

I flip the page, something like hope fluttering in my heart. "Upon consuming his heart, Maria Azucena became nearly unstoppable. Her strength quadrupled. Her senses heightened. Even her hunger grew. It took a High Circle and a dozen more brujas to sever her head, but not before she killed dozens. They burned her body parts in separate pyres. El Corazón claimed both their souls."

"It's good to know gods only care about souls and blood." I half cry, half laugh. "Well, if Maks eats *my* heart, he gets superstrength."

"That's not going to happen, not while I'm still breathing." She grabs the book from me. "We'll find a way to save you."

"Save me? What about Maks? What about the others? Are we going to burn New York to the ground? Alex, this is hopeless. It's called *The Accursed Book* for a reason."

I hunch forward and grab hold of my side. The pain is back with a vengeance. I bite back on the cry and breathe until it subsides. I have to keep Alex focused.

She flips back to the beginning. "There has to be something on how to kill them without calling in the National Guard."

I take a deep breath and fight through the pain. Snatch the book back. "Let's see. More anatomy of a heart. Bones. Eyes turn white or yellow when they're consumed with hunger. Death, death, death. Ah."

I flip the final page. "Typical methods of zombie exterminations do not apply to casimuertos, as decapitation will only slow it down. A single casimuerto can be killed by destroying its heart. A horde can be eliminated by using a divine weapon to kill the—"

"What is it?" Her voice a whisper now.

"The human they are bound to."

She looks confused, then frowns with the realization. "So—"

"I have to die."

21

A casimuerto is neither living nor dead, but something in-between. Created by a deep bond of love, the heart is the only food that can keep them in a state close to human.

—THE ACCURSED BOOK/
EL LIBRO MALDECIDO,
FAUSTO TOLEDO

There's always another way," Alex says, but her voice is distant. "I know there is."

I press my hands on the uneven cement floor. That's what Lady de la Muerte meant when she spoke to me. *Destroy the heart and make the sacrifice.* I hit my head on the wall behind me. I'm an idiot for thinking the sacrifice would be only Maks.

"Lula, get up," Alex tells me.

But I'm not listening to her. I'm staring at the statue of Lady de la Muerte. At the skulls at her feet, eye sockets stuffed with white peonies.

"Lula."

"Stop!" I shout. "Gods, Alex. We are infinitely patient with *you.*"

She gets down on her knees so we're eye level. "I'm sorry. I don't want you to go down that path. Once you start thinking you've failed, you already have."

"I really screwed up."

"So did I. But here we are."

I nod, take her hand. She helps me up. My head spins, and I have to hold on to her arm to stabilize myself.

"Hang on," Alex says. She opens the book and snaps photos of the pages with her phone. "She didn't say anything about phones."

We shut the door behind us and hold our breath as we race to the other side of the greenhouse, past the kitchen, and to the front of the bakery.

Angela is placing sweets in a white box. "Find what you were looking for?"

"More or less," Alex says evenly.

"Where did you get that book?" I ask her, walking around the glass counter, holding on to Alex for support.

"Nena, don't take this the wrong way but you don't look good," she tells me.

It's my turn to laugh. "Well, I feel as good as I look."

Angela moves slowly, methodically, taking her time. She cuts a piece of string. She ties it neatly around the box to keep it closed.

"The book," she says, "was written by an old friend. Fausto was obsessed with finding the cure for death."

"There is no cure for death," Alex says.

"Doesn't mean we don't still try to find it. Most of the time, the good people, the rare and truly good, don't want the cure for themselves. They want to save someone they love, isn't that right?

But when Fausto started to research successful attempts, he came across incidents like this."

"Seven of them," I say.

"Seven that were recorded," Angela corrects me. "Death makes people desperate, and our history is long."

"What about Death herself?" I ask.

"What about her? She's a goddess, born from the shadows to keep the world in balance. Even from the gods themselves."

"The Book of Deos doesn't have much information on Lady de la Muerte, but you have a whole shrine devoted to her. Your statue is closer to her likeness than any I've seen."

Angela watches me for a moment as if seeing my future right before her eyes, and by the look on her face, it doesn't look good. "Lady de la Muerte has collected so many lives as a product of my work, it is only fitting I choose her as the patron of my magic. She is a reminder that everything ends, even the reign of gods. Even this world."

"She wants me to find her spear," I say. "In *The Accursed Book*, it said she used it to kill some casimuertos. It's a divine weapon, isn't it? Where did it come from?"

"Her spear was made from the dregs of the elemental Deos. There's a rhyme about it in the Book of Deos, if I remember correctly. As for your other problem, here."

She takes something out of her pocket and sets it on the counter beside the pastry box.

"What's this?" I ask. The tiny bottle is corked tightly. The liquid is black with tiny flecks of silver.

"An elixir for your pain."

Alex takes it from me and sets it back on the counter. "We can't. My mother will make something when we get home."

Angela turns her dark gaze on my sister. "That is not for you to decide. It's for her. She said it herself. She has to free La Muerte. Can't do that *and* walk around the city almost dead herself. Besides, I grow the kinds of herbs your mother, La Mama bless her many talents, has never heard of."

"I have nothing to offer you," I say.

"You don't have to. La Muerte and I have a score to settle and I can't do that if she's trapped. Consider it a gift."

I want to say that when it comes to magic, nothing is *just* a gift. Gifts of power come with blessings or curses or sometimes both. I want to say that I'll return her kindness by being nicer to Nova. But my insides are as twisted as my tongue, and so all I can do is take the tiny glass bottle and say, "Thank you."

"Just remember," Angela says. "The casimuertos consume because they are never sated. It's the thing that makes them the most human, even though they are unnatural to this world. Do not fail her."

So I've been warned.

"Thank you, Doña Angela."

"Don't thank me yet." She pushes the pastry box toward Alex. "Take this for your parents with my blessings."

Alex doesn't talk back.

We're halfway outside when the bells jingle overhead. Outside the sky is darker. The streets empty. An unseasonable chill in the air.

Angela calls out to Alex one more time, and we stall at the doorway.

"Tell Nova to come home. When he's ready."

We take the train back home. We don't talk. Alex holds the pastry box in her lap and stares out the window at the graffiti on the subway walls. I reread the pictures of the book she took on her phone but nothing stands out. Then I take out the small potion and shake it between my fingers.

"Are you going to drink that?" Alex asks.

"I'm still feeling the side effects from the other potion," I say, clearing my throat in the process.

Alex nods quietly. There is nothing quite as sobering as the truth. "I can keep healing you. You don't have to."

I can't keep having my sister suffer the recoil of healing magic for me. "I will. I just…I think it's going to get worse, and I want to save it for when it does. I can manage this."

She looks at me like she wants to disagree, so I change the subject.

"Find the spear, free La Muerte, destroy the heart, and make the sacrifice." I rest my head on her shoulder, a hard weight pressing down on my chest.

"I'm going to save you," Alex says. "This isn't how your story ends."

I don't want to tell her that she's wrong about one of those things. "Until we can find the spear, we need to make sure no one else gets hurt. We can't tell anyone about what we read. Especially not the parts about me dying."

"Agreed."

The train rattles more than usual, and the b-boys jumping

190

around in the car rethink their busking strategy. I'm afraid Lady de la Muerte is going to appear out of nowhere again, but the last time I saw her she looked about as healthy as I do. At the next stop, the car empties out.

"I should've listened to you." I rest against her because my body feels drained. "To Ma. To everyone."

Alex sighs. "You don't have to do that to yourself."

"I can't help it. I did this, Ale. I was just so angry. I thought I could take control of everything I wanted. I even used my power to make Maks want me again. Maybe the Deos caused that accident because I tried to use my power on me and Maks." I lick silent, salty tears from my lips. "I made him kiss me because I couldn't handle us being apart. What kind of a monster does that?"

My sister brushes my hair away from my face. She holds my face gently in her hands but her eyes are fierce. "You're not a monster. The accident wasn't your fault. The Deos didn't punish you. You of all people know that your power doesn't work like that. If Maks kissed you, it was because he wanted to. You were hurt and confused and you messed up. But you're also loyal and kind and good. You've never been afraid to bare yourself. When I needed you, you were there, in Los Lagos, guiding me. Because you *loved* me. All my life I've wanted to love as fiercely as you love. So when I say this isn't how your story ends, I mean it."

I hold her hand tighter and take the strength she offers just by being with me and don't let go until our stop.

When we get home, I'm half expecting the place to be wrecked. Nova and Maks aren't exactly compatible. But when Alex and I walk through the front door, we hear the strangest sound.

Laughter.

"We have a PlayStation?" Alex asks.

Rose, Nova, and Maks are sitting on the couch.

"Bro, she is kicking your ass," Maks shouts. He runs his fingers through his hair in a motion so familiar it brings butterflies to my stomach.

Rose's thumbs move fast across the controller buttons. Every few seconds she grunts, like she's coaching her player in real life.

"Yes!" Rose yells. She smiles so hard her eyes are nearly swallowed by her cheeks. "In your *face!*"

Nova curses but then laughs and hands the controller over to Maks.

I turn to Alex. "Is this more or less weird than the poison greenhouse we walked through?"

"For us?" she says, scoffing. "More. Definitely."

The trio on the couch look over at us, like *we're* the ones acting strangely.

"I didn't know you had *Street Lighting*," Maks tells me. "Your sister kills at it."

"I didn't know we had it either," I say, walking around and sitting on the couch arm beside him. He places a hand on the small of my back, and for a moment, it's enough to forget everything Alex and I have learned.

A moment.

"I found it in the basement," Rose said, typing her name as the new top score.

"From the look on your faces," Nova says, "my gran didn't exactly have good news."

He stands, and the smile vanishes from his beautiful face. I feel like I'm Lady de la Muerte herself, sucking the life out of a room.

"Any word from Mom and Dad?" Alex asks Rose, ignoring the question for now. I wonder what Nova would say if he knew the deal Alex struck for him.

"The baby won't come out," Rose says, turning off the game and switching to the local news. "I don't know when they'll be back."

"At least they'll be safe out there," I say.

"What's up?" Maks asks. "What did the witch lady say?"

Then Nova, Alex, Rose, and I say, "*Bruja.*"

Maks holds his hands up. "My bad, jeez. Sorry."

Alex pushes aside the PlayStation on the coffee table and sits. She sets the bakery box beside her.

"Angela let us read a book detailing past incidents with casimuertos." Her eyes flick to Maks. "It's called *The Accursed Book.*"

"And?" Nova asks impatiently.

"She gave Lula a potion for her pain."

Nova makes a face, supersuspect of us. "She just *gave* it to you? On top of letting you read that book?"

"No," Alex says, but won't meet his eyes. "We paid."

"What did you give her?" Nova stands abruptly.

Alex blinks but doesn't react to his outburst. She closes her hand into a fist to hide the index finger with the promise mark. "None of your business."

"You don't know her, Alex." Nova shakes his head and paces

193

across the living room. "Everything she says has a loophole or a trick. Trust me."

"We got what we needed. Let me handle this."

"What's next?" Maks asks. "Is there a way to reverse this?"

I can't look at him. I can't tell him that there's no way to reverse this. That the only way he'll feel better, stronger, is if he consumes my heart.

"We're working on that," Alex lies for me.

"Wait, turn that up," Nova says, pointing at the screen.

For a few seconds, I'm thankful for the break in answering questions. Alex raises the volume. It's the same reporter we saw a few days ago except now his eyes are bruised with sleepless dark circles.

"Is that by your school?" Rose asks.

The reporter glances warily at the house across the street, and bright-yellow police tape ripples in the breeze. A dozen cops gather on the front lawn, one of them taking a witness statement.

"Behind me is Detective Hill," Adam reports. "He has not confirmed the cause of death of the Maguire family, allegedly attacked by a group of assailants in the neighborhood just behind Thorne Hill High School. A neighbor reported hearing screams, but when the police arrived, the perpetrators were gone. The medical examiner is on her way, but sources confirm that there are no survivors. Police are canvasing the area. Detective Hill advises all to stay in their homes—"

"It's the casimuertos," I say, rubbing the painful spot building in my chest. "It has to be."

Nova looks worried but not convinced. "There are tons of murders in this city."

"It's right by our school though," Alex says. "What if it's the others who went missing? We have to at least look into it."

"What are we going to do if we find casimuertos?" Nova raises his voice. "If I see *Vino*? Smash his brain out or ask him to come quietly? Do we even know how to stop them? Because stabbing him sure didn't."

"We could—" Rose starts to say, but her voice is drowned out by Alex.

"Anything can be killed," Alex says, and Maks flinches at the hardness in her voice. "I can sedate them with my power."

Maks tugs on my arm. "We aren't going to try to find a cure?"

"That's not what Alex meant," I say, rubbing the hand he rests on my knee.

"You shouldn't be using your power out in broad daylight anyway," Nova says. "We don't need the THA or the hunters coming after us."

Maks's eyes dart from Nova to me. "What's the THA?"

"Thorne Hill Alliance. It's a supernatural group that's supposed to keep the peace," I say quickly.

"What if " Rose says again.

"Also, I'm a little uncomfortable with the whole 'smashing their brains out' part," Maks says, fidgeting on the edge of the couch.

"Where are we going to put them if we can't kill them?" Nova claps his hands, frustrated. "I'm pretty sure your parents are going to notice a living room full of undead baseball players."

"Soccer," Maks corrects indignantly.

Rose stands up and stomps to the living room entrance. She takes a geode from a side table and slams it on the ground. The crystal splinters into pieces and leaves a fist-size scuff on the wooden floor.

"Can you all be quiet long enough for me to talk?" Rose asks.

"Then talk, kid," Nova says, holding his hands up defensively.

Rose looks pleased with that, but Alex still frowns.

"Where did you park your car before you got on the bus?" Rose asks Maks.

He squints, struggling to search for the memory. The last time we were in that car, he was breaking up with me.

"School," I say. "We parked in the lot and then got on the buses."

"We can take his car," Rose says. "We can put them in the garage."

"And what, keep them hostage?" Maks asks. The pink is gone from his cheeks, and his eyes are starting to fade to a milky blue. He's going to need to eat again and I can't help but edge away from him.

"Keep them where they can't hurt anyone else," Alex says, and her body tenses like she can read my thoughts. "There were twenty-five bodies missing from the hospital morgue that day, and you're the only one whose location we know."

Maks breathes hard and fast, opening and closing his fingers into white-knuckled fists. "I don't understand why this is happening."

Nova leans forward, rubbing his hands together as if he's getting ready to fight.

"I think I can," I say, and all eyes are on me. "Every story in *The Accursed Book* starts with a bruja or brujo trying to save someone from the dead. I know the way our magic works, and the combination of our three powers, the binding canto I used to tether your life to mine, and Lady de la Muerte appearing—it all just clashed."

"But why are there others like me?" Maks asks, and it pains me that he looks so lost.

"Because they were all supposed to die too," Rose says. "Everyone that was supposed to cross over got pulled into our canto."

"I can end this," I say.

"How?" Nova asks. "I thought you said there was nothing in the book."

"*There wasn't,*" Alex cuts me off, the anger in her eyes silencing me. "What she means is *she* has to be the one to free Lady de la Muerte. That's how we end this. But right now, we have to do what we can, and that's get the casimuertos off the streets."

"Can this Lady Muerte bring me back?" Maks asks.

"I don't know," Alex lies again.

There's a static quiet—Rose cleaning her glasses, Nova cracking his black-inked fingers, Maks scratching his chest raw, and Alex's pleading stare transfixed on me.

"Let's start with Rose's idea," Nova says. "It's the best plan right now. Follow the places where the latest attack reports are." Then something dawns in his eyes. "Better yet, how did you find Maks in the first place?"

"A thread," I answer, placing my hand over my chest. "I can't control it. It hasn't happened since."

Nova scratches the back of his neck and looks at Alex. "Without your power, we'll need weapons."

"Not my first magical rodeo," Alex says and leaves without another word. She takes a right in the hall, toward the kitchen. I can hear the squeaky basement door open and slam, followed by her heavy footsteps going down.

"What did Alex trade with my gran?" Nova asks me, looking over his shoulder like he expects my sister to materialize at the sound of her name.

"That's for Alex to tell you, if she wants," I say, leveling my eyes on his. "You really think I'm going to betray my sister for you? Boy, bye."

Before he can respond, Alex runs back in, a black sports duffel slung over her shoulder and Dad's old machete in her hand. She lets the bag drop on the ground, metal clinking and clanking against the floor.

"Where did all this come from?" I ask.

"After my mess last year, I've been trading cantos for weapons." Alex unzips the bag. "Take your pick, y'all. We're going zombie hunting."

22

El Papa was no fool.

He noticed the way La Mama pulled away.

The way she leaned into El Cielo, unburdened by shadow.

And so his jealousy gave birth to La Amargura.

It was the beginning of the end.

TALES OF THE DEOS,
FELIPE THOMÁS SAN JUSTINIO

The five of us take the train to Thorne Hill High. Maks watches me as we catch the N train and sit down. Aboveground, the sunset casts an orange glow over the city. It even makes Maks look less gray, less undead.

"Is this what you do all the time?" he asks me.

"No," I say, placing my hand on his thigh to stop it from bouncing nervously.

He twitches slightly every few moments.

"I just remembered something," he says. "I dropped you off at that yoga place in Williamsburg. Were they really yoga classes?"

I turn on the yellow subway seat to face him. "You have to understand. We aren't allowed to tell people about our secret."

"Why?" He isn't defensive. He's calm. Too calm. The calmness of when I discovered him and brought him home. "With your powers, you could help people. Like, the way they healed you? What about the people who can't find a cure elsewhere? Alex is like a superhero. She could catch bad guys. She—"

"It's not that simple." I drag my thumb gently over his cheek.

"I don't understand," he says. "How come you made the exception to heal me?"

"You weren't the exception," Alex says.

I turn my head so fast I almost give myself whiplash. "No one is talking to you."

"He has to know," she says. "He's part of this."

"Wait," Maks said. I asked you for the truth, Lula. I deserve to know. What does your sister mean that I'm not the exception?"

Rose pushes up her glasses and bites the already-raw cuticles on her thumb. Nova looks away, and Alex, well, I'm going to kill her.

"We weren't supposed to heal you. No one believed you'd come out of the coma. But I did it anyway because I couldn't lose you."

"Maybe you shouldn't have brought me back," Maks whispers. For a painfully long couple of minutes, he turns his face to the window, watching the tunnel zoom by. When he finally looks at me, his brows are knit close together, and his eyes search my face. So much pain marks his features, and I hate that I'm the one who put it there. "But I'm glad you did."

He kisses me hard, and I don't care that we're in a train with my sisters and Nova. I kiss him back harder because, when this is all over, I want to remember the feel of his lips.

Destroy the heart and make the sacrifice.

"This is our stop, lovebirds," Nova says.

When we get off the train, Alex and Rose walk up front, and Nova brings up the rear.

"Will you stop looking around?" I tell Nova. "You look suspicious."

"You kidding?" Nova adjusts the bag of weapons and flashes me a smile. Even in the dark, his Caribbean Sea eyes are bright. "This is the safest I've ever felt. We got a get-out-of-jail-free card." He winks and points at Maks.

I laugh, but Maks doesn't. He's stares at the red hand at the crossing light.

"Anything in my grandmother's zombie book about when he spaces out?" Nova whispers at my ear.

The light changes over to white, and we move.

Maks's milky blue eyes swivel toward Nova, and for all of his bravado, I see a nervous flicker in Nova's face. Maks's mouth widens into a smile.

"You okay, bro?" Nova asks him.

"I'm just trying to remember," Maks says. "Whenever I try, I see splotches. Even before the accident."

"It'll take time," Nova says. "Your mind is probably trying to protect you from the trauma you suffered. That mixed with mad magic, boom! Memory loss."

"Thanks for the lesson in Nova-science," I mutter.

Maks and Nova do that thing guys do, when they lift their chins and nod in solidarity. When we reach the high school, we stop. The tall, Gothic spires create long, pointed shadows on the ground. But that isn't the arresting part.

The entire steps are covered in flowers, candles, and wreathes with pictures of the dead. Ramirez. Kassandra. Maks. Twenty-two faces, smiling and alive. A shrine as big as I've ever seen. The ache in my chest strengthens, and Maks squeezes my hand hard. It can't be easy seeing himself there.

"How long has it been?" Maks asks. "Time is one of the many things I can't keep track of."

"Seven years," Rose says, walking ahead of us. "Welcome to the zombie apocalypse."

I glare at Rose, but Maks just laughs. There's something frightening about his laugh, especially here in front of a shrine dedicated to the dead. Or undead, I suppose.

We keep to the side of the building as we walk toward the parking lot. Alex breaks the lock with her magic, and we zigzag between cars until we find Maks's. His parents have been too busy to pick it up. I want to believe it's a sign the Universe is in our favor. I want to send a prayer to the sky, but I just keep walking. The Brooklyn lullaby of sirens fills the air. Past the parking lot, behind a row of houses, the red and blue lights whirl where the cops are at the crime scene.

"Anyone bring the keys?" Nova asks, looking over his shoulder. With the sunset, there is only the bright streetlamps that make shadows jump out around us.

"Move over," Alex says, pushing him out of the way. She presses her hand over the car door. Her eyes darken as she summons her power, and then there's the *click*.

"Okay, now does anyone know how to hot-wire a car?" I ask.

"I got this." Maks cracks his knuckles.

"You do?"

"Yeah, remember my cousin Rome?" Maks pulls a plastic cover from the underside of the front seat. "He works at a garage. The summer I was benched after my surgery, he had me work there so I wouldn't go nuts in the house."

"I didn't know that," I say.

He pulls at some wires and starts to twist them. "I'm glad after two years of being with me I can still surprise you."

When he winks, I get butterflies. I haven't felt this way in so long. I press my hands on my abdomen, like I can feel real wings unfurling.

"Guys," Rose says, craning her neck around another parked car. "I think we're being watched."

"I'll go check it out," Alex says.

"I'll come with you," Nova says.

"No," Alex says harshly. "I'm stronger than you. You'll just get in my way."

Nova looks like he's been punched in the gut, but he doesn't follow my sister as she runs out of the parking lot.

"When did Alex get so mean?" Maks asks. He jumps as something shocks him. He undoes the wires again and mutters something about color schemes.

"She's not mean," I say. "She's stressed."

"Did my gran say something to her?" Nova asks, crossing his arms over his chest and leaning against the front of the car.

"Yeah," I say. "She said to tell you to stop whining."

Nova kicks the tire and sucks his teeth. "Forget y'all. I'm going to see what I can get from the crime scene."

"Shouldn't we stick together?" Maks asks, frustrated.

But Nova's already gone.

"Do you see anything?" I ask Rose.

"No. All I see and hear is static. Like when we—" She stops abruptly and looks over at Maks. "At the hospital."

I nod, understanding what she means. The night we tried to heal Maks, she said the same thing. It has to be up to me to sense the casimuertos. But I don't know how I made the thread appear when I was looking for Maks.

The roar of the engine is followed by the beam of headlights. Maks dusts off his hands and smiles victoriously. He pumps a hand in the air, the way he did when he saved an impossible goal and basked in the uproar of the crowd. *Maks will never play again*, I think.

He climbs out of the car and grabs me around my waist and lifts me into the air, bringing me back down slowly, so we're close enough to kiss. His cool breath is on my lips, and I shiver under his cold touch. *Maks will never be warm again*, I think.

Then, clouds roll in with a gust of wind. Lightning crashes all around and wrenches us apart.

23

La Mama and El Cielo gave birth to
El Viento, Lord of Flight. They didn't stop there.
Flowers and trees rose across hilltops,
leaning toward their mother's light and their father's sky.

—TALES OF THE DEOS,
FELIPE THOMÁS SAN JUSTINIO

I push myself off the ground, and tiny pebbles stick against my palms. I touch my chest, expecting to see the thread of silver, but there's nothing there besides a deepening ache.

"Rose?" I call out.

There's a dent on the door where Maks was slammed into the car. But if he feels pain, he shrugs it off and stands.

"You guys okay?"

"That's Alex." Rose appears from around the back of another car, a bloody cut on her forearm. "I recognize her power."

"I'll go find her," I say, unzipping the duffel bag of weapons and retrieving a machete. "Stay here, both of you."

I run in the direction Alex went, ignoring Maks's and Rose's protests.

"Alex!" I shout her name. The block is completely deserted. When I run around the corner I have to stop. My insides seize with a stabbing sensation, and my legs threaten to give out under my weight. I crawl on the sidewalk toward the lamppost, scraping my knees as I dig in my jacket pocket. I knew it would get worse before it got better. I pull out the glass bottle with the elixir, but my hand cramps, and I look down to see the veins beneath my skin roiling like black snakes. I take a swallow, leaving some for later.

I breathe deep, aware of every inch of my body, every spark of agony. It's like my guts are threaded with live wires. But I keep breathing, the elixir burning cold in my belly until the pain ebbs to nothing. When I can stand, I look up at the sky to search for Alex's lightning, but there are only thick rain clouds. I keep running, but this street turns into a dead-end alley.

"Lula! Stay back!"

It's Alex.

I hear footsteps behind me, but when I glance over my shoulder, the street is empty and pitch black. I run into the alley, follow the sound of fists pummeling flesh and bottles shattering.

Alex is surrounded by five figures. She's conjured an orb of light overhead, but she can't seem to hold it and fight at the same time, so it pulses like a strobe light.

"Sorry about the lightning," Alex says, looking at me past her attackers, hands up in a fighting stance. "It was supposed to be a little warning thunder clap."

A guttural growl comes from the shadows that surround my sister. I shake out the cramp in my hand and grip the machete tighter.

Casimuertos.

I pick up a bottle from the pile of garbage and throw it at them. "Hey, over here!"

Two of them turn on me.

"Oh no!" I cover my mouth at the familiar faces staring at me.

Raj and Dale. Or what's left of them after the accident. The skin around Raj's jaw is missing, exposing the white bone and bloody mess of his gums. Dale's sickly gray skin is covered in burns and bruises. There's a long gash on the side of his head where the stitches are coming undone.

"I don't want to hurt you," I say, losing my nerve. *You already have*, a voice growls in my thoughts.

They answer with unintelligible grunts. Raj lunges for my chest, but I kick out and throw him off balance. Dale grabs ahold of my jacket and pulls hard. I swing the machete upward, hitting his side.

But when I pull the blade back, he keeps charging for me and knocks it out of my hand.

"They're not stopping," I shout at Alex. "Remember the book—"

"The author of that book never met me."

Despite the confidence in her voice, she's panting and clutching what must be a cramp at her side. She shuts her eyes, a hard breeze picking up dirt and garbage around us. Her magic gives me vertigo, and I stumble to the brick wall for support.

She raises her fists into the air and shouts above the whistling wind.

"I call on El Terroz, Lord of the Earth and Its Treasures. *Quiebra!*" Then she punches the ground with bare fists. The ground trembles and bucks, knocking all of us over, expect for her. One of the brick walls crumbles on top of three casimuertos.

Her victorious grin is gone as her eyes fall on something moving behind us.

Dale and Raj are standing back up.

"I can't knock them out long enough to rip out their hearts," Alex says. "I'm fading."

She picks up two bottles from the floor. Shatters the ends and holds them up as weapons. I can't leave my sister to fend for herself. I push myself off the wall, screaming, and shove Dale down. He slams his head on the corner of a metal Dumpster. I roll on my side and scrape my knees as I stand.

"Raj," I cry, every breath coming labored.

For a moment, he looks at me. His eyes are unnaturally white, and red veins run from the dark center. But there is no recognition there, and he snaps back to Alex. Beside them, Dale rises again.

Raj lashes out, his fingers curved into claws. Alex leans back to dodge, then kicks him in the solar plexus. He curves forward, holding his middle as he falls to his knees. Before he can stand, she thrusts the glass through the gaping hole in his jaw.

Alex dusts off her shaking hands. "One more."

"Dale," I say. "Remember me? I introduced you to Lonnie. Remember?"

"That's not working!" Alex grunts.

Dale bares his teeth and snarls. There isn't any recognition in his eyes. Just hunger.

But as he reaches for my chest, Raj sits back up too. Then, bricks tumble where the other three casimuertos rise from the rubble.

"I'm going to summon fire," Alex says. "Run. Get the others and go. I won't be hurt."

"I'm *not leaving* you alone."

We're side by side now, facing five casimuertos that block the alley.

"I know you," one of them tells me, her voice warped and deep. Her hair is burned off, exposing bubbled skin. One of her eyes is missing, and flesh dangles where the hollow space is. The other is white and red.

"Kassandra?"

"You were next to me." Her bottom lip is split and green with infection. "You should've died."

"Kassandra, listen to me." I hold up my hands. But what can I say? What can I offer them except death? "I'll fix this."

"Do you know what I saw just before I was going to die?" she asks me. "I saw my family. They were waiting for me. My grandmother. My dad. I was walking toward them. And then, I saw you. Ripping me away and bringing me back here. You ripped me out of Heaven."

"I'm so sorry." But I know if I were her, I wouldn't want an apology. I would want revenge. "I'm going to make this right."

Another lie. I can't make this right. I can't bring them back. My eyes burn hot as I realize there is nothing I can do for her—for all of them—expect sacrifice myself. And that feeling of helplessness is worse than anything else.

"No," Kassandra says. "You're going to die."

She lunges for me. I shut my eyes and put my arms up. I should move, but I can't.

There's the whistle of wind. The sound of Kassandra grunting. The gurgle of something wet.

I open my eyes. A long, curved blade splits Kassandra in half, carving her down the middle from head to throat.

I blink, my lashes heavy with sweat and blood splatter. I try to breathe, but my chest feels tight. I follow the sword from the hilt to the black-gloved hands that hold it, all the way up to an unsmiling, half-masked face. Eyes dark as ink look down at me.

"I gave you twenty-four hours," he growls. "You didn't listen."

He grabs my shirt and drags me away from the casimuertos. I trip on a pile of garbage and fall forward. I want to shout, but I'm too stunned, a rag doll in his grasp.

"Lula!" Alex shouts. She sends a blast of energy at the guy holding me, and a few moments later, she's helping me stand.

She revives the orbs of light overhead. We stand before a group of newcomers, three imposing figures dressed in black, brandishing long swords with curved edges and handles that glisten like obsidian.

Though I've never seen them before, I know who they are, and my heart thunders. *Hunters.* The Knights of Lavant.

The guy who spoke to me recovers from Alex's attack, but he doesn't advance on us again. His posture is predatory but rigid, as though he's holding back. His shoulder-length hair blows around his face, and even though he's masked, his dark, disapproving stare is unmistakable.

"Finish these," he tells his companions in a harsh voice. "I'll get the witches."

The three of them move fast as the wind. I blink, and the next moment the casimuertos are hacked into pieces, fingers still twitching and eyes still blinking.

"Stand back!" Alex holds up her hand up, and the hunter hesitates.

I pick up a brick and fling it as hard as I can. As Alex yanks my hand to retreat, I can't see it hit the mark, but I hear the hunter grunt.

Headlights beam and a car skids at the alley entrance in front of us.

"Get in!" he shouts. I never thought I'd be so relieved to see Nova. Alex runs around to the front passenger seat.

Maks opens the passenger door and gets out to reach for me, but he freezes at the scene behind us.

"We have to go!" I press my hands on his chest, but he won't budge.

"Stop right there!" one of the black-clad hunters shouts.

When I turn around, the long-haired hunter is running after us.

"Maks!" I slap my palms on his face and he starts, coming out of his shock and climbing back into the car.

The hunter punches the window on my side, glass fractures, and whatever the hunter shouts is lost in the rev of the engine. Nova hits the gas and doesn't let up until we're far out of their reach.

24

When he learned of La Mama's betrayal,
El Papa cried so long his tears gave birth to
the oceans, drowning La Mama's other creations.

—TALES OF THE DEOS,
FELIPE THOMÁS SAN JUSTINIO

Nova runs a red light. He hands a metal rectangle to Alex in the front passenger seat.

"Is that my license plate?" Maks asks.

Nova looks up at the rearview mirror with humor in his blue-green eyes. "Yeah, I didn't want the hunters to get a read on that. Though I'm pretty sure they already know who we are."

"Hunters?" Maks asks.

"Welcome to our world, little zombie," Nova says.

"Don't call me that," Maks says, voice dripping with disgust.

I could explode right out of my skin right now, but Rose places her hand on mine. She always has a calming way about her that's hard to understand. But the calm doesn't last. Nova drives as recklessly as a yellow cab, and I grip the handle above the window as he makes a sharp turn on the highway. Traffic is light, so we coast most of the way south. I keep looking back to see any cars following us, but so far nothing. There is only the river and bridges connecting us with downtown Manhattan, lights sparkling like stars.

Alex rests her head back and clenches her jaw as the recoil of her magic hits her system. She arches her back, and her arms tremble with seizures. When it passes, she breathes long and slow, then wipes away the black soot on her palms.

"I've never seen the hunters before," Rose says, a little too enthusiastically considering they're now hunting *us*.

"Who are they?" Maks asks.

"Ma never really talked about them," Alex says.

"They're called the Knights of Lavant." When he says their name, Nova grips the wheel harder. "They've been hunting magical beings for centuries. Mostly were-beasts and vamps. Witches were harder to find out, but they have no love for us."

"Why doesn't anyone know about this?" Maks asks, frustrated. "I mean, regular people deserve to know what's out there."

Those words coming from him bother me more than I'd ever thought. *Regular people.*

"Because the *regular* world can't process anything outside of their comfort," Nova says. "The Knights of Lavant existed to rid the world of evil and keep the supernatural hidden. But not all things that look monstrous are evil."

He and Alex share a quiet stare, and I wonder if they're remembering their time in Los Lagos.

"So this happens all the time?" Maks asks, and his incredulity is so naive. "How do you live?"

Alex cackles humorlessly. "You being a casimuerto has something to do with their interest in us."

"What, they don't hunt witches?"

"It's complicated," Nova says, glancing over his shoulder at the empty road behind us. "The abridged version? When the underworld leaders banded together to form the Thorne Hill Alliance, the Knights had no choice but to stop hunting without probable cause. The Knights didn't even sign the Alliance treaty until three years after its inception. They didn't want to give up their authority, but that was the good thing about the Thorne Hill Alliance—the vamps, the weres, the witches—we have our differences but we outnumber the Knights."

"Wait, Thorne Hill? Like our school?" Maks asks.

"Yeah, the founder of the school was a hunter," Nova says. His eyes catch mine in the rearview mirror.

"I didn't know that," Alex says, frowning. "How do you?"

"I told you once, Ladybird," Nova says, leaning forward on the wheel to reach for his seat belt. "I make it my business to know things."

"The hunter who saved me from Kassandra said he gave me twenty-four hours," I say, and in this moment, I wish everything would slow down. That I could get lost in the dark of the city and have all of this fade into a dream. "They gave me the heart. They know where we live."

"I can't believe I'm saying this, but we were lucky the Knights showed up," Nova says. "They must've been hunting the casimuertos. When I went to investigate the crime scene behind the school, the EMT said the whole family had their hearts ripped out. That could've been you."

Alex looks at me and the secret between us is a chord around my neck.

"Lucky," I say bitterly.

"That girl was going to *rip* out your heart," Alex shouts, turning around in her seat. "You weren't even going to fight back. I know you feel guilty, but you have to fight back. You were stupid and reckless. You can't free Lady de la Muerte if you're dead."

"Whoa, easy," Nova says.

"No, she's right," I say softly.

"Isn't this one less problem?" Rose asks. "We can concentrate on the spear, and the Knights of Lavant can hunt the casimuertos."

"Not if they want to kill Maks too," Nova says.

"So where do we go?" I ask.

"I know a shifter," Nova says. "He's THA so if we explain what's happening, they can give us sanctuary. The Knights can't touch us if he lets us in. We can let the heat die down tonight and go from there."

"And you're sure we can trust him?" I ask.

Nova nods as the car flies down the highway. "As much as I can trust anyone."

"T-H-A?" Maks spells it out.

"Thorne Hill Alliance," I say.

Nova flicks the turn signal and takes the exit to Coney Island. "I forgot I love driving. I should really get my license."

The crumbling art deco building on West Twenty-First Street faces the ocean. I've walked past it a million times and never thought

215

of it as much more than another bit of decaying property in New York's forgotten corners.

But now, standing in front of one of the four archways, I can feel the glamour protecting it. When Nova lifts the rusted knocker on one of the doors and slams it, the illusion crackles and fades away, and I see the building for what it truly is.

Terracotta tiles cover every inch of the exterior. Sandstone carvings that mimic rolling waves decorate the top of each archway. Blue-and-gold mosaics depict breathtaking renderings of Poseidon and his trident, the night sky, a wolf howling at the moon, and a woman wielding magic.

"What if he's not home?" Maks asks.

"What if he won't let us in?" Rose asks.

The door swings open, and the soft light from inside the building is the brightest thing on the boardwalk. A young man with messy, brown hair peeking from the edges of a black Yankees baseball cap stands at the door. He has a twisted smile, like he finds everything in the world amusing.

"What's the brouhaha, kids?" he says, mischievous, brown eyes taking in the harried sight of us.

Nova shakes his head and takes the hand the shifter extends. "You're still corny as hell, McKay."

"You look familiar," Alex says, squinting at his face.

"I just have one of those faces." McKay lifts his cap up at her and steps aside to let us in. "Sorry about the mess. We've been out in full force thanks to an increase in otherworldly attacks. But I suppose that's just a regular Tuesday night."

"It's Thursday," Rose points out.

"Scorn the calendar gods!" McKay shakes his fist at the ceiling in faux rage. He shuts the door and it locks automatically. "I'd ring for tea, but this doesn't seem like a social visit. Also, we don't drink tea. What's up, Nova?"

"Trouble," Nova says. "You mentioned an increase in other-worldly attacks."

"Yeah," he says, his curiosity piqued.

"We know what they are," I say.

"Say no more," McKay says, lifting his hands. "My partner will be here shortly, and he'll want to hear this. Follow me."

We follow the shape-shifter through a living room area littered with clothes and books and dozens of coffee mugs. It looks more like a laid-back office space than the headquarters for a super-natural organization. Then, he leads us down a hallway to a metal door with a closed eye embedded at the center. When McKay gets closer, the eye opens up and blinks twice. McKay lines up his eyes to the one on the door, a bright yellow light scans his retina, then the eye shuts. The metal door swings open.

"Is that a real eye?" Maks asks.

McKay sort of shrugs and turns the light on in the white room. Rows of tables project holograms of public spaces: Times Square, the World Trade Center, Coney Island, Central Park, the airports, the seaports, and Long Island City. Every few moments, the holo-gram zooms in on a face. Information scrolls up in neon-green text. Name: Melanie Alacran. Category: Solitary Ada. Species: Fae. Threat: Minimum.

"What is this?" Alex asks, touching one of the holograms.

When she does, the picture zooms in to Central Park. A group of teens are drinking in a field. It takes a moment for me to realize that they aren't human teens. Their ears are pointed and their faces impossibly beautiful.

"Fairies," Rose says, a smile rounding out her apple cheeks.

"London's got nothing on us," McKay says. "We monitor all magical activity in the tristate area."

"Is this even legal?" Alex asks dryly.

McKay looks from Alex to me and back to my sister. "As legal as the infirmary on the second floor of your house. And no, we weren't spying on you. Your mother healed my friend and me last year."

"That's how I remember you," Alex says, snapping her finger. "You and the vampire. You showed up skewered by a dozen arrows."

"The shish kebab look didn't really suit us," McKay says.

"And I prefer Frederik to 'the vampire,'" a deep voice says from the corner of the room. If he'd been sitting there this whole time, he must've been incredibly still or invisible.

"Actually, he really loves when people call him Count Sparkle Pony," McKay says, winking at Rose, who proceeds to turn a fiery red.

Frederik moves faster than I can blink. In a fraction of a second, he's standing beside me, arms crossed over his chest. His face is the white of moonstone, with endlessly black eyes fringed by darker lashes. His elegant features conflate with his simple, dark clothes, as if he were pulled out of time and never acclimated.

"I don't believe our guests are here for a comedy routine," Frederik tells McKay. The edge of his mouth quirks up to reveal a glistening, sharp fang.

Is that supposed to be a smile?

When Frederick looks at me, I feel like I'm actively shrinking to the size of a speck of dust. "Why have you come here?"

"We—we were attacked," I say. "The Knights of Lavant are after us."

"But *why* are they after you?" Frederik asks me, and I wonder if he can hear the way my heart speeds up.

Alex, who's been shifting her weight nonstop beside me, leans into Nova and mutters something in his ear. Whatever she said has the brujo smirking and nodding.

"I speak twenty-seven languages, Miss Mortiz," Frederik tells my sister. "And I can hear anything within a ten-block radius."

"Plus, whispering's just rude." McKay winks at her.

Alex stammers. "I'm sorry. I just want to be sure we can trust you."

"You're in my house," Frederick says, and even though his face is calculated steel, his tongue is sharp. "The Thorne Hill Alliance is willing to help everyone from the magical community who comes to our doors. And we owe your mother a debt. But I need the truth."

There is so much I want to communicate to Alex. Nova turned on her once, and even though I want to believe he's trying to do better, there's a part of me that doesn't trust his intentions. But we need their resources.

In one breath, I tell him everything. The healing canto, the tethering spell, Lady de la Muerte, the other casimuertos in the alley, the heart in the box, our visit to Angela Santiago. When I get to *The Accursed Book*, Alex's stare never wavers from my

219

face. But I keep my promise and only tell them about the other recorded accounts. At the end of it, I'm breathless and the aches in my side and my chest pulse with pain. I grab hold of one of the tables for support.

Frederik's face is unmoved. It's like looking at a marble sculpture. Then, he looks at Maks, who visibly shrinks back from the dark stare.

"You're one of them?"

I shield Maks by stepping in front of him. "He doesn't remember. He hasn't fed since the Knights left the heart on my doorstep."

Frederik looks at McKay, a ripple disturbs his chiseled jaw, and a hot flash covers my body from head to toe out of fear I have said the wrong thing. "The Knights gave you a heart?"

"It had to be. In the alley, one of them told me that he gave me twenty-four hours," I explain. "That's what it said on the note in the box."

"What I don't get is how that hunter knew Maks was in our house," Alex says. "Why help Maks and not the others?"

"Do the Knights go rogue?" Rose asks. "You seem surprised."

"The Knights of Lavant are assisting in cleaning up the dead bodies," McKay says, as if they're picking up a wreck after a frat party instead of cleaving bodies in half. "They never said they knew the source of all this or that they'd made contact with you."

"Why would they keep that from you?" I ask.

"Oh, don't worry. I'll get answers," Frederik tells me. He keys something on the hologram and a map of the city covers the entire far wall. "As for the other issue at hand, we've been trying to pinpoint the source of these zombie—*casimuertos* by following the murders in the city. The blue dots are bodies with missing hearts. The red dots are what we believe to be the culprits."

There's a smattering of glowing black dots on the screen. I ask, "What about the black ones?"

"Just run-of-the-mill murders," McKay says, winking his big, brown eye.

I have the strangest feeling of déjà vu, but I focus on the images on the projected map. "The boys and the family behind my school were the only ones on the news."

"Plus the other fifty-seven that have gone unreported."

"*Fifty-seven?*" My voice is so high-pitched dogs can probably hear me.

McKay looks down at his feet, his smile gone for the first time since we arrived. "We protect the people of this city. This news could spread untold panic. But every time one of our witches tried to pinpoint the origin, this happened."

McKay zooms in on the map to highlight downtown Manhattan and Brooklyn. Bright-red dots glow where we are in Coney Island, flickering like fireflies. Dozens of them—in Prospect Park, around Thorne Hill, and a horde clustered on the Brooklyn Bridge, moving toward Manhattan. Thin, red lines connect them all, zigzagging in a tangle all over the city.

"Oh, dear gods," I manage to say.

"That's not all," McKay says, pressing another button. "At the rate they're multiplying, this is what the city will look like."

The red fireflies spread over entire parts of the city. My heart beats so fast I can't breathe. I dig in my pocket for the elixir and

221

pop off the cork with my thumb. I drain every last drop, until I can stand on my own and my body doesn't hurt anymore.

"Last summer a sea witch tried to decimate this coast," McKay says, "and now this. It's like the magic of the world is pushing back against everything that's kept it hidden for so long."

"Even with the Knights of Lavant," Frederick says, "we don't know how to contain this. I've been developing a serum to sedate them. They're stronger when they feed, but we haven't been able to catch one to run any tests. Now they seem to be gathering in packs."

I don't know how to contain this, but I know one way of ending it for good. I try to keep my voice from trembling. Panic twists in my gut, like a hand wringing around my insides. "How long until the city is overrun?"

McKay lifts his cap to smooth out his hair. He sighs uncertainly. "A week? If we're lucky. It's not viral, but they're still multiplying somehow."

This is the future I've given my city. I look at Alex, and she shakes her head slowly, her lips taut, her eyes pleading.

Frederik doesn't miss the movement. "What is it?"

"*Lula.*" Alex says my name like a warning.

"Lula, something's wrong." Maks reaches for my hand, but a pain makes him double over. His eyes flash white and then back to blue. He's going to turn. He's going to turn in front of everyone the way Raj and Dale and Kassandra did. I tell myself that Maks is different. Because I healed him before he died, before I tethered him. The others didn't get that kindness.

"What aren't you saying?" Frederik's posture becomes predatory as he turns to me.

Alex tries to reach for me just as Frederik fades into a blur. Alex hits him with a ripple of magic, and the vampire bares his fangs and punches against the inviable barrier she creates between me and the others. "Lula, run!"

"Fred—he's turning," McKay says as Maks falls to his knees.

And in this moment, I know I can't watch what he'll become.

I run out the room and out the way we came. Red dots dance in front my eyes, residual lights from staring at the screen McKay showed us. My legs move slower than usual, but I keep going until there is only the ocean and me.

The night sea breeze hits my face as I hurry down the board-walk, away from the lights and the rides, away from the Thorne Hill Alliance building, away from my family and Maks.

A cramp works its way back into my chest and sides, and I stop. I grip my knees and wait for the dizziness to pass. I look up at the night-blue sky, dotted with speckles of stars and a waning moon, hoping to find the answers there that no one has been able to give me—not even La Muerte.

Where are the Deos? I asked her.

In the place where you least expect them, she said.

You must free me, she said.

All I wanted was for my life to go back to the way it was. All I wanted was for Maks to live.

Emergency sirens blast in the distance, and I have to wonder if they're going to find a heartless body when they get to where they're going. I press my hand over my heart. When I read *The Accursed Book*, I knew my fate. Despite what Alex said on the train, this *is* where my story ends. Maybe not in this moment, standing on this boardwalk in the dark, facing the ocean, but I can feel it drawing near, and I don't know if I can right the wrongs I've set in motion.

"How am I supposed to do this?" I shout at the sea. The sky. The empty space that surrounds me. "Answer me!"

I breathe sharply, but my insides tighten like rusted springs and I can't exhale. A thread pierces the core of my heart, and in that moment, the agony is so acute I can see only darkness.

Everything fades, and the same room in which I last saw La Muerte comes into focus.

She's thinner than before. Her skin is the translucent slickness of an amphibian. A black ooze drips from the edges of her twisted thorn crown, and her cracked, blue lips pull back over glistening yellow teeth.

"How can you speak to me this way?" The accusation is drenched with melancholy.

I press my hand over my heart. There's nothing there.

"Am I dead?"

"Do you want to be?"

"Why can't you just give me a straight answer?"

"Why can't you see that I have? You cry for our absence, but we are where we've always been."

She points an accusatory finger at me as I pace around her. In this in-between, I am weightless. There is a rushing dark, like a swarm of bees, but after a moment, you stop noticing it.

"You have seen the outcome of this. The casimuertos are tied to you, and you are tied to me."

"You could've told me there was only one way to end this."

"It is not the only way. Find my spear—"

"But *where* is your spear? If you're here, then where is it?"

"I was born at the edge of this world. It is where I always return; it is where I should be now." Lady de la Muerte turns slowly, following my quick pace with her molasses-dark eyes. "Do you know why mortals pray?"

I stop in my tracks. Why do I light my candles and sing rezos and keep my altar to the Deos? Why do I scream at her now? "Because we want something."

"If the Deos had all the answers," she says, "we wouldn't have created you."

I laugh. My heart has stopped beating and back home my undead army is wreaking havoc all over the city. But here is the lady of death, asking the world of me and all I can do is laugh.

"You don't know," I say. "You don't know how to fix this."

"Lula, you wanted something I could not give you. You didn't ask for life and here you have it. But you did ask for this burden, and you *must* free me."

She extends her long, bony arm, and fissures of light erupt from the tip of her finger, stabbing the bare skin between my breasts.

I start awake on the boardwalk. Whatever Lady de la Muerte did, the silver light appears over my heart once more. This time, there are more threads than before extending in dozens of directions. Except for three of them. They wrap around my shoulders and tug me backward and across the boardwalk, toward an empty lot full of overgrown weeds that are lit by my silver light as I draw closer.

Three figures emerge from the shadows. They squint against the bright threads that pierce their hearts. One of them I recognize as Derek Ferreira, number five on the team. His pale skin is shiny with sweat, and his once-brown eyes are covered by a milky-white film. He takes a step forward, and I can see that his mouth is red with dried blood. He's wearing a letterman jacket with nothing underneath, displaying a canvas of pink scars.

"Derek?" I say his name, because part of me still doesn't believe that he's here. When I blink, I can picture him getting thrown from one end of the bus to the other.

The other two boys are Dylan Monroe and Paul Gopal. Paul doesn't look like he has a scratch on him. His dark skin is smooth and unblemished. He looks completely alive, and if it wasn't for his colorless eyes, I wouldn't be able to tell he's a casimuerto. Dylan is another story. His pale-gray skin is badly bruised over the right shoulder, where a nasty scar was stitched up and never healed properly. Again, my mind flashes to an image of the bus tumbling and flipping over. A pane of broken glass wedging itself deep into his shoulder.

"I know you," Paul tells me, blinking a few times.

"You're Maks's girl," Derek says, stalking toward me. He's my height and made of lean muscles that ripple with each step he takes. He extends his bloody fingers toward the silver thread that links us, but they touch only air. "You're the one who's been calling out to us this whole time."

"Me?"

"Haven't you felt it?" Derek quirks up a dark eyebrow. "That tug in your heart. That's all of us."

I look on either side of me, but the boardwalk is dark. Other than the waves, we're alone.

"I have," I say, trying to stop myself from running. If I run, they'll follow and I don't know how much longer the elixir can sustain me. "I'm here to help you."

"Help us?" Paul says. Thick, black hair falling over his stark-white eyes. "I've never felt better."

"It was weird at first," Derek says, his mouth spreading into a wicked, wide smile tinged with blood as he gets closer. "I couldn't think straight. It wasn't until we ate that I felt like myself again. The more we eat, the better we feel. I can smell things I never could. The fear on someone's skin. How sweet it turns the blood. Like you…"

"There's a moment," Dylan says, "right after we eat. All the pain, all the confusion goes away. But beneath that, you know what I feel? What all of us feel?"

I take a step back and hit the metal railing separating the board-walk from the sand.

"Your heart."

"Speaking of." Derek breathes the air around me, dark eyes falling to my chest. "We don't have to hunt tonight."

I swing my fist, colliding with his nose. There's the crunch of cartilage and a soft trickle of blood, but the other two grab my arms. I kick frantically until my knee hits flesh. One of them lets me go, and I pull the other to the ground. They growl like wolves and look up behind me as the sound of footsteps draws nearer.

Derek snarls, and when he lands on me, I grab him by his throat.

"I don't need to breathe." He laughs and threads his arms between mine to break my hold.

I scream as his nails rake across my chest. The metallic scent of blood sends him into a frenzy.

I realize *he's going to rip out my heart*. I think of my family scattered around the city, my sisters fighting alongside me, La Muerte waiting for me to free her, Maks—and I know, I know I can't let this happen. If they consume my heart, they'll be unstoppable, and the city falls. If I have to die, I'm taking them all with me. A primal instinct within me ignites. I punch and thrash and I fight back.

There's the stampede of footsteps and my name on the wind. A blast of light hits the casimuerto in the face and he flies backward with a thud.

"Alex!" I shout, scrambling to my feet.

But it isn't Alex. It's Rose. And her entire body is bathed in light.

25

El Terroz rose, lifting the earth
above La Ola's drowning waves,
forever scorned by his sister's wrath.
—TALES OF THE DEOS,
FELIPE THOMÁS SAN JUSTINIO

How did you do that?" I take her hands and she helps me up.

"I don't know." She trembles in my grasp. I brush her hair back to examine her face. She wraps her arms around me and holds me tight. "Are you okay?"

Behind her, Nova's arms are shaking as he holds a phone to his ear. "Come west on the boardwalk."

"Is that Alex?" I ask. "What about Frederik?"

"He wasn't going after you. He could sense Maks's change," he says. "That's what set him off. After we calmed Frederick down, we split up to find you. What happened?"

"I needed space," I say, the adrenaline in my veins causing me to shake. "I spoke to Lady de la Muerte again. Then I found them."

I keep a tight hold of Rose and think back to the night of the spell—the way her power shined brighter than Alex's and mine. The strength of it was raw and pure. Could our canto have changed her power too?

"Since when can you conjure light?" Nova asks Rose.

She shakes her head and says nothing.

We turn around at the moaning sound of the casimuertos getting back up. A hard breeze blows my hair back. When I blink, Frederik is here with a silver tube in his hand. He injects the casimuertos in the chest with a needle.

"What is that?" I ask.

"A serum." Frederik's voice is the calm before a storm. "But it won't last long. We need to go."

When we get back to the Alliance building, Alex sees me and it's like the tension in her whole body unwinds. She runs across the room and pulls Rose and me into a hug. I've never been happier to just be together.

"What happened?" she asks.

"Before I get to that, we have to talk," I say.

Alex stands back and looks between Rose and me. "What?"

"Rose conjured light."

Rose walks around us and sits on the sofa. She takes off her glasses and examines a long crack in one of the lenses before placing them on the table. Her round cheeks are pink from running back and forth, and there's a layer of soot on her palms. She rubs a hand on the knee of her jeans, darkening the denim until her skin comes away clean.

"How?" Alex asks.

"I said *I don't know*," Rose shouts.

Nova walks in, sits on the edge of the sofa, and puts his hand on Rose's shoulder. In a way, it feels like he belongs here. "It'll be okay, kid. We'll figure it out."

"We need Mom and Dad," Alex says. "I tried to call them but got voice mail."

"Rose," I say, "has this ever happened before?"

She stares at her hands. "I'm not sure. During the healing canto in the hospital I felt something strange. It was like, when I touched Alex, my power was as strong as hers."

"Have you ever heard of something like that?" I ask Nova.

"No, but right before Rose conjured, I was trying to access my powers as well. The casimuerto was on top of you, and I was getting ready to blast it, but then Rose did it first."

"I grabbed on to you," Rose says, balling her hands into fists. "Just for a moment to steady myself because we ran so fast. I put my hand on your arm. It was this surge, like my whole body was—"

"Lit up like Christmas," Nova finishes. "That's what I feel like when I use my power."

"Try it out," Alex tells Nova. "Light it up."

"I'm not a circus act."

Alex shrugs. Nova looks like he's about to protest some more, but then looks at Rose and his features soften. He holds out his hand and conjures three balls of light that flitter around the room.

"No, I'm a seer." Rose shakes her head. "That's what I've

always been. This is just a one-time thing because I wanted to save Lula. Just leave it, okay?"

"But, Rosie—" Alex presses on.

"I said leave it!"

Nova extinguishes his conjured light.

"It's fine," I say, pulling Rose closer. "We don't have to figure this out now."

Alex holds her hands up in defeat, but I know she isn't going to drop this completely. "You're right. You saved Lula, and that's what matters."

But Alex gives me a look that says this isn't over.

"Wait," I say, looking around the room. "Where's Maks?"

"He freaked out and went full casimuerto," Nova says.

"I think it's the hunger," Alex says. "Frederik put him in their containment unit."

"What?" I shout, but she places her hands on my arms and shakes me.

"He's fine now. They got him something to eat."

And I swallow the choking doubt in my throat when I say, "I need to see him."

"Lula," Maks calls out for me behind a glass wall. He sits precariously on the edge of narrow metal bench. Seeing him this way, seeing him at all sends a current through my body. How could I have run from him the moment I was too afraid?

He presses his hands on the glass, leaving red prints. His eyelids flutter closed, hiding the pale blue of his eyes. He slumps down to the floor and whatever they used to keep him sedated knocks him to sleep.

"What have I done?" I ask myself, but I realize I've said it out loud. McKay is the only one in the holding area with me.

"You wanted to save him." McKay lifts one shoulder and drops it. "You might possess magic, but you're still human."

Everything from the last couple of days makes my chest tighten, and I can tell the elixir is wearing off because the pain in my abdomen returns. "I'm going to end this," I say.

"Let me guess, we throw you in the volcano in which you were forged?" His lips don't smile, but his coffee-brown eyes are bright, like there's a well of hope inside of him. "It's a fight against magic, witchling. The biggest sacrifice is always the answer."

At that I have to laugh because I've always been so confident in my knowledge of magic. Turns out I don't know anything.

"In *The Accursed Book*," I tell him, "it says the only way to stop the hordes of casimuertos is to destroy the heart of the source with a divine weapon. They're tethered to me. La Muerte says there's another way, but I'm no closer to finding her spear than I am to finding a cure for this."

I both hate and appreciate the sympathy in his eyes as he sighs deeply.

"I've seen people come back from worse," he says. "Frederik was turned into a vampire by his own sister six hundred years ago. Took him three centuries and he nearly lost his soul, but he killed her before she could set the world on fire. Your own sister gave up her magic for her girlfriend and still saved you all *plus* all of Los

Lagos. I went vegan and I'd thought I'd never come back from a steak taco bender. I'm telling you, witchling. You'll get through this. The THA helps people, just like you and your family do. If there's another way to save you, we'll find it."

"Will he be okay here?" I ask, looking back to where Maks is asleep.

"We have two stars on Yelp. Most of our prisoners don't really like the cells." McKay rings his arm around my neck and leads me back to my family. "Come on, Lula. The night is young, and there's a whole mess of magic to unravel."

26

La Ola swam across the seas a thousand times,

the oceans too wide and not wide enough.

—TALES OF THE DEOS,
FELIPE THOMÁS SAN JUSTINIO

McKay and Frederik bring out a spread of cold pizza and chips, but I can't stomach much of it. I guzzle soda because it's the only thing that doesn't make me want to retch.

We're back in the surveillance room with the eye on the door, and the monitors are being closely watched for new movement. For every red casimuerto dot that vanishes, another one pops up somewhere.

Members of the Thorne Hill Alliance walk in and out, seeking orders from McKay and Frederik before heading out to help hunt casimuertos. They steer clear of us. Though I suppose if there were strangers in my house, I'd be wary too.

"Mom and Dad just texted," Alex says, tucking her phone in her back pocket. "They'll be home in the morning."

I'm dreading seeing my parents, especially my mother. But at the same time, I long to see her just to hear her voice, even if she'll be yelling.

One of the hologram displays has a live feed of the holding cells. Maks is still knocked out. But Derek and the other two casimuertos are banging on the walls, leaving their bloody handprints everywhere. There's a tray flipped over on the floor in a clear rejection of the cow hearts Frederik procured.

"How can you eat at a time like this?" Alex asks Nova, watching in amazement as he pounds on his chest and belches.

"With my mouth?" he responds.

"I guess the cow hearts aren't working," Rose says.

"Neither did the synthetic hearts," McKay says, pulling up another hologram.

"The hunters gave you a heart before," Nova says with his mouth full. "Why can't they do that again?"

The hair on my arms stands up. "I don't know who it was from."

"More of a reason to act fast," McKay says. "We have only one lead on your lady of death."

He uploads Alex's files of *The Accursed Book* onto the screen so we can study it. He keeps rubbing his temples as if the answer will manifest from the friction, but all it does is upset the vampire even more.

"Go over everything again," McKay tells me.

There's a collective groan of frustration, but I do it, retracing my steps from the very beginning with Alex's glamour on my scars and ending with my last visit from La Muerte. I can't help but trace the length of my scars across the side of my face as I realize this is the first time I've thought about them in days.

"If there's one thing I've learned," Frederik says once I'm done, "it's that gods never say what they mean. They don't see things the way humans do. Every divine text is a human interpretation of forces they can't even begin to understand."

"But 'find my spear' is pretty literal," Rose says dryly.

I think back to the way Lady de la Muerte kept pointing at me. *The Deos are where they've always been.*

"What? What are you thinking?" Alex asks me. "You only make that face when I tutor you in math."

I rub the spot on my chest. "Every time La Muerte has appeared to me, she points She tells me that the gods are where they've always been."

Nova cocks his head and looks me up and down. "I don't think you're tall enough for the spear to be literally in you."

I ball my fists and step to him, but Alex holds me back. "Stop. Maybe we're looking at this the wrong way. Do you remember when I was in Los Lagos and you helped me heal for the first time?"

"Of course I remember," I say. "The root of healing is love. Our gifts are natural, but magic has always been about belief." My thoughts spin around that. "The Deos are where they've always been," I say, and I realize that Lady de la Muerte was never accusing me. I turn to my sisters. "Do you guys remember the rezo we found in *Tales of the Deos*?" I snap my fingers, unable to recall the passage line by line.

"The Deos too learned their limits," Nova says. When he speaks of the gods, his body becomes haloed by a faint light and his eyes shut in reverence. "El Fuego extinguished into ash. La Ola crumbled into salt. El Terroz clove the earth in pieces. El Viento fell and kept on falling. But from their limits, Lady de la Muerte was born."

"Can we commune with these Deos?" Frederik asks. "If you spoke to Lady de la Muerte, surely we can seek help from the others."

I shake my head, but my body sighs with a new realization. "Lady de la Muerte has a function in this world. She collects souls. The other Deos don't exist in this realm, but they are where they've always been—"

"They exist in our power," Alex says, the corners of her eyes crinkling with a smile.

The past months, I wondered where the Deos went, why they abandoned me. But they didn't. I've always had my power, and in my power I finally have some hope.

"The Deos act through us," Rose says, quoting one of my favorite lines from our Book of Cantos.

McKay raises his hand. "So, we're going with the spear *isn't* inside you."

The ember in my heart grows brighter. "No, but think about it. *From their limits, Lady de la Muerte was born.* She was created from the dregs of their powers! She is the end of everything! If we combine the same powers that were used to *make* her, perhaps we can use that to find the spear."

"Can you do that?" McKay asks. "I mean, flame, water, wind, earth—those are the Deos mentioned in the poem, right?"

"It's not a poem!" Nova shouts. "Do we even know brujas strong enough to conjure elements? I mean, other than Alex?"

I turn to my sisters and propose the one thing I've been avoiding.

"We need Mom and Dad. I'll petition the High Circle again. They can't turn me away this time. Not when the whole city is in danger."

I look at the screens projecting holograms of the city. I can't tell if I'm simply exhausted or if the red dots are increasing at a faster rate. Alex stands closer to me as my body sways with exhaustion. I lean on her.

"They're going to be so mad," I say, hands trembling.

Alex tries to smile. "It's still not as bad as what I did."

"Actually, yours had a lower mortality rate," Nova says.

Alex punches him in the shoulder, and in this moment, I wonder what it would've been like if we'd had a brother.

"It's nearly sunrise and you look like you're going to fall over," Frederik says.

"Yeah, you can't release a goddess and save the city on zero sleep," McKay adds. "I'll take you to our guest rooms."

Then Frederik is gone in a black blur and McKay is leading us through the winding hallways of THA headquarters.

After we say our good nights, my sisters and I climb into a four-poster bed that'd be too big to fit into any room in our house. Alex and Rose manage to fall asleep instantly. Lying between them, I feel a comfort I haven't had in a long time.

And yet, the tug at my heart is ever present, keeping me all too aware that I am untethered to this earth but bound to the undead hordes I raised. I trace the scar on my belly, thick and jagged. It aches more than ever, but at least it isn't splitting open like before, and I send a silent thanks to Angela Santiago.

As exhausted as I am, I know I need to take care of one last thing. I resign myself to another sleepless night, because I have to see Maks. All of this started with us, and it has to finish with us. During every step I take, I play out scenes in my mind where he comes back to life for real. Where his life isn't linked to mine, a parasite draining me down to the marrow. Where Maks is the boy I fell so in love with I couldn't let him go. The boy I wanted for keeps.

When we release Lady de la Muerte, I'll have to end this. *Destroy the heart*, she said. I owe him the same comfort my sisters gave me. I owe him the truth.

I find my way to the holding cells in the dark.

"Maks." I hate that my voice sounds so small. I press my hand on the glass.

Maks paces around the room but stops when he sees me. Presses his hands against the glass. The blood on his hands and mouth is brown in the UV light. The heart on the tray gone.

"You shouldn't be here."

"I had to see you," I say.

"I don't want to be like those things in the alley. I don't want to be like the others. But I was so hungry." His eyes are lighter now, the pupils like pinpricks against the bright sky blue of his irises. He's there, holding on.

"I'm coming in."

"Don't."

"You won't hurt me." I push the lever to unlock the door.

He reaches for me, and I can feel how tired he is too. He threads his fingers with mine, and I let a pulse of my magic flood through him. It isn't the same magic I use to heal cuts or bruises. It's more like a feeling, a part of me I've pulled back because

I was afraid. Knowing what has to come next, I can't imagine being afraid of anything before this. For a moment, his skin is warm again. He gasps as the magic traces his skin. I can even hear the hushed beat of his heart murmuring against my own.

No, not his heart. I shut my eyes and tears spill at the corners. It's my heart. *My heartbeat.* It's been my heart the entire time because Maks is dead and I couldn't bring him back.

"I'm scared, Lula," he says.

I rest my head on his shoulder. But the magic leaves quickly, and the cold returns to his hands.

For a long time, we stay like this. I drift in the terrifying place between sleep and consciousness. I remember the Knights of Lavant dressed in shimmering black, the point of a sword coming inches from my face as the hunter cut Kassandra in half.

The image in my mind flickers, and then I see Derek. His eyes are as white and clear as quartz. Red veins spread across the white of his eyes. He moves like his joints are rusted, hands stretching out toward my face.

"*Lula,*" he sings my name.

Wake up, I tell myself. But I feel like my body is pinned down by an invisible force.

"*Lula,*" someone else calls out my name.

In the shadows of my dream, they are only silhouettes. But as a white light shines over them, I can see their faces. Derek is joined by others. I recognize the dead from the accident and so many more. There's a man with a bullet hole in his forehead advancing with the other. A woman with both eyes missing. A man with a kitchen knife stuck in his chest. With every step they take, more of them appear.

Someone else calls out my name.

Maks. His voice travels through the darkness like an echo. He is everywhere and nowhere.

"Maks?"

"Lula." The way he says my name, like a curse, makes my skin crawl.

My dream changes.

I'm pulled up higher and higher into the ether. We're on the beach. The wind blows sand into my eyes and the waves almost reach the boardwalk.

Maks is facing away from me. He's hugging himself, a terrible shake racking his body.

"Maks?" I edge closer to him.

"You did this to me," he growls.

"I was trying to save you. All I wanted was to save you."

He whips around, and when he does, the sight of his eyes is startling—the blue has faded to ice white. The jagged scars that cover his body are pronounced and red. When I look at him, I don't see the boy I loved. I see his walking corpse. A casimuerto.

That's when I notice it. The thread that binds us together, a silver thread coming undone. Maks puts his hand around it.

"No!"

And he tugs.

The pain makes me fall to the sand. He tugs again, and this time, white-hot pain floods every part of me.

"Why won't it work?" He grabs me by my shoulders and shakes me.

"Why are you doing this?" I ask him.

242

"Because I remember now." His hands trace the sides of my neck. "I remember everything."

My scream dies in my throat, but I can hear another in the distance. My face feels red and my thoughts darken with a lack of oxygen.

"I remember it all, Lula!" Maks shouts, his grip crushing my windpipe.

Wake up, wake up, wake up.

I open my eyes.

But his hands are still around my throat. And I can't breathe. And I can't call for help. And I'm not dreaming.

Maks is killing me.

27

The world burned and splintered and drowned.

To save their creations, La Mama and El Papa

let La Muerte rise.

—TALES OF THE DEOS,
FELIPE THOMÁS SAN JUSTINIO

The air sparks with electricity. Maks's skin is covered with pinpricks of currents that bring him to his knees. Then rain falls from a dark cloud that blankets the ceiling. Maks's body is flung to the side, but his nails still rake across the thin skin of my throat.

My dad's hands hold spheres of electricity. His eyes are black as night.

My mom runs to my side and presses her hand against where I'm bleeding. When I try to talk, my throat burns worse than ever. Even the breath I take is jagged and small.

"Rose," Alex shouts. "Help me carry her out. Pull the door lever!"

They shoulder my weight and carry me to a bed.

"It's okay," Mom tells me. The sight of her face is calming.

Her magic floods through me, finding the places that hurt the most. I wince as a bone snaps into place. "It's okay, nena. We're here."

I know this won't last. They're going to find out what I've done and be angry with me. But for now, I let my mother hold me and brush my hair away from my face. I let her mend the skin around my neck and press kisses on my forehead just as she did when I was a little kid. I let her thank La Mama that I'm alive and threaten to kill me in her name as well. I let her be my mother.

"Lula," she says, her voice pleading. "What did you do?"

"Yell later," Alex says. "First, we need to summon the High Circle."

"No," I say, trying out my voice. "I should explain. About Maks and the others."

Dad rubs the soot off his hands on his sweatpants, his gray eyes like perfect storms. "Others?"

I take a deep breath and sit up to face them. "I messed up."

The important moments in life always seem to happen around kitchens, from holidays and parties to everything in between. So I'm not surprised that, somehow, we end up in the THA kitchen to talk about how I cast a spell that will destroy our city.

Ma makes a strong black tea with Frederik's herbs. She slams the kettle on the stove. She cranks up the flames. She sets the jar of loose leaf so hard on the counter I'm surprised it doesn't shatter. The entire time she mutters in the Old Tongue.

"You have no idea what you've done." Her voice is tired and angry.

I stay quiet. Alex and Rose are busy examining the dirt under their nails because they know Mom's anger is coming for them too.

I'm prepared for her to scream, to tell me how much I've let her down. I even brace to have something flung at my head.

Instead, my mother sighs deeply. It's like a weight pushing down her thick, strong body. She shakes her head from side to side and pours the boiling water into the teapot. She sets the tray on the table between us and I breathe in the scent of bitter roots and jasmine.

I fear I've broken more than just the balance of the world. I've destroyed the trust my mother had in me.

She just sits there and stares at the door, waiting for my father to return. Dark circles ring her eyes, but her plum lipstick is still somehow unblemished.

As the day breaks and the sunrise shines into this strange, metallic kitchen, a shadow spreads across her neck in the shape of handprints—the same ones she healed from me. And seeing my mother hurt is worse than anything else in the world.

Dad and Nova walk in, a draft following at their heels. My father is still shaking from having used his power, and his face is scrunched up with ire and worry. There's a brownish-red smudge on his cheek that at first looks like dirt, but when I look at Nova, he too has a bruise on his face. I wonder if we are ever going to be more than a pile of broken bones and bruises.

Dad and Nova exchange glances and something passes between them, something untold that the four of us aren't privy to. I envy Nova for this.

"The casimuertos are down," Nova says. "For now."

My mom gets up and hands them both a cup of tea. Dad shuts his eyes before drinking it, and I don't know if he's cursing the Deos or praying to them.

"What happened while we were gone?" Dad asks quietly.

"I wasn't completely honest about the canto we used on Maks." I take a sip of tea to wet my dry tongue. Then I confess. "When the bodies went missing, I thought that was the end of it. But they just reappeared in different parts of the city. The day I left the house for a walk, I really went to the boardwalk. That's where I found Maks."

"How did you find him?" Mom asks.

"I'm connected to them. Tethered. That's why I haven't been healing properly." I explain about the threads.

"Lula—" Mom starts to say.

"Let me finish," I say. "Please. Otherwise I might not be able to say it again. La Muerte told me I had to free her, but when I found Maks, I felt like finally something had gone right."

My lips are so dry I feel like, if I start to cry, they might bleed. So I hold it in. "Alex and I went to see Nova's grandmother. She let us read a book she had on casimuertos."

Dad is pacing in a circle around the table. He touches his bottom lip with his fingers, face sunken in with so much burden it makes him look like he's aged a decade.

"The book," he says. "*El Libro Maldecido*?"

"Yes," Alex says. "How do you know that?"

"Patricio?" Mom asks.

Dad frowns the way he does when he struggles through his memory. "Remember Fausto Toledo back in our circle?"

"That was twenty years ago," Ma says. "The circumstances were different."

"Raising the dead is raising the dead. He wanted to create an army to fight against the Knights of Lavant."

At their name, Nova, Alex, Rose, and I exchange a not-so-secret glance. But we're not about to interrupt my dad, so we let him keep talking.

"But he failed," Ma says. "The bodies were taken out to the island and dumped in the sound."

"That wasn't in Angela's book," I say.

"It wouldn't be," Dad says severely. "Fausto wrote it. After his army failed, he started to die. Not even sinmago doctors could treat him. He simply withered down until there was skin and bones. It was his punishment for what he'd done. He tried to figure out a cure for death. Spent years gathering up stories about the undead. You see, casimuertos aren't created by a virus. They're bound by magical blood. And the only way to kill them all is—"

He freezes, stormy-gray eyes glassy when he looks at me, like he's only just remembering the cost. "No. I'm not losing you again. Lula—"

I can't stand the hurt there, the way my mother presses her hands against the table for support as she stands to wrap her arms around me. They squeeze me, gently but firmly.

"The Alliance is helping," I say in an attempt to assuage their fear. "La Muerte told me there was another way. I think we've figured out a way to break her free, but we have to find her spear first."

I explain to my parents about the elements.

248

"We need the High Circle and we need them here now," Alex says. "The casimuertos are multiplying faster than the THA and Knights of Lavant can kill them."

Glass shatters. Mom's dropped her cup on the floor.

"What did you say?" Dad asks.

Alex looks stunned, blinking too fast. "Knights of Lavant?"

"You spoke to them?"

"They showed up," I say. "We were being attacked by casimuertos in an alley and they were just there. Why?"

"I want you to stay away from them."

"But why? We want the same thing—to destroy the casimuertos."

"Patricio," Mom whispers, placing her hands on his shoulders. "Be calm."

Dad looks down at the ground, then fixes his gray eyes on me. "One day I will have the answers you want, something that makes me worthy of you, all of you. But for now, please listen to me and stay away from them. They hunted our kind for centuries. They—"

Down the hall, there's a knock coming from the front door, and since it's not our house, we're unsure if we should answer it.

"Anyone expecting company?" Nova asks.

But after the third knock, I see McKay dash past the kitchen in his boxers. I need an out, so I get up and follow him.

A tall, young guy walks right in, past McKay, whose grimace has nothing to do with the two hours of sleep he got last night.

"Good, McKay," the stranger says. "Should've known. You're all here. Saves me a trip."

His face looks familiar, but I can't place it. He wears a white shirt, jeans, and motorcycle boots. He keeps walking in until he stands in front of me, all up in my space.

"Lula Mortiz."

Where do I know him from? His serious face brightens with a smile. Memories rush at me. Dark eyes framed by darker lashes. A square jaw tallied with thin scars that could be from shaving or from a fight.

"Who wants to know?" I ask.

He smooths the top of his hair, tied back in a knot. He stands tall, over a foot taller than me. His dark eyes take in every one of us, and he smirks.

"Lula Antonietta Mortiz, you are guilty of endangering the life of the humans of the tristate area slash the world, and are in violation of the Thorne Hill Alliance, Treaty of New York, section six: the reanimation of corpses."

"What the hell are you talking about?" I shout.

"I am here to arrest you on the authority of the Knights of Lavant."

28

The monsters, the monsters,
they crawl in the night.
The monsters, the monsters,
they hide in plain sight.

—WITCHSONG #33,
BOOK OF CANTOS

know you" is all I can say to that.

He ignores me and reaches around to his back pocket and pulls out a black chord that he winds around his hand. "You know the drill. I'll have to search the premises, McKay."

"Listen, Rhett," McKay starts. His bare feet slap on the ground as he makes to stand in front of me. "You clearly waited until Fred was knocked out. You don't want to do this. I'll take you to the zombie heads, but leave the girl alone."

"We can't contain the threat," the hunter says. "There are bodies piling up, and the human authorities are panicking, and nothing good happens when they panic. Someone has to answer for it. You can't save everyone."

Strands of Rhett's brown hair fall out of place. His attention is drawn to my family, who emerges from the kitchen and surrounds him. Something like amusement lights up his deep-brown eyes.

"If you think you're taking my daughter, you're going to have a lot more to worry about than the undead plaguing these streets," Dad says.

"Patricio, stand back," Mom says, but I can feel the air thicken with magic.

"I don't care who you are," I tell the hunter. "I'm not going with you."

He turns toward me on his shiny, black shoes, then lowers himself so we're face-to-face. "You will."

My heart thunders in my chest. It's like a flash going off in my head. His tenor voice, like a warning, conflates with his face. A face that's so clear and bright in this memory. *You're stronger than this.* "You're the nurse from the hospital."

"Oh yeah," Rose says behind me. "But he doesn't seem as nice right now."

He smirks. "I'm actually disappointed it took you so long to remember me. But I suppose you've been *busy*."

"We thought you were the one who took the bodies at first. What the hell do you want with my sister?" Alex asks. She keeps her hands behind her back, but I can feel the pull of magic in the air, a living thing grazing against the back of my neck.

"I *just* said," Rhett snaps at her. "Do you know how many of these creatures we've had to put down? And I know you're harboring four more. The only way to solve this is for the witch to *peacefully* come with me and turn over the undead."

And just like that, something snaps within me. The rage, the fear, the hopelessness I've felt for the past few days, even the past few months, bubble up inside me. I slap him across his smug face, and he stumbles back. "I am a *bruja*."

"You're the reason all of this is happening," he says, cradling his now-reddened cheek.

"Please," Ma says, the portrait of civility. Her dark curls are pulled into a bun at the top of her head. Amethyst crystal earrings swing against her brown skin as she holds her hands up in supplication. "We're on the same side. We know how to fix this."

"Carmen Mortiz," Rhett says, raising his brows at her. "Healer to the poor souls of the city. How was the sea creature's delivery last night? I do hope the sea princess has a speedy recovery."

My mother's face hardens, but her brown eyes don't hold any anger. She's afraid.

Dad, on the other hand, is less successful at containing his disdain for the young hunter. Dad's white skin is stark against his salt-and-pepper mustache, and his eyes are narrow slits, waiting to attack until Rhett puts his hands on me.

"Don't you need an arrest warrant?" McKay asks, snapping his fingers like he just figured out a riddle. "If we wake up Fred, I'm afraid for your life. Treaty or not."

"I'm not afraid of a vamp." Rhett looks at McKay with a challenge in his eyes as he pulls out a square piece of parchment from his back pocket. He glares at my dad as he hands it to me. The card stock has an aged quality and is velvety to the touch. There's a scarlet wax stamp at the corner with a coat of arms, the same one he wears on his belt buckle.

The letters are finely written in stark black ink. My eyes go blurry, like a camera coming in and out of focus, but I can still recognize my name.

"Lula?" my mom says.

I hold the card in front of Rhett's face and tear it in half. "Why wait until now? You're the one who was stalking around our house and left a human heart on our back porch. You have no right to be here."

"I have every right," he says. "I gave you a chance to handle this yourself. Now it's our turn."

"You're one of the hunters from the alley," Nova says. "I recognize your ponytail."

"*Get out*," my father says. He hasn't moved, hands still on his hips. But he annunciates every word, baring his teeth.

"I don't think so," Rhett says, losing his cool. "The Knights of Lavant assist the Thorne Hill Alliance. You, on the other hand, keep creating messes for us to clean up. So, you see, I have every right to be here. Nothing changes the fact that your daughter has broken several of the laws of the treaty."

"Did you see her break the law, ponytail?" Nova asks.

Rhett turns his attention to Nova. His body posture changes from confident to predatory. He takes a single step in Nova's direction, and Alex puts a hand up. An invisible force ripples, stopping him from moving any farther.

"You can call me Rhett," he says, retreating a step. "Not *ponytail*. Look, I know I'm the bad guy to you. But I'm following protocol. There are rules in place for a reason."

"Hypothetically." I meet his dark eyes. "Did you see me raise the dead?"

254

"We don't follow human law and order," he says. "But if we did, you know I saw you and your sisters go into Mr. Horbachevsky's room just before he died. When I went to inspect his body in the morgue, he was mysteriously gone."

"So what?" I ask and hope I'm convincing enough that he doesn't call my bluff. "You're going to put me in a cell? Without our help, you'll spend the rest of your life hacking away at casimuertos. Let us help. You were willing to before. What's different now?"

Rhett lowers his lips to my ear. "What's different is that I lost two hunters because of you. Because I gave you a chance. Because I felt sorry for you. Their deaths are your fault just as much as they are mine."

"Back away from my sister," Alex tells him.

Rhett shrugs. "You won't hurt me."

Alex's eyes flash with pinpricks of lightning. "You want to test that theory?"

"Don't threaten me, Alejandra Mortiz." Rhett sets his briefcase down. He opens it and pulls out a black metal handle. I recognize it as the hilt of the sword, but the blade is missing. Strange. I can't even sense the magic that cloaks the blade. "Very well. You'll assist with the larger problem. But for now, I do need to dispose of the abominations in your possession."

Maks. It wasn't supposed to be like this. My stomach drops. I've known the end has been coming for us. But the thought of him being cut down by a stranger who thinks he's a monster makes me want to hit something—someone. It can't happen—not like that.

"And if we refuse?" Alex asks, reading the panic in my face. "Do you know what I am?"

"Yes." Rhett settles a cocky stare on my sister. "What do you call it? An all-powerful encantrix. Nice job you did on that tree in your backyard. We had quite a time covering that up from the cops. How's Rishima Persaud, by the way? I do hope she's enjoying her cousin's wedding in Fort Lauderdale. She looks lovely in that violet dress."

Alex's face is ashen with fear, which is swiftly replaced with fury. The pull of her magic feels erratic, and I force her to look at me so she won't act on her anger.

"The Mortiz sisters," Rhett says, setting his eyes on Rose. "I sure hope you're the good one."

Rose doesn't react to him. She tilts her head to the side. Her hair rises with static the way it always does when she's seeing beyond the Veil. Her eyes go completely black. Dad holds on to her shoulders. Then Rose speaks to Rhett in a strange whisper.

"*Follow the path, son. Make me proud.*" She clears her throat. "Do you want to hear from him, Rhett? You're not the only one who can make threats."

Rhett's face blanks and his eyes widen. I allow myself a moment of pleasure at his discomfort. But as Rose recovers, so does he. He cracks his neck, and his full lips press together into a scowl.

"I'm not the enemy," he says.

"Tell that to our ancestors your kind has slaughtered," Dad says. "You might've signed the Alliance's treaty, but that doesn't erase centuries of bloodshed."

"Of course it doesn't, Mr. Mortiz," Rhett says, and his voice is unwavering. "We don't want to erase it. But there are laws for a reason. Lives are at stake, and your daughter is the one who put them in danger. But I can tell you haven't been yourself since you've returned from, well, wherever you've been."

Dad moves so quickly all I see is a blur. He charges at Rhett and slams him into the wall.

I've always thought of my dad as the biggest, strongest man I've ever known. But Rhett doesn't even flinch. My dad's arm is pressed against Rhett's chest, but he pushes my father away like he weighs no more than a bit of lint.

Mom and Alex catch him as he stumbles.

Rhett pulls back the glamour around his sword, revealing a silver blade glinting in the morning light.

"Believe me, Mr. Mortiz," he says, "I do want to help."

"Wait." I stand between Rhett and my father. The blade is inches from my face. A new, wrenching pain twists at my insides. The threads unfurl, and by the looks on their faces, I know everyone can see them now. Rhett stands back and McKay curses.

"Lula—" Dad says, reaching for me, but Alex catches me first.

"Something's wrong," I say. I lock eyes with Alex.

Rhett keeps one hand on his sword. "If this is a trick—"

"It isn't!" I shout, holding on to my sister for support. "I'm connected to them. It's like...they're moving."

"Oh gods," McKay mutters, and runs up the stairs to where the holding cells are.

Rhett is right behind him, his movements too fast to be human. An alarm goes off. Doors lock and windows slam shut. People start to come out of their rooms, most of them rubbing sleep out of their eyes at the same time they brandish weapons.

I grab hold of Alex, climbing the stairs one at a time. Bloody footsteps lead out of the open holding cell door. McKay watches footage replay on a screen, and Rhett punches his fist through a wall.

Maks and the other casimuertos are gone.

29

*They hunted us across
every land that we claimed.
But we are resilient
as great kapok trees.
But we are as vast
as earth's brutal blue seas.*

—WITCHSONG #1,
BOOK OF CANTOS

R hett turns around and shouts at the room, a vein in his throat bursting against his skin. "Where are they?"

"I don't know!"

He closes the distance between us and grabs for me, but a forceful wind knocks him back. He slams into the bloody room and rolls over. I scream, turning my face away as his head makes a terrible cracking sound.

"Run," Alex tells me. She holds her hands in the air, eyes completely white, fingertips sparkling with electricity. "Run!"

I run past the crowd gathered in the halls. I'm sure the front door is locked, but I follow the bloody footsteps that get lighter and lighter as I reach a bathroom at the end of the hall. The window is shattered, and there's blood on the jagged glass, as if they struggled to fit through the window. I go through, scraping my legs and palms along the way.

When I hit the ground, I'm disoriented by the bright morning light. The beach is to my right and the crowded avenue to my left. A bicyclist shouts at me, nearly clipping my hip with his handle. But I keep running left until I pick up the footprints again on the sidewalk.

A young woman screams at the sight of me emerging around the corner of the building. I don't need a mirror to know what she sees. My face streaked with sweat and dirt, the scars on skin, my bare legs freshly bloody. She sees me and runs.

I look behind me once, expecting to find Rhett.

But there's no one there.

I cross the street, following the faint footsteps that jaywalk to the other side. Cars honk and drivers curse at me as I sprint to the sidewalk.

I have no idea what I'm going to do when I find Maks, but I push forward anyway.

My heart is like a fist trying to punch its way out of my chest. I turn another corner, but the bloody prints have stopped at the intersection.

"Where are you?" I whisper.

I close my eyes and search for the thread that links me to the casimuertos. The connection comes easily now. Dozens of silver and iridescent threads appear from my chest, stretching in different directions. Which one is Maks?

I think of him and the way we were before all of this. Before the accident that claimed his life. Before the one that changed mine. I search for those memories. Maks taking my hand and pressing a kiss into it. Maks reaching for a coil of my hair and threading it around his finger. His lips pressing against mine, soft as rose petals.

Then, his thread pulses, flickering like a firefly.

I follow it for blocks and blocks, past rows of homes covered in ivy, until I fear my legs will crumble into nothing. The thread grows brighter and I know I'm getting closer until, suddenly, it disappears at the steps of a familiar brownstone.

I wait a moment for my heart and head to catch up with me. Sweat drips down my face and back. The white metal fence is smeared with blood, and the gate is ajar. I look toward the front door and see another dark smudge on the doorknob.

There's sobbing coming from somewhere in the house.

"Maks?" I call out for him.

My heart beats against my eardrums as I inch inside. The white carpet is thick with blood, oozing with every step I take. All the walls are covered in it.

I turn and walk into the living room, at the center of which is a beautiful leather couch holding the most horrific scene I've ever witnessed.

An older man sits on a high chair, the skin of his face ripped to shreds. A woman's body is laid on the couch, carefully arranged so that her head faces the ceiling, blood on her temples, as if he brushed her hair back once he was done feeding.

Both of their chests are ripped open to expose the cavities where their hearts once were. All that's left is a mess of dangling tissue and the cracked, white bone of their rib cages.

My eyes blur and I fight the urge to vomit. I grab a picture frame from the grand fireplace mantel, hoping that the faces in the photo will be foreign to me. But instead, I find exactly what I expected to—Maks, his sister, and their parents smiling at the camera. I drop the frame when I hear footsteps upstairs. I climb the winding stairs two at a time, tracking blood and dirt.

I swing open the first door on the landing and peer inside. It's Maks's sister Irina's room.

Unlike her parents downstairs, Irina isn't dead. She's sitting in the fetal positing at the far end of her room, a kitchen knife in her fist. Maks is down on his knees, staring at his open hands.

"Lula!" Irina cried. "What's going on?"

At the sound of my name, Maks snaps his attention to me. His eyes are the white and red of casimuertos, and he growls at me.

I take several steps back, hitting the railing. I nearly lose my balance and fall backward, but I hold on.

"Maks?" I hate the way my voice trembles.

Maks moves swiftly, closing the distance between us and grabbing hold of my shirt in his fist. "You did this to me."

"Maks, please don't," Irina cries from within her room.

"I didn't want to hurt you, Lula. But you should've let me go when you had the chance."

"If you don't want to hurt me, then don't. I know you, Maks. I know a part of you has to be in there somewhere."

"Lula." Maks shuts his eyes, holds on tighter. He grinds his teeth and his eyes phase from white to blue and then back to white as he struggles to hold on.

I need him to hold on, so I say, "I can help you."

"That's not what you told the shape-shifter," Maks says, his voice unnervingly calm. He grabs my shoulders, sounding like himself again. But the red veins in his eyes darken as he inhales my scent. "What were your exact words? I'm having a hard time recalling them from the *prison* you were going to leave me in. Tell me, Lula. Were you going to kill me yourself or have your witch sister do it?"

I grip his arms and try to catch his gaze, hoping I can coax him into calming down. "Maks, you said you'd never hurt me. You can fight it. You did it before."

"It's over, Lula. Stop trying to save me!" He digs his dirty nails into my shoulders. "Do you know what it's like to tear out your mother's beating heart?"

As I look into Maks's feral, white eyes, I see the last of my Maks fade away, replaced by desperate hunger. How long has the boy I loved been gone? There's nothing left to save here, but there is back at the THA headquarters. I need to get back to my family, and fast.

I take a swing at his face, but he catches my fist with his open palm, squeezing until the bones in my hand crunch. I scream and raise my knee, driving it into his groin. He grunts and lets go of me. I cradle my hand against my chest and turn around to run.

He grabs my arms and yanks me back. I lash out with all my fury, channeling every bit of anger and insecurity I've felt in the last eight months into a punch that connects with his chin.

His head snaps back, but only for a second. When he rights himself, he is angrier. Meaner. He is every bit the monster I created when blood vessels thread his white eyes and a terrible cry comes from his open mouth. It makes me jump back. I hit the railing on the second landing and panic as I think about the marble floor at the drop behind me. I shut my eyes, clutching the banister as hard as I can.

"Sweet Lula," Maks murmurs, each step cutting off my escape.

A shiver runs through my body when he's a breath away from me, and when I look up, I see a pair of familiar blue eyes behind Maks. Irina's eyes.

She charges us, her scream piercing as she stabs him through his shoulder and then again and again. Maks punches her back onto the floor.

He whips around and digs his fingers into my arms, lifting me off the ground.

"Don't!" I scream. I yank on his hair, his shirt, his skin, trying to hold on to whatever I can as he pushes me over the banister. Because now more than ever, I want to live.

I want to live.

PART III

THE SOUL

30

La Mama's love burned brighter than ever,

her rays too strong for anyone to touch.

—TALES OF THE DEOS,
FELIPE THOMÁS SAN JUSTINIO

This was never a love story.

I realize that as I fall.

I close my eyes, and to my surprise, my mind is completely blank. I don't see my past. I don't see my family. I just wait for the impact.

But instead of hitting the marble floor, something crashes into me. A body?

The force of him is like a wrecking ball pushing me to the side. We slide and slam into a wall. I'm half in his arms and half on the floor.

"You're heavier than you look," he says. He half smirks and half grimaces as he tries to sit up.

I blink a few times, and my heart pounds so fast I'm afraid it'll run laps around the room on its own. Rhett's earth-brown eyes look down at me, probably checking to see if I have any life-threatening injuries. Then I grasp what he just said to me and I manage an indignant grunt.

"I'm small but mighty," I say.

"Right, you're okay, then."

I try to stand up but it's a struggle. A wave of vertigo keeps me in his arms even though I'm trying my hardest to stand up. I scream as I accidentally place my weight on my bad hand.

"Nothing about this is okay," I say. I look back up at him through the dark shadows at the edges of my vision. "Maks is still upstairs. His sister is alive. You have to help her!"

"Stay here." Rhett sits me up against the wall. "I'll go find him."

Where would I go? I want to say. But I can't talk anymore. I can barely move.

"No need," Maks calls out from above, his voice a deep growl. He jumps over the railing and lands in a crouch. He pushes himself up gracefully and looks the hunter up and down. "Who the hell is this? Another monster to add to your collection?"

"I'm the last person you're going to see." Rhett reaches for the sword at his hip but grabs at empty space.

Maks lands a solid punch in Rhett's face. The hunter spits out blood but swings and misses. Maks dodges him and staggers back with a cruel grin on his face. He cracks his knuckles, ready to attack again, when a shuffle draws our attention to the living room door. My heart falls when I see her.

"You dropped something," Irina says, her voice like syrup. Her eyes are fading from blue to white, blood trickling from the knife wound at her neck. She picks up the sword lying at her feet.

"Irina—" The words die on my tongue. What can I say? I'm sorry. I'm so sorry. As my heart seizes painfully, I know it won't be enough.

Rhett's features are tight, like he's combing through every scenario in his playbook. Maks has casimuerto strength and Irina has his sword. Rhett has a messed-up shoulder and no weapon. He's taller and more muscular than Maks, but Maks doesn't back down.

Instead, he takes a step closer. His snowdrift eyes are open wide in amusement as Rhett puts his fists up.

"Stop, please," I manage to say. I cough up blood and my heart gives a few painful lurches.

"Maks," Irina whispers, raking her fingers across her chest. "I don't feel well."

That's when I notice Irina and Maks both wince. It's the tiniest flicker across their gray, undead faces. But it's there. They can feel the pain I do. Rhett seems to notice too.

"Keep the sword," Rhett says, and pulls a slim, black box from his pocket. "See this? It's an alarm. My unit is coming and you two won't make it out of here alive."

"I guess we're not done after all," Maks tells me, and runs out the door with his sister.

Rhett looks back at me. The corners of my vision are dark, but I focus on his face. I remember him better now. At the hospital, soft and kind. Then, his voice in the alley and at headquarters. I can see him struggle between going after Maks and staying with me.

He stays.

Rhett groans as he lets himself collapse and take stock of his injuries. His nose bleeds freely from Maks's sucker punch, and he presses the back of his hand to his nostrils to stop the flow. The skin over the ridge of his nose is split open and bruised around the bone.

I crawl over to him.

"Stop moving. You're barely alive," Rhett says. His voice is a deep, angry thread in the ringing in my ears.

I don't know much about hunters, but I'm sure they don't like when they get knocked to the ground by a member of the undead. He scoops me up and carries me into the kitchen, setting me down on the marble island. The cool stone is refreshing on my hot skin.

"I'll be right back." He hops on his good foot and stalks off toward the bathroom.

I assess my injuries with a weak pulse of magic. My left shoulder is dislocated from the impact against Rhett and the wall, though it would have been worse if I'd hit the stone floor. There's a warm trickle of blood running down my temple. I touch it with heavy, trembling fingers. It's a small relief that only the skin was broken when I slammed into the wall. I press my hand on my abdomen, where the injury that was healing has reversed again. Blood soaks through my cotton shirt. The skin around the stitches is hot and I'm sure if I look, I'll see it's splitting open again.

I pat down my pockets for my phone, but remember it's plugged in the surveillance room at headquarters. Rhett's heavy boots announce his return before I can see him turn the corner. There's a first aid kit in his hands.

"What's that going to do? Sinmago medicine doesn't work on my kind." I ask, laughing even though it hurts.

"Yes, but bandages will stop the bleeding until help gets here. I can't exactly carry you in this condition on the subway."

"How far away is your unit?"

He scoffs and pulls out the black device he showed Maks. He flicks the top off and pulls down on the wheel, igniting a small blue flame. I string together a series of curses at him.

"I'm glad our lives depended on your *bluffing*." I lean my head back, dizziness taking hold of my sight. "Is letting people get away what the Knights of Lavant do best?"

"Look at me," he says, voice deep and commanding. "Help is coming. All hunters have tracker implants. They'll come for me."

"That seems wrong somehow." I try to breathe through the new swell of pain. "I need to get back to my family. They can heal me."

"Don't close your eyes. Not yet."

I curse him because it's the only thing that feels good. "If I have a concussion, it's because of you."

He opens the kit and riffles through Band-Aids and gauze pads. "You're the one who ran off to find your precious zombie boyfriend."

"You tried to *arrest* me." I pull my hand away from his.

"Lula, please." He takes hold of my wrists softly. "I promise, I'm not going to hurt you."

My heart is racing too fast and I want to throw up and pass out and cry. But he's the only one here and even if I can't trust him, I at least know he wants to put an end to this.

"Fine," I say.

Rhett works quickly, cleaning my wounds with alcohol and peroxide. He bandages up what he can, but I need more. I need my family.

"Are you really a nurse?"

"All the Knights of Lavant receive medical field training." The muscles on his face relax and a smile accentuates his sharp cheekbones. This close, I can see how deep his brown eyes are, like I'm being swallowed up by their darkness.

"Lula?" His voice is frantic. "Stay awake."

When I breathe in, I inhale chemical fumes that burn my senses awake. I blink rapidly, willing my eyes to focus on his face. The broken ridge of his nose, the fierce frown of his brow, the raven-black hair that falls over his face when he leans closer to me.

"Lula, Lula, stop," he tells me. "Help is on the way."

A hot flash racks my body and nausea hits me in an unrelenting wave. I lean forward and get sick all over his lap. Because I haven't eaten much the last few days, I throw up bile and the remnants of the black-and-silver-flecked elixir I've been drinking.

Rhett audibly groans. Still, he brushes my sweaty hair back and dabs at the corners of my mouth with a cloth.

"Tell them to hurry," I say.

His hands reach for me, and for the second time today, he catches me.

31

Silver flecks and kraken's ink,

weary bones and orchids pink.

Shake under a crescent moon to drink.

—THE ART OF POISON,

ANGELA SANTIAGO

Cold air burns my throat and my nasal passages. I'm on a hospital bed surrounded by bright-white lights that force my eyes shut.

"It takes some adjusting to," Rhett tells me.

He's beside me, dressed in that black leather suit he wore in the alley. I reach out and touch the sleeve. This close, I can see the scale pattern that makes it look like dragon skin.

"What are you doing?"

"I just wanted to see what it felt like," I say. "I'm not sure if you're a vigilante or a scuba diver."

"Funny," Frederik says, appearing as if from thin air. "I see why Marty likes you so much."

It hurts to laugh, but it's also satisfying. Maks tried to kill me and would've succeeded if it hadn't been for the hunter who wanted to arrest me. I sit up and take inventory of the various needles hooked into my veins. They're connected to thin tubes that pump an iridescent liquid into my bloodstream. It makes me feel like an experiment.

I take note of the black hospital gown I'm wearing and, all at once, feel exposed.

"Your mother changed your clothes," Rhett tells me, like he's reading my mind. "She's downstairs with everyone else."

"Did they heal me?"

Frederik steps forward, his presence comforting for someone so undead. "They couldn't. They need to save their strength for the Circle."

I wade through my clouded memories. Before Rhett showed up, we were going to summon the High Circle. I glance at the hunter, but he's avoiding my stare.

"What is this stuff?" I ask of the liquid.

"It's what's healing you," Frederik says. He disappears in a blur, then reappears holding a familiar flower in a glass vial filled with glowing blue water. "I've been working on a serum that can heal supernatural beings."

"In your spare time?" I take the vial from him.

"I've found some time in three hundred years since I took up the endeavor, yes."

"It was you," I say, touching the deep-plum petals. The same flowers are in a vase in my house. "You left the bouquet at my doorstep. The flowers were just like this."

Frederik's dark eyes look confused. Then he looks at Rhett.

"It wasn't *this* flower," Rhett says, annoyed. Then turns to

Frederik and says, "It was the batch you couldn't use because the soil samples weren't correct. It was meant to be a gesture of peace before all of this."

I pause for a moment over the fact that Rhett left me flowers. But something far more important pushes the thought aside and I instead turn to Frederik. "Could the serum heal the casimuertos?"

"I'm sorry." Even for a vampire, he looks somber. "I tried before they escaped. It didn't take."

"Why didn't you say something?" But even I know the answer.

"I didn't want to give you false hope. Even now, your body is burning right through the serum. The way the casimuertos are multiplying, it's taking an unsustainable toll on your body."

I banish the spark of hope that was starting to form.

"I developed it to cure almost any creature on this earth," he explains. "It affects species differently, of course. It's a temporary cure. It won't stop or reverse death. It's healed your flesh wounds. But there's still the abnormality here that is completely untouched."

He points to the X-rays. Right over my heart is a black, misshapen mass.

"It's grown a centimeter in diameter since Rhett brought you back in. It's nearly the same size as your heart."

I touch my chest right over my solar plexus. This is the very thing that tethers me to the casimuertos. When I look at the black mass on the X-ray, I shudder.

"This whole time I've thought that the silver thread that appears is linking me to the casimuertos. But it's not a link. It's a parasite."

I start to stand, but Rhett stops me.

"I know you're upset, but you need to let the serum finish working."

"Upset?" I pull the tubes out and shimmering liquid spills down my arm. "The city is crawling with an undead swarm that *I* raised. The goddess of death is between realms and only I can break her out. On top of that, my ex-boyfriend just tried to kill me. So tell me, Rhett, how *upset* am I?"

"I just—"

Frederik presses his hand on Rhett's chest. Rhett tries to push forward but the vampire is freakishly strong.

"Now, take me to my family. I need to speak with Alex."

"As you wish," Frederik says. He leaves a plain, black shirt and jeans on the exam table, and they wait for me outside.

I dress quickly, giving one last look at the X-ray of my chest. This leech—it's impervious to magic and science because it was born out of death. And I know the only way to get rid of it.

I follow the vampire and the hunter through a long, narrow hallway. The florescent lights above flicker in time to our steps, and the walls tremble as if an earthquake is hitting us. Then we hear yelling.

Frederik opens a door, and I see my family gathered around.

"Alex!" I run up to where her hand is pressed against a glass wall.

I snap my head around to look at Frederik. "You locked my sister up?"

"She couldn't contain her magic," McKay says, standing behind the control panels.

"Let her out!" I shout.

"She's been like this for hours," Rose says.

I run up to Rhett and shove him hard. There's a flicker of

shock on his face as he stumbles backward, but he catches himself quickly.

"We had no choice but to contain her," he shouts back. "She attacked me. Besides, this isn't jail. It's a time-out unit. The real jail is in the Hudson River."

"Let her out," I say. "We need her." *I need her.*

"It's hard to convince me that you're willing to work with us when your sister is trying to fry us."

"Why do we have to convince you?" I ask. I mean, he did technically save me and bring me back. But that doesn't give him the right to do this. "*We* protect our magic."

"Tell her to kill the lightning, and I'll let her out," Rhett says. "We're on the same side."

"What's the *magic* word?" I ask.

He takes a deep breath and mutters, "Please."

I go to the glass wall keeping Alex contained. I press my hands on it and she lines her palms with mine.

"Are you okay?" she asks, dodging one of her own lightning bolts that bounces from wall to wall. "I can't stop it, Lula."

"I'm fine," I say, and I can't help but glance back at the hunter. "He tried to help with Maks but he got away. I need you, Ale. Please, you know how to contain your power."

Alex takes a few steps back. She stands in the center of the small room and holds her hands out. Dozens of bolts bounce off the walls, leaving behind giant burn marks. She closes her eyes and inhales until the lights stop flickering and the walls stop shaking and there is only stillness.

"Thank goodness. The electrocuted look does not work for me,"

McKay says, and punches in a code. The glass wall slides open with a *whoosh*.

I run in to hug her, not caring that I get a shock of static when I do. Her body relaxes against mine, and when she holds me, I start to shake. She smooths down my hair and rubs a hand on my back.

I wipe at the tears on my face. My entire life I've watched my mother hold back her emotions. I wanted to be like her. Strong. Resilient. Like steel made flesh. I hated crying. But I'm not like her. My strength is different from my mom's. It's different from my sisters' too. And maybe that's okay because everything I've done has led me back to the place where I belong—with my family.

I steady myself and say, "I'm ready to call on the High Circle."

Dad pulls on the whiskers of his mustache. "They would never come to this place."

"They have to," I say. "Because right now we're the only hope for this city."

The surveillance room is full of faces both strange and familiar.

The High Circle showed up, along with some of the younger brujas and brujos of the community. *Pleased* is not the first word that comes to mind to describe their attitudes, but at least they're here.

Mayi and Emma sit at the edge of the couch, unable to hold back their excitement. When you're a bruja, it's rare to be included in grown things, though I wish the circumstances were different.

Two young brujos, Adrian and his older brother, stare at the members of the Thorne Hill Alliance and the scale-leather worn by the Knights of Lavant.

"Why don't we have hologram screens?" Adrian asks.

"Do you have hologram-screen money?" Lady Lunes mutters.

Rhett introduces himself as Garhett Dulac of the Knights of Lavant. He names Frederik Stig Nielsen as the High Vampire of New York, and Marty McKay as the representative to all solitary fey and supernatural creatures without nations. Because it's an official meeting, one of the THA takes minutes in the corner, her fingers moving at a dizzying speed.

"This is a live feed of the Brooklyn Bridge," Frederik says, pointing at a projection map of the city. He's turned the volume off, but I can imagine the screams of the stampede taking place. Three casimuertos are feasting on fresh kills. The Knights of Lavant descend on the scene, evacuating as many people as they can. The Knights fight fast, but the casimuertos are fast too. They bare their bloodied teeth and fight back. We watch, horrorstruck, as it takes three knights to bring down one casimuerto.

"Turn it off," Valeria says. She holds her eyelids shut with her fingertips. "I can't stand that and the pull of the Veil. Don't you feel it, Rose?"

Rose looks down at her feet and gives a gentle nod. I realize we haven't talked about her new ability, if it's a new ability, at all. But there will be time for that later.

Rhett pulls up the hologram map that estimates the spread of the casimuertos and their victims. "This is what the city will look like this time tomorrow. We've dispatched a team to work with our branch of the NYPD, but it isn't enough. We need to work together in this, or the city falls."

A chatter starts among the magical beings and swarms into a loud buzzing.

"Those zombie things attacked my pack in the park two nights ago."

"This city will have to burn again, won't it?"

"They don't seem so hard to kill."

"I mean, decapitation has never not worked."

"Please, listen!" I stand in the middle of the room. A mix of angry and curious faces stare back at me. Frederick's serum is starting to fade, and a dull pain starts to pulse at the base of my heart, right around my ribs. "I'm Lula Mortiz. I'm the one responsible for raising this undead army, and I called you all here because you are my only hope to stop them."

"You went against our word," Gustavo says, staring at me like he might commit murder himself. His wife, Anna, clutches her amethyst prex, trying to get Adrian to sit back.

"I know—" I start, but he interrupts.

"You violated our most sacred laws. Now you seek our help *again* to clean up your mess, and you put us in the same room as the people who have hunted us for eons."

"This concerns us all," Frederik says coolly. "The Thorne Hill Alliance is a neutral place. The Knights of Lavant are bound by the same laws as the rest of us. No one will harm you here."

Gustavo makes a distasteful noise in his throat, but Rhett ignores the outburst and gives me the floor again.

"What do you propose?" Lady asks me, her head wrap twice as

tall as usual, and her neck adorned with polished gems and a tiny clove of garlic that rests in the dip of her clavicle.

"I don't understand," Elisabeth, a witch from the Thorne Hill Alliance, says. "How did you create these zombies?"

"They're called *casimuertos*," I explain. "It means *almost dead*. They're literally straddling the line between living and dead."

"What's keeping them alive?" Elisabeth asks. "I mean, our magics are different, but all magic needs an anchor. Something must be tying them to this realm."

There's a flurry of discussion and suggestions. Beheadings and fire and a quest for a magical spring that cures everything.

I bring my fingers to my lips and whistle hard and loud.

"I am the anchor." When I speak those words, it silences them. I wonder how many are thinking it would be best to kill me right here and now. "The casimuertos are feeding on my life force. Our magic can't heal it and potions won't help. There's a weapon that can sever the tie and destroy all the casimuertos bound to me. But this is bigger than just the casimuertos. La Muerte is trapped. The balance between the living and dead is broken. Spirits can't be collected or cross over. Our world can slip into that in-between space."

"What do you need to do?" someone asks.

"I need to call upon the elements to retrieve the Spear of Death."

"Even if we gathered every witch on this continent," Valeria says, "what's to say we can summon the power of the Deos?"

"This is a fool's errand," Gustavo mutters.

"You can think that, but it's the only option we have," I say. "Lady de la Muerte needs the spear. I trapped her, and I have to free her."

"Isn't that a good thing?" Mayi asks quietly. She shrinks back a bit when all eyes turn on her. "No death, I mean…"

Lady pulls out a cigar from her long skirt and lights it. Her fingers are trembling. I've never seen her scared in all my life. "In a perfect world," Lady says, her eyes lingering on the vampire for a moment. "Immortality is for the gods. This world needs a balance of life and death. Without it, there is no renewal. There is stagnancy and chaos. Look at all those bodies out there."

"You really think you can conjure the elements?" Helena of the High Circle asks. "Conjuring is rare magic in our times."

"I'm an encantrix," Alex says, standing beside me. "I was blessed by the Deos. I can summon all the elements."

"No," my dad shouts. "That'll kill you before Lula has a chance to see the spear, let alone get to it."

"Yeah, you'd die from the recoil, even if you could survive conjuring," Mayi says.

"McKay, can you put up the texts on the screen?" I ask.

The shifter pushes a button and the rezo for Lady de la Muerte appears. I read it out loud.

"El Fuego extinguished into ash. La Ola crumbled into salt. El Terroz clove the earth in pieces. El Viento fell and kept on falling."

Nova steps forward, resolution in his Caribbean-sea eyes, as if daring anyone to challenge him. "I'll be your light, Ladybird."

"No," Alex says, taking his hand. The magical burn marks work their way up to the knuckles now. "The recoil will literally kill you. You're not—"

"That's for me to decide." He yanks his hand back.

"Sit down, son," my dad tells Nova. "My lightning, it can substitute fire as well. I should be the one."

"Dad—" I start to say, but whatever is going to come next gets caught in the cry I silence.

"I can summon wind," Adrian shouts excitedly. He runs up to me, pulling out of his mother's and father's grips. He stands in front of me. "You remember, right, Lula?"

"You're doing no such thing," Anna tells her son.

Adrian doesn't look at his mother, but at me. "My mother asked me to keep my power secret because of what happened with Alex. She thought you guys might be bad influences on me. But I am a Son of El Viento, Lord of Flight, and I can do this."

"Thank you," I say, gripping his hand in mine as he stands beside my father. He's half the size of my dad and thin as a lamp-post, but there is more bravery in this kid's eyes than in most of the people in this room.

McKay holds his hand out. "Okay, so fire and wind. What about one of the mermaids? They might be able to be one of your water witches."

My mom speaks up from her seat. "Unless they can command the sea itself, conjure it to move with the others, it wouldn't work."

"I think I can," a voice comes from the crowd.

I'm not sure it's even her until she stands. Rose. Her long, brown hair is a tangle of waves. Her chest rises and falls quickly, a nervous shake in her usually still hands.

"That is not your power," Valeria says. "That's impossible."

Rose shakes her head. "It isn't. I don't know how or when, but my power has changed."

"Rose?" Ma steps forward to touch Rose's round cheek.

"It happened once last year," Rose says. "I healed a cut on one of the patients. I thought I imagined it, so I ignored it. But during the healing canto, when we tried to heal Maks, I felt stronger. It was like…this energy coming awake."

"That doesn't mean anything," Gustavo says.

"Of course it does," I tell him, standing in front of him so he won't look at Rose with the same disdain he looks at me with. "The other night, when I left headquarters, Rose saved me. She conjured light, just like Nova."

"What makes you think that means you can conjure water?" Lady asks, more curiosity than doubt in her sultry voice.

"Every time, there was one thing in common." Rose walks to the center of the room and takes Nova's hand. "I was touching another bruja."

An understanding passes from Rose's eyes to Nova's. A radiant orb forms in his free hand, dragging across his body like a rope, and down his other arm. Rose raises her arm and a beam of light radiates from each one of her fingers.

There's a series of gasps in the room.

I can't stop smiling.

The old brujas and brujos of the High Circle press their thumbs to their lips, then foreheads, and whisper a rezo to the gods. None of them have ever witnessed this kind of magic.

"Can I try something?" McKay asks Rose.

"You're not a brujo," Rose says.

"No, but I'm still of the magical variety. I want to see something. May I?" She nods and they hold hands like they're about to arm wrestle. "Close your eyes and think about the most beautiful person in the world. Think of their face. Then slowly, think about seeing that face when you look in the mirror."

Someone tries to protest, but another person shushes them.

Slowly, Rose's hair darkens and coils like Christmas ribbon. Her skin darkens to a milky brown, she's taller by an inch or so, and her waist narrows. But it's her face that startles me. Rose is wearing my face.

I let go of a shuddering breath and touch my sister's face. *My face.* She's even wearing my scars.

"Oh, my Rosie."

She lets go of McKay's hand and shifts back into herself. I hold her as tight as I can, and I wish I didn't have to let her go.

"Holy t—" Nova starts to say.

"How did you do that?" Mayi asks Rose, eyes lit with wonder.

"The other times, I wasn't aware of what I was doing. This time, I knew what I wanted. I wanted to use his power."

McKay grins widely. "It felt like I was being hijacked. Like something about you was hacking into my *being.*"

"Does it hurt?" I ask.

McKay shrugs. "Tickles actually."

"Try me!" Adrian says, and Rose touches his arm. This time, she lets go and uses both hands to create a cyclone. They test out the theory by having her touch a mermaid and a werewolf, but it only seems to work with magic.

"You're a magical hacker, Rose," Nova tells her, slapping her on her back.

She stares at her hands. "I think I like the sound of that."

"All this time," Ma says, tears in her eyes. When she blinks, they fall long and hard, and there's something about seeing my mother cry that makes me want to come undone. She brushes her hands along Rose's blushing cheeks. "I thought you had the gift of the Veil."

"Valeria *was* the first person to ever hold her," Alex says. "And your power is always stronger after your lessons. I can't believe this. You know what this means? You could be stronger than me."

"I think we can be glad for this," I say, then repeat what Lady de la Muerte told me. "The Deos are where they've always been."

"You can tap into my power," Alex says, cracking her knuckles. "That will help you conjure water and I won't have to worry about that recoil. That leaves me with earth."

"I'm glad you've got your circle," Rhett says. "But where do you suppose you're going to do this?"

"The roof?" Nova asks.

Frederik wags a finger. "We just rebuilt half this building."

I scour my thoughts for every word La Muerte spoke to me. She's in a dark in-between, but her spear is elsewhere. I slap my hands together, recalling my last meeting with her. "Lady de la Muerte told me she was created at the edge of the world. But in our stories, there was one land and then just the sea."

"The beach," Alex says triumphantly.

"What about the casimuertos that are out there right now?" Emma asks, sitting closer to Mayi.

"That's where we come in," McKay says.

"While you guys head down to the boardwalk," Rhett says, "we'll send more teams to hunt the casimuertos."

"If I were an undead army of teenage soccer players, where would I go next?" McKay says, drawing his fingers together like an evil villain. He turns back to the screen on the main wall and pulls up the map of the city again.

"School," Rose says. "That's where we found the first nest in the alley. Most of the bodies found with missing hearts are around there. Plus, the school closed early this year after the accident. It's empty now."

"I think they've grown out of high school," McKay mutters.

Everyone faces the wall. The red dots of light are less spread out than before.

"Are they moving?" I ask.

"They're migrating," Frederik says. "Prospect Park?"

I follow the slow movement of red dots. The lines that connect them seemed random before. But now I see something that I didn't before. There's a red dot, fainter than the rest, but right where this building is. I shouldn't be surprised. It was Rose who told me my soul was detached. How can I be touched by La Muerte and be claimed for anything else but death? That red dot is me.

"They're coming here," I say.

"Call Camillia and tell her to bring the weapons truck to the THA back entrance," Rhett says to another hunter. "We leave on my go. We have to clear the beach from all ends to give Lula's circle time to retrieve the spear. I want groups of three at every street entrance."

Lula's circle. The thought of it makes me smile for a moment. Just one.

The living room is a flurry of activity. The witches of the

Thorne Hill Alliance introduce themselves to Lady and my mother. Frederik becomes a blur as Mayi approaches him. In the maelstrom of it all, Rhett watches me from the other end of the room. Rose and Adrian talk about their newfound powers and Alex and Dad stand together in their usual silence.

I know I'm not going to get another moment like this, so I take it all in—their faces, their fight, and their hope.

That all vanishes when Gustavo walks up to me.

"This won't work!" He grabs my arm and squeezes. "You. You and your sisters. All you do is bring trouble to our people. You've allied with our enemies. You've brought shame to your ancestors. Chaos kissed the lot of you. I will not be a part of it and neither will my son."

The prex I'm wearing—the one my mother made to protect me against bad intentions and curses—breaks apart and falls to the ground.

"Get your hand off my child, Gustavo," Mom says. She's standing so close to him that it takes me a moment to see the blade she's pressing against his ribs. There's a deadly stillness to her face, a resolution that frightens me. My mother is a healer. Her hands have saved countless lives and brought so many souls into this world. That same woman is willing to hurt someone for me. And I know I can't let that happen.

"Ma, I got it," I whisper, aware that dozens of eyes are on me.

"I made the wrong choices," I tell Gustavo. "But your son has the opportunity to help me make things right."

Gustavo takes his wife and son by their hands. "Adrian, we're going."

Adrian shakes his head, feet firmly planted on the floor. "I can't. I have to do this. You're the one who taught me that our power is greater than ourselves. Please, Pa."

Gustavo takes a long look at his son, then turns to me with fury in his eyes as he holds a finger to my face. "You still have to pay a price, Lula Mortiz. You can't get out of paying it. And by the Deos, I hope that day comes quickly."

I stare right back into the hate in Gustavo's eyes.

All I can say to him is, "I know, Gustavo. But that's between me and Death herself."

32

For eons, the Deos slumbered.
La Ola in her sea, El Terroz in his mountains,
El Viento in the skies, and El Fuego at the heart of the world.

—Tales of the Deos,
Felipe Thomás San Justinio

The Coney Island boardwalk is deserted. The shops are closed up for the night. Neon graffiti on the metal grates is the only color against the gray darkness that takes hold tonight. Thick, black clouds carry the beginnings of a storm toward the shore.

I take a moment to let the drizzle kiss my face, feel the wind in my hair. The Deos are where they've always been and, more than that, are all around me. In this moment, I am ready.

Out on the water, tall waves swallow up the jetties and lifeguard towers, licking the edges of the boardwalk.

Dad, Adrian, Rose, and Alex gather around me and we go over the conjuring one last time.

"Alex, we need light," I say, and she conjures a glowing orb over each of our heads. "Dad, can you bring the storm closer?"

He holds his hand with the other to stop it from trembling but nods wordlessly.

"Are you sure you can handle this?" I ask.

He takes my face in his hands. It's been so long since I've really looked at him. I see myself in his weather-gray eyes and the fine curve of his nose, in the way my brow furrows when I'm quick to anger or worry, and in the curl of his hair.

"I know I can never get you girls back. Too much time has passed. But I'm going to be here now, and I'm going to give you everything that is in my power to give."

My thanks is lost as the sky thunders, a sonic boom I can feel right at my core. The pain around my heart is getting stronger. I can feel the dark mass growing, a life-sucking leech.

"Let's go," I shout over the gale, and they follow me onto the beach.

I hold my dad's hand the entire way, and he only let's go when they form a wide circle with me at the top.

I am at the edge of the world, I think. Looking into the black horizon, it truly feels that way, as if there is nothing but the engulfing power of the sea at night.

"The waves are getting closer," Alex says, reaching for Rose's hand. "Rosie, you ready?"

"If by ready you mean terrified, then yes," Rose says before letting go of Alex. She's a natural at wielding this unknown power, moving her hands like she's decoding the language of gods with her fingertips. As a dark wave threatens to crash over us, Rose faces the approaching wall of water and holds her palms up. Salt water sprays around us but she steadies the wave with the motion of her hands. Her force field twists water into a rope and lassos around the Circle.

Dad goes next. The salty air is charged with magic. His eyes are threaded with pinpricks of lightning. Every lamppost on the board-walk shatters as he pulls that energy into his fist, twisting it into a ball of electricity high in the air.

He calls on La Tormenta, Lady of the Storms and Wife of El Cielo. Dad shuts his eyes, and despite the ring of water spinning around us and the black cloud that he's pulled directly over our heads, he's never looked so peaceful. When he raises his fist into the sky, a silver-white light fills the Circle from the inside out, so bright we all have to look away momentarily.

In his fist is a bolt of lightning.

"Adrian, go on!" I shout.

Adrian's eyes flash white, and my heart skips at the thought of Maks's eyes. But I have to focus, so I concentrate on the crash of the waves and the howl of the wind. Adrian spreads his arms open as air funnels around him and he rises six feet off the wet sand. As if he can't believe his own strength, he hollers into the sky.

I look to Alex, who goes last. She rubs her hands together and bends down to press them against the sand. Her face is stoic, as if she's turned to granite herself. It's then that I feel the rumble beneath the ground racing toward us.

Alex is like a maestro conducting an orchestra. Her hands pull Rose's rope of sea and shifts Adrian's tornado up high, forming a twisting cylinder of water and wind with us at the center. The earth still trembles beneath us, closer still.

"On your signal!" I shout.

Alex takes the lightning from Dad, and he makes a terrifying cry as he lets go. Alex shudders as she holds the bolt in both hands, weaves it like a webbed dome around us.

The force of the elements pushes and pulls on our bodies, threatening to carry us away. I grab hold of Rose and Alex. They grab hold of Dad and Adrian, who close the Circle, each one of their arms a lifeline to mine.

My face is wet with sea spray and cold from the wind. The ground vibrates faster and harder beneath our feet, and then, when I think the earth will split open and swallow us whole, Alex smashes her fists into the ground.

The blast rebounds, and together, the elements break through the waves, carving a path through the sea.

"I don't know how long we can hold this," Alex shouts. "Go now!"

As the ocean parts, split by wind and a ripple along the sand, a narrow rock formation appears in the distance as tall as the waves. Electricity winds itself around the spear, which is wedged into the very top, shimmering like a beacon of light.

I race along the path. Pinpricks of pain stab at my heart and my lungs burn as I put them to the test. I want to extend seconds with my bare bands to give myself more time. There's never enough time. The lightning lets me see the way ahead, framed by the debris and stones encased inside the parted sea. There's a ripple on either wall of water and I pump my legs harder and faster than I ever thought I could go.

My heart soars with hope when the boulders get bigger the closer I get. When I stop, I grab hold of the base. I was wrong. It isn't one large rock, but lots of boulders wedged together, a stairway to the skies. There's only one way up.

The parted sea is taller than the tower. Wind whistles like sirens singing, but I keep going up. Cramps dig at my sides and my legs tremble. My foot hits a loose stone wedged between two boulders, and I start to slip and fall.

I grab at the slick, wet stones and hold on for dear life. The wall of water is inching closer around me, the power of the Circle weakening.

I shake and I scream and I curse at the sky and sea and wind that pushes against me like the weight of the heavens is slamming me down. But I think of my family waiting for me, the whole city waiting for me to right my wrongs, and I can't let them down. Inch by inch, I pull myself along the boulder. My frigid skin finds comfort in the warmth of the blood trickling down my legs.

When I reach the top, a gale almost knocks me back. I hurl my weight forward, my nails scrabbling against the rock as I claw my way to safety. I only take a moment to stare at it—the Spear of Death wedged cleanly into the stone. I touch it, but sparks burn against my skin.

"What am I missing?" I whisper.

I think back to the time I saw Lady de la Muerte wield it. But she's a goddess and I'm just mortal. We cast cantos and sing rezos. Why do we pray? Because we ask something of the gods, and in return, they ask for sacrifice. I did it when I tried to heal and tether Maks to me. We do it when we ask for blessings on our Deathdays. Then it hits me.

Blood. It's always blood because blood is life. The Deos ask for it.

I rub at the open gash on my thigh and smear blood across my palms. Then I grab the center of the spear, expecting electric shocks. I let out a victorious scream as my hands close around the shaft, and I'm able to pull upward. I raise it up to the sky, a lick of lightning sending a jolt down to my arms.

Somehow, the wind carries the screams of the Circle to me.

I hold the Spear of Death in my hands, and the power is unlike anything I've ever felt before.

But when I look up, I no longer see sky, just the ocean closing over me.

33

She never asked for this, but she bore the weight
of the world in silence, her strength reaching all
those souls who didn't know where to find her.

—REZO OF LA FUERZA,
LADY WHO CARRIED THE EARTH ON HER SHOULDERS,
BOOK OF CANTOS

The waves spin me around and around until I can't tell which way is up or down. My chest is tight from holding my breath, and my eyes burn against the sting of salt. But I hold on to the spear and nothing, not even the sea itself, will rip it from my hands.

I try to kick, but my muscles ache from running and seize up in the frigid water. Bubbles leave my nose and mouth too quickly as every impulse in my body is begging to open up and breathe.

Something hits my side, and I scream as a hand colder than the sea itself grabs me around my waist, dragging me down to what I'm sure is the bottom of the sea.

Instead, I break the surface and gasp for air. I breathe it in hungrily, choking on salt water that splashes its way into my mouth.

"You really shouldn't drink the water anywhere around here," Mayi yells.

I cough and laugh and cry as she hooks her arms under my armpits and pulls me back to the shore. The entire time I keep a solid grip on the spear. I have *the spear*.

A wave pushes us closer to the shore. When we hit land, I could bend down and kiss the sand. But my sister runs over and pulls me into an hug first.

"Lula!" Alex shouts in my ear. "Thank the Deos."

She helps me stand and climb over the metal railings of the boardwalk. Dad wraps an arm around my shoulders. He hunches over, the recoil taking hold of his body. With one arm, I keep the spear upright. It even helps to lean against it.

"You did it," Adrian tells me, mouth open as he turns to stare at the calming waters.

"Because of you. All of you. I couldn't have gotten this far without your help. Mayi, where did you come from?"

She's a wonder to look at, her glamour gone to reveal her true face. Every imperfection uniquely, wonderfully hers. "I couldn't stay back, not while you were willing to risk your life. Alex guided me."

The clouds still cling to the sky in every direction, a light rain falling across the city. I take in the boardwalk. There's some damage, but it can be blamed on the storm.

"Should we get back to the headquarters?" Rose asks.

"The hunter said to wait here," Mayi says. "He said the building's compromised. They're going to take us somewhere else."

But there's only one place I want to be.

Home.

Rhett parks the Knights' black car in the driveway and goes around back to make sure the coast is clear. My mother takes my arm to help me walk up the front porch.

I take a second to memorize our house. On a block full of newly renovated houses and brownstones, ours has a roof that leans a little to the right after weathering too many storms. Its windows are shaded by a sturdy oak tree, and the paint on the sides peels off in long streaks. A poor house. A loved house. A house full of brujas. My home.

I brought death here and I'll take it out.

"Lock the door behind you," Ma tells me as she opens the door to let everyone in. I can practically see the checklist going off in her mind. "I'll go prepare the infirmary."

"Out of the way," Alex shouts, helping Rose up the stairs, followed by Mayi and Adrian. Nova lets my dad lean on him as the recoil fully sets in. Dad's skin is covered in painful blisters. Even from out here, I can hear the sounds of retching and groaning that fill the house.

"Coast is clear," Rhett says, coming up behind me on the porch. He walks the length of it, searching every surface, like a casimuerto is going to be hiding between the potted plants. When he stands in front of the window, a memory flashes in my mind.

"You were the guy," I say, and I laugh even though my abdomen hurts. "I chased you that night with the hose."

He grimaces but doesn't deny it. "Not one of my better moments. I needed proof the casimuerto was in your house."

298

"The Knights of Lavant are officially creepy in my book," I say, trying for humor but it doesn't make either of us laugh. "Kitchen is down at the end of the hall and bathroom is to your left. But you probably already know that."

"I won't be long," he says, and disappears down the hall, balling up fists covered in dirt and blood.

I close the door behind us and lock up tight. When I turn, I'm face-to-face with our altar for La Mama. The hand is still broken and tucked into the decaying flowers around the base. I grab three tea lights, a stick of greenberry incense, and strike a match. It's been so long since I attempted this, but I know if I can't find the words now I never will.

"I ask for strength I probably don't deserve," I say, using the spear to lean against. "Strength to do whatever it takes to keep my city safe. In the name of La Mama, Mother of all the Deos, and La Fuerza, Lady Who Carried the Earth on Her Shoulders."

"Lula?" Rhett clears his throat behind me.

I jump and swing around.

"Careful!" Rhett jumps back. His eyes flick up and down the spear. "Isn't that thing supposed to sever souls from the living?"

"Sorry," I say, and actually mean it.

Rhett looks at me with a curious smile on his face.

"Your scuba suit came in handy," I say.

"It's *dragon skin*," he says, all indignant. "At least call it a dragon suit."

"Pass." I shrug. "Any word from the others?"

"We were trying to corral them before they hit headquarters, but there are too many."

We have one spear and hundreds of undead. *It won't be enough*, my dark thoughts chime in.

"It will be done," he assures me.

"Rhett," I say, a question I've held for a long time finds its way to my lips. "How long were you following me? Did it start at the hospital?"

He looks startled, like he didn't think I'd ever bring it up. "We were following your family."

"But you didn't have to talk to me at the hospital. You didn't have to feed Maks. Why do that only to show up at the THA trying to arrest me?"

"There was a detail placed on your family after the accident months ago." Rhett absentmindedly touches a thin blade tucked under his left sleeve. "We were making sure nothing went in or out of what's left of the portal in the yard. We wanted to make sure people were safe."

"Safe from us?" I ask, affronted by the thought that we could be considered dangerous. Though, after everything I've done, I suppose he was right. "And this whole time we were worried about us being safe from the world."

"I determined your family was not a threat. We've kept tabs on Nova Santiago as well, but he doesn't cause any harm to anyone but himself."

"Don't try to change the subject," I say. "Why did you lie to the Alliance? You gave me a head start with the box…"

"It doesn't matter now."

"It matters to me! Where did that heart come from?"

"I didn't rip it from someone's beating chest, if that's what you're asking," he says, raking his fingers through damp, long waves. "We have our own morgue of bodies that can't go to the human authorities. I broke protocol. I knew I'd made a mistake, but I left the box that night because I saw how much you were suffering, both before the accident and during. I wanted to help you, Lula. When we stopped being able to contain them and Knights were killed, I was so angry at myself that I acted like an idiot."

"I'm sorry about the hunters you lost," I say, my breath hitching in my throat. "I'm sorry I couldn't let him go."

"Lula—" His eyes follow the arc of my cheekbone, tracing over the scars. His lips part, starting as his phone buzzes. He gives me his back and listens intently. "No, they're safe here. I'll meet you there."

"Was that McKay? Where are they?"

"He's with my unit. The casimuertos are using the subway," Rhett says, taking several steps away from me. "All hands on deck."

He runs out the door, and the scent of the ocean lingers in his wake.

I lock the door and walk down the hall to join the others. Every step I take is like walking on hot coals.

In the living room, Ma, Nova, and Mayi are tending to the recoil Rose, Dad, and Adrian are suffering. The place looks like a war zone with buckets of water, bloody bandages for Dad's blisters, and the bag of weapons Alex has been collecting massed in piles everywhere.

Alex looks up from sharpening her favorite dagger. "You realize you haven't let go of that thing once, right?"

"Can I touch it?" Adrian asks.

I move the spear out of his reach.

"I can't lie," Nova says. "I thought that when you pulled the Death sword from the stone that it would make Lady de la Muerte appear."

"Where's Sargent Scuba Suit?" Alex asks.

"The casimuertos have gone underground, literally, so the Knights are regrouping. In the meantime, I have to figure out how to use this thing to free La Muerte."

"She's between realms," Ma says. "That would mean we need a portal."

I wonder aloud, "Is the portal in the yard *really* closed?"

"Yep. Total dead zone. Besides, La Muerte isn't in Los Lagos," Alex says. "I'd know."

The living room lights short-circuit.

"Alex!" Ma yells.

"That wasn't me!" And for a moment, our house feels the same as it always has.

"I got it," Nova says, making soft orbs of light appear all across the ceiling.

"It's the storm," Rose says, still coughing up water into her closed fist. She pulls back the curtain and looks out. "The house next door is dark too."

"I'll check the breakers," Mayi says. "And bring up candles."

"I'll go with you," Adrian says. "My dad says they kept a dead body down there once. Is that true?"

It's just the six of us in the living room. Even with Nova here, it feels right.

Ma presses her healing compresses on Dad's welts. He explains what it felt like to hold the lightning in his hand again. Nova keeps calling Rose a *magical hacker*, and she kicks his shin. All the while Alex watches me, like she's afraid I'm going to spontaneously combust. I know she's only worried, but for now, all I want is to bask in this moment.

I want to tell my parents that I love them. I want to tell my mom that when I felt like I needed strength, all I had to do was think of her. I want to tell my dad that I'm grateful that he used his power. I want to tell Nova that he needs to be careful, that he's got family if he wants it.

But I'm stopped by the sound of breaking glass.

"That came from the back," Mom says, picking up the machete on the coffee table. Dad gets up and goes with her.

"Stay here," they tell us.

Rose and Nova pick up weapons from the table too.

I hold the spear spike-side out and go into the hallway.

"Lula," Alex tells me. "Stay together."

"I have the spear. I'll be fine."

A cold draft blows in from the front door. I locked it after Rhett left. I know I did. I head straight for it to slam it shut, but a chill runs along my arms.

His voice behind me stops me cold.

"Hey, baby."

I spin around, holding the spear out as a threat I fully intend on carrying out.

Maks stands in the entrance of my home. His skin is the palest gray, crisscrossed with scars that run along his face and arms like eels skimming beneath the skin. His eyes are stark white with bright-red veins.

I pull the spear back, ready to plunge it into his heart, but then I see them just over his shoulder.

My sisters and Nova held captive by casimuertos.

"I hope you don't mind," Maks says. "We dropped by unannounced for dinner."

34

El Odio could not stand the world
but left his discord buried like seeds.
Beware the souls who eat his fruit.

—TALES OF THE DEOS,
FELIPE THOMÁS SAN JUSTINIO

I should've let them kill you when you turned," I say, and the bitterness on my tongue tastes so good.

"You're not strong enough for that, Lula," Maks says. "Isn't that why you locked me up and then dragged me all over the city trying to keep my memories from me?"

"I didn't keep your memories from you," I say. "That was the magic."

"Liar!" When he yells, his breath washes over me, rank and metallic. "Everything that's ever come out of your mouth is a lie, Lula. You lied about being a witch. You lied about what you did to me."

"Let them go," I tell him.

But he just looks at me and laughs. "You did do one thing for me, Lula. You freed a part of me I didn't know was there. That will always belong to you."

"Screw you, Maks," I growl. It's clear he's not going to play along, and I need a new plan. I turn to the other casimuertos and say, "You want the truth? Maks has been lying to you all. He brought you here to die."

"What's she talking about?" Derek asks, his rage deepening the red in his eyes. Beside him Irina cocks her head unnaturally, her white eyes boring into her brother.

"I can make you human again. Maks knew all along."

All the humor drains from his face, and he growls at me. "Don't listen to her! She said it herself. There's no reversing this."

"Lula," Alex shouts. "Stop it! I can fight them."

I look at her and shake my head. She's still recovering from conjuring the elements. And this is a battle I have to fight myself.

"Nope. That's what I've been keeping from you. In order for you to live again, you need one thing." I tap the center of my chest.

There's desire in their eyes. Longing. Not just for my heart. But for life. They shake with the need to consume. A casimuerto is never sated.

"You're going to have to catch me first," I say, and I run out the door.

"Good plan, Lula," I mutter. "Have your psycho, dead ex and friends chase you around the yard."

As I sprint down the porch and up the driveway, there's a shock of white light from the inside of the house followed by a series of blasts. *Dad and Alex*, I think. I want to picture them fighting side by side, holding back the other casimuertos. We have always fought. They will keep fighting long after I'm gone.

When I look up to the window, I see more casimuertos flooding the house. I want to scream, but I see others too. Hunters and brujas and the blur of a vampire. My heart soars at the sight of them fighting back, and I use that momentum to keep running.

"You can't run from me for long," Maks shouts. "I can feel your pain, you know. That's got to be, like, poetic or something."

In the dark, I can hear his fists bang against the side of the house. I slip into the garage and hide beside a metal rack.

"Lu-la." My name is a song on his lips. There was a time when he sang my name, when he sought me out because he missed me, when we couldn't imagine being apart. That Maks is long gone.

I grab the rack and pull it forward as hard as I can. It falls with a loud crash that shatters the car's windows and pins Maks to the floor. He groans but doesn't stay down.

"You're going to regret that." He takes out his rage on the car, ripping the door off its hinges. He throws it in my direction but misses.

"All that strength and you're a terrible shot. What happened to the MVP?" I don't wait for him to answer and wedge myself through the back door.

Maks smashes his way after me, breaking through wood and glass with his fists. I sprint across my yard but I've got nowhere to go. I need a portal and I need one now. *Find the spear. Free La Muerte. Destroy the heart and make the sacrifice.*

It's too quiet out here. I look over my shoulder to search for Maks, but he's gone. I spin back around. A crushing pain fractures across my face. I try to hold on to the spear, but I fall backward and hit grass and loose stones. When my head stops spinning, I focus on getting my hands back on the spear. Maks swipes it in one fluid motion, his knuckles dripping with blood.

"You hear that?" Maks asks, his blue lips bleeding where the skin cracks. There's the sound of thunder clapping and windows shattering. Someone screams, and I don't know if it's from my side or his. "That's the sound of you losing. Isn't that what you're most afraid of?"

As if responding to him, my heart gives a terrible squeeze. I dig my fingers into the grass at my sides because it's the only thing I can hold on to.

"I figured out why I was having all these weird emotions." Maks taps his chest right where the white T-shirt is splattered with blood. "After the switch went off in my head and everything became clear, I could still feel you. Even after death, I was tied to you."

"You're nothing but a leech, Maks." I push myself off the ground and keep a distance from him.

"*I'm* the leech?! I tried to get rid of you first. *I* tried, and still, we're connected. You were so afraid of being left alone that you *brought me back to life*." He flips the spear to examine the sharp, curved end. "I suppose I do owe you some gratitude. I loved you once, Lula. But between you and me? I'm too young to die twice."

The fight inside the house is getting closer, moving toward the kitchen. A body crashes through the window and rolls across the back porch. Maks looks at the body facing down on the ground and shrugs. His face contorts as he puts all his strength into stabbing the spear through my heart.

Run. Fight. Hit. Scratch. My mind is a flip book of scenarios, but all I know is I can't let him touch me.

There's a scream, but it isn't mine.

A blur runs past Maks. I feel the wind it trails on my face. Maks and I both stare at his arm, raised toward the sky. There's a red bracelet where there didn't used to be. The bloody blade of a machete follows its downward motion, and then my mother rights herself, her face streaming with sweat and tears.

Maks screams. His severed hand falls with a faint thud onto the grass. I'm too stunned to move, but I watch my mother. My mother covered in blood and sweat. My mother shaking with adrenaline. My mother saving me. My mother.

She takes my chin in her hand, runs her fingers across the tears on my face. "The others might have physical powers. But you and I must have a different strength."

I press my forehead to hers. "I'm so sorry."

"Fuerza." She presses her palm on my chest. "This is the heart you were born with and you have to decide how strong it will be."

"I know, Mama. I know."

Behind us, there's another blast coming. She looks torn between staying and going, so I make the decision for her.

"Go. I've got this."

She gives me her blessing, pressing her thumb to her lips, then to my forehead. And then she's gone, running back into the fray inside our house.

I want to run after her, but I know I have to be here.

Maks holds his arm around the wrist and screams. His eyes go completely red and he charges at me. Knocks me on the ground and chokes me with his good hand. I kick my legs but hit air.

This is the heart I was born with, and I have to decide how

strong it will be. And though it's being consumed by the darkness I unleashed into this world, it has never been stronger.

I lash out, dig my fingers into Maks's red eyes. I feel him blink around my fingertips, slick and wet. He growls, nearly rabid, and rolls off me.

I grab the spear from the ground and get up. Maks's severed hand is still wrapped around the middle. I try to pry the fingers off but they won't budge.

Maks shudders, and I realize he isn't crying. He's laughing. When he looks up to me, he softens his eyes and puts on a sweet smile. My heart twists and turns, remembering the boy he was. Eyes blue as wild flowers.

"You'd never hurt me, Lula. Deep in your heart you know that."

"You're right, Maks," I say. He's weak and desperate, swaying on his knees in front of me. "I did love you. I loved you so much I thought it was the only good thing that had ever happened to me. I did everything in my power to save you.

"But between you and me?" I plunge the spike into his chest. "I love myself more."

I stare into his eyes and watch them change from red to crystal to dark blue. He gasps for air and hits the ground. The spear trembles in my grasp, and suddenly, there's a golden glow coming from my chest. The threads that spooled from my heart are dimming. Maks's severed hand falls off the spear and lands on the ground with a final twitch.

I hear the whispers, hundreds of them, all at once. They buzz around my head like a colony of wasps. I can feel the power of the spear coming alive, and I know what I have to do. It isn't a portal that will free La Muerte. It's me—it's always been me. I flip the spear, line it up with my breast.

The back door swings open and my family runs out. Flames rise behind them in the kitchen and spread quickly. Destroy the heart and make the sacrifice. I take a deep breath.

"No!" Alex shouts, her hand reaching for me.

I thrust the spear into my heart.

35

Esa brujita con

ojitos luceros.

Con ella me entierro

sin ella me muero.

—WITCHSONG #33,
BOOK OF CANTOS

The light burst is blinding. It spills in a beam of silver from my chest.

I can still see Alex, running down to catch me before I fall. She will always catch me. She pulls the spike out of my chest and throws it on the ground, repeating my name over and over and over again.

"Stay alive, do you hear me?" She shuts her eyes and fat tears slide along her lashes and then onto my face. "This is not how your story ends."

Rose sits on the other side of me. She takes my hand in hers. "She's free."

For a moment, I think she's talking about me.

I don't feel free. I feel numb. Cold. Broken. I feel like my world came undone and fell back together in different places. I feel like every breath I take hurts more than the next. But I don't feel free.

"Step aside," says Lady de la Muerte in her deep, shadow voice.

Alex and Rose scramble away from Lady Death.

La Muerte takes her spear back and holds it with a firm hand, and I don't know if I'm hallucinating, but I think she is smiling.

"This is not the sacrifice, Lula Mortiz." Her skin is no longer translucent, but back to the bone white of the first time I saw her. Her crown of golden thorns is no longer bleeding. Her long, slender fingers twitch as she kneels beside me and shoves her hand into the bloody gash in my chest. The pain is so fierce my vision turns red. I shut my eyes, sure she's ripping my heart out. I can hear Alex and Rose crying. My parents screaming. Sirens in the distance. Always sirens, the Brooklyn lullaby.

And then, silence.

A serene quiet unlike anything I've heard before. I open my eyes expecting to be in a dream, the in-between where La Muerte and I used to meet when I was close to death myself.

But I'm still in my backyard, surrounded by family and friends and allies. The wound on my chest is healed, leaving a scar in the shape of a ring between my breasts. Lady de la Muerte squeezes a slithering black mass in her hand.

"Is that an octopus?" Rose asks.

I would laugh if it didn't hurt too much.

"This was how the dead were feeding on you. It started off the size of silverfish."

The thing has dozens of tentacles with pointy suctions. It slithers them in the air, trying to grab at something.

"Shouldn't we kill it?" Adrian asks.

Lady de la Muerte turns her head slowly in the direction of the boy. The crowd parts, just as the sea parted for me when I went to retrieve the spear. Adrian gulps, but other than that doesn't move an inch.

Lady de la Muerte bows her head once, then throws the creature on the ground, and before it has a chance to slither away, she stabs it right through its center. Then again and again until it cannibalizes itself and melts into the earth, killing the entire patch of grass it touched and turning dirt to sand.

"That was inside of your chest?" Alex asks. "Gross."

When I stand, I feel lighter than ever.

"What did you mean when you said that wasn't the sacrifice?" I ask La Muerte.

"All the lives that were taken as a result of your betrayal," she tells me, staking her spear in the earth and lifting her chin up. "I will require a year off your life for every person that was taken."

"The bus accident was not her fault," Alex says.

"That may be so. But the others. The ones killed by the casimuertos. Those deaths were robbed from me."

"How many years?" I ask her, afraid to hope.

"One hundred and six."

I have to laugh. "I'm not going to live that long."

Lady de la Muerte walks in a slow circle around me. "I know how long every single one of you is going to live. You, Lula Mortiz, could have had a very long life."

My great-grandfather lived to be one hundred and twenty. Even if I'm meant to live to ninety, it wouldn't be enough. As much as

314

I want to think I'm ready, I'm not. I look around the backyard full of brujas and hunters and the THA. I look at my sisters and my parents and Nova.

"Then what are you waiting for?" I take a steadying breath.

"Lula, no," Mom snaps at me, then softens her voice when she turns to Lady de la Muerte. "Please, My Lady. I beg you. Take years off my life instead."

"No, take mine." Dad steps in front of my mom.

"What about a deal?" Nova asks. He weaves through the throng of people in the backyard. "How about years taken from some of us?"

Her black line of a smile is terrifying as she sets her sights on Nova. "Not you, Noveno Santiago. With your gift, you do not have enough years to give me."

Nova's face blanks, and the bravado he had moments ago is gone.

"But I consent to your proposition," she says. "Only, I get to choose who gives me their life years."

"No," I say. "I have to do this. I have to pay this price."

"Lula, we don't agree all the time," Mayi says, "but any of us would have made the same mistake."

"Most of us have," McKay says, and my heart feels a familiar joy when I see him.

"Enough," Lady de la Muerte says, her voice deeper, a darkening cloud. "I grow tired of this realm. You and you." She turns to my father and Alex. "You are the souls I choose."

"Dad," I say. "What if she takes your life and then you drop dead? I only just got you back. And, Alex. I'm sorry I made you do my half of the chores. I swear, I forgive you. Just let me do this—"

Alex places a hand on my shoulder and looks at Dad. "We have to. In a way, this all started with us."

Lady de la Muerte pushes me aside and presses a long, thin finger on Dad's cheek. "Your timeline is strange. I cannot read you. You've been to a realm I cannot follow." Then she sets her eyes on Alex. "So have you. Brave girl. Powerful girl. I want your years for simply fighting against me."

"It's done," Alex and Dad say at the same time.

Lady de la Muerte raises her hands and makes a pulling motion with her fingertips. Three threads, one from my father, Alex, and me, wind around her wrist and burn into her flesh, a silver tattoo against her porcelain skin.

"Good-bye, Lula Mortiz," she tells me. Though it's already dark, her shadows pool around her, twisting into a cloud of smoke. "I don't want to see you for a very long time."

36

El Fuego, most misunderstood of his kin,

sought the dark refuge beneath the earth.

Don't you know?

His flame is destruction.

His flame is rebirth.

—TALES OF THE DEOS,
FELIPE THOMÁS SAN JUSTINIO

The fire spreads faster than we want it to.

It starts in the kitchen, eating its way through layers and years of paint and old curtains. Jars of oils and elixirs blow up like grenades. The stove blows a hole clean through the second floor and into the attic.

Dad and Alex run inside, conjuring rain. But they only needed to get one thing. Our Book of Cantos.

Rhett makes his way through the cleanup and stands in front of my parents.

"I know you don't want to hear this," Rhett says, "but it will be safer for you to let it burn. We'll take care of the bodies."

"What will we tell the police?" Mom asks, her eyes flooding with tears that reflect the red flames.

"I'll stay," Rhett says, starting to retreat. The shadow boy who watched over me like a dark angel. "I'll take care of it."

My mom pulls him into a bone-breaking hug.

"The sun is rising," Frederik the vampire says. "Some of us must go."

"I'm starting to wonder how many so-called accidents are actually THA cover-ups," Alex says out loud. She rests her arm on my shoulder and leans her head against mine.

McKay and others of the THA pile as many casimuertos as they can into the back of a black SUV that pulls into our yard. The Alliance works quickly. Expertly.

When it comes to Maks, I ask them to wait. I take his severed hand and place it on his chest. I press my fingers to my lips and carry that kiss over to his. My eyes sting at seeing him like this. In spite of everything, I loved him, and the last memory I want to have of him is on that bus as he tried to save me.

"I'm sorry," I tell him one last time.

When the bodies are all gone and the fire reaches Alex's room in the attic, we finally hear sirens.

"That's our cue to go," McKay says, adjusting his black baseball cap and hopping into the driver's seat. He points a finger at Rose. "Be good, little magical hacker."

I try to thank everyone here. But the Alliance is hard to thank. They brush it off like it's just another day.

"Got all the weapons?" Rhett asks one of his hunters. They pack up anything that might look suspicious when the NYPD does their sweep.

"I guess a living room full of daggers and machetes was going to raise a lot of questions," I say.

"We'll try to replace what we can," he assures me.

I watch my house go up in flames. This is the place where I was born. I broke my nose sliding down the banister and Rose wore a permanent spot on the carpet in the nook where she liked to read. We celebrated our dead in there. We ate and drank and gossiped in the kitchen. I snuck out the window and broke my ankle. Twice. We saved lives and lost lives, and we laughed and cried and whispered our secrets and fears into every corner we could find.

We lived.

Mom sits on the tree stump that was once a portal, clutching the Book of Cantos to her chest. Dad rubs her back. I hold my sisters' hands. Nova takes a power nap on the grass but wakes when a car door slams.

A black cop car pulls up on the front yard. We know what to say. Rhett told us to talk about the electricity going haywire, which is true. And the fire, which Alex technically started when she was fighting off a casimuerto. But that's always been our lives—half-truths and half-lies.

"You've got to be kidding me," I say, then sling a string of curse words that feel so good to say out loud.

"Ms. Mortiz," Detective Hill says as he walks toward us across the lawn. His face is like a melting candle and his leather jacket smells of cigarettes and bourbon. "The fire department is on their way."

There's nothing left for them to save.

There's a fresh gleam in his eyes, like he's excited about what he might find. When he looks over my shoulder, something he sees upsets him. *Someone.*

"Mr. Dulac," the detective says, a scowl on his face. "I'm surprised to see you here."

Rhett. He's dressed differently. In a plain, long-sleeved shirt that looks soft to the touch and dark slacks. He holds his hand out to Detective Hill, who stares at it longer than is the custom before shaking it.

"I'm sure *surprised* isn't the word you really want to use." Rhett pats the detective on the back and leads him back to the front of the house, a silent understanding between them I can't fully grasp, but perhaps I don't need to yet.

For now, I have to be present.

I join my family.

We gather around and watch our home burn.

37

She lives in the glimmer of dawn.

And when the night is weak,

and when the light is gone.

—REZO FOR LA ESPERANZA,
GODDESS OF SIGHS AND
ALL THE WORLD'S GOODNESS,
BOOK OF DEOS

Graduation isn't something I thought I'd get to have. After they closed the school early because of the accident, they discovered a pile of dead bodies in the school basement, which the casimuertos used as a hideout, and so, my entire class graduated automatically. I was probably one credit away from failing, but here I am in my cap and gown, sweating under the July sun.

The first half of the evening was a memorial for the students killed in the accident. They wanted me, as the sole survivor, to give a motivational speech. Something that would make people feel hopeful. But I couldn't bring myself to do it. And so Dante Ramirez, Ramirez's little brother, gave a speech he could barely get through.

As I watch our valedictorian give her speech, I can't help but focus on the knight sigil that's on the podium and think of the THA and the Knights of Lavant.

When each student walks across the stage, the applause is subdued, respectful. They call out my name, and I go through the motions. I shake the principal's hand and the hands of local councilmen and women who came to pay their respects. I don't miss Detective Hill in the audience. Even McKay and some of the THA showed up. They wave at me as I make the walk across the stage.

When I step out of school, I breathe in the midsummer air. It's over—the casimuertos, Maks, high school. And I let myself bask in this moment of calm. A couple of friends invite me to graduation parties, but I'm not in a party mood. My family and Rishi's family are in conversation when I find them.

When I get closer, I can see my reflection in Rishi's sunglasses—my dark curls made unruly by the summer breeze, my red lipstick to match my dress, my scars uncovered and for everyone to see.

"You look beautiful." She pulls me into a long embrace. While her parents are busy talking to ours, she stomps her feet and playfully slaps my arm. "I can't believe I missed the zombie romp across town. I feel like Alex needs to take me ghost hunting for winter break."

Alex laughs and threads her fingers through Rishi's. "I promise, it was just a regular Tuesday night."

"What about you, Lula?" Rishi asks, her nose ring catching the bright sunlight. "Are you okay? I know how *verbose* you Mortiz sisters can be with your feelings. Spare no details."

I chuckle and look down at my shoes. Am I okay? I feel so many things. Weary. Relieved. Guilty. Free. Sometimes I feel everything all at once and sometimes I don't feel anything at all. But my family is helping me deal with everything. I just have to ask for help.

My body, on the other hand—there are some things that science or magic can't fix. In the evenings, when it's cold and damp, the pain in my hips comes with a side of angry tears. Even now, I have to reach for Rose's arm for balancing support. My body is different and strange and new to me, and I have to be kind to it. I have to learn this version of myself and love her like she deserves.

But now, I know I'm telling the truth when I say, "I'm going to be fine."

Queens Village, Queens, is a strange place.

It definitely isn't Brooklyn. Our neighbors want to talk to us, which is weird, and the house feels too new. Too freshly painted. Too straight. Too big.

The Knights of Lavant bought the house. They didn't have any properties in Brooklyn, because Brooklyn real estate is somehow worse than Manhattan these days.

Dad didn't want to take the house. But McKay convinced him that it was the least they could do after they burned ours down. I didn't tell Dad it was Alex who started the fire.

Half-truths and half-lies.

That night, after graduation and the memorial and dinner, we

323

set up our new altar in our new house. Mom ordered a new statue of La Mama from a botánica down in Florida. There's a built-in shelf in the entrance wall where she fits perfectly. Rose and Nova are in charge of candles. Alex and I string flowers together with white thread.

"What's Dad in charge of?" Rose asks.

"Finding a good angle for the TV," I say.

Mom hits me on the back of my head.

"*Ma*," I groan.

She strikes a match and starts lighting the sage bundles. Even new houses need to be cleansed. "Let your father be. Nova, honey, set a pot to boil."

"Actually, Ms. Carmen, I wanted to talk to you guys about something."

"Did you leave a red sock in the laundry again?" I ask, which garners another smack to the back of my head. Everything is almost back to normal.

We sit around the living room with Nova on the couch across from us. He's trying to let his beard grow out, and I think he's trying to emulate my dad. The marks on his hands are getting longer, and we try to act like we aren't worried.

Ever since that night, I have a mark on my chest too. Just like Nova does on his heart and hands, and just like Alex does on her palms. Mine is in the shape of a star, burned right over my solar plexus, at the center of my scar.

"I was thinking about what Lady de la Muerte said," Nova says. "About how you've been in a realm she can't reach. I think that might help in getting your memories back."

324

Dad sits up on the couch. He smooths his mustache down around the corners of his mouth. "What did you have in mind?"

"You've tried potions and cantos, and nothing works," Nova says. "But I think we're missing something from the realm you were in. I can find something that can help us."

"On one condition," Dad tells him.

"What?"

Mom and Dad sit closer to each other than they have in the last few months. Dad puts his arm around her and she sinks into him.

"We've talked about it," Mom says. "We want to have a Deathday for you to stabilize your power."

"I couldn't," he says, blue-green eyes glassy and I never thought I'd see the day when Nova Santiago was bashful. "That's too much."

"You already live here," Rose says.

"And you're already a pain, like a brother would be." Alex smirks.

"What they mean," I say, "is you did so much for me. You stayed, even though you didn't have to."

"Family isn't just blood," Dad says. "Sometimes you get to choose your family. And you've earned a place here."

The middle of July is scorching. I miss Coney Island. I miss the beach and the noise. But Queens is okay. I sit in the front yard on a lawn chair. Light breaks through the large tree in front of our house and makes patterns along my skin. Alex and Rose lie down on a blanket. Rose reads from *The Kingdom of Adas*, and Alex tries to find a canto for Nova in a large, unmarked text.

A black car pulls up right in front of our house.

"Here comes your *boyfriend*," Alex singsongs.

"He's not my boyfriend," I say calmly because I know they're just trying to get a rise out of me. "I'm not ready for boyfriends."

"Hey," Rhett says, approaching the brick gate. The ends of his dark hair curl at his shoulders, and he blows a strand away from his deep brown eyes. It's strange seeing him in broad daylight. He's holding a plant with dark-purple flowers, and it makes him look like a normal guy, instead of a hunter. "I should get you one of those 'number of days without an incident' signs."

"Do *not* get us that," Alex says without looking up from her book.

"Right," he says. "I just wanted to drop by a housewarming present from the THA. Frederik grew it."

Rose lowers her sunglasses and tells him, "Half-truth."

Rhett smirks. "Charming. How's your new power working out, magical hacker?"

She pushes the lenses back up with a dismissive finger. "You can't call me that."

"Stay there," I say, and I get up from my chair to save him from my sisters. Close the distance between us. I favor my left leg, which hurts less, but I'll always have an ache in my bones. Even now, the scar on my chest burns.

I lean my elbow on top of the brick gate. A part of me likes the way his Adam's apple ripples when he swallows, the blush that creeps up to his cheeks when I look at him.

"These are beautiful. Tell Frederik thanks." I touch the gauze-like petals that remind me of butterfly wings. I grab the pot by the base. "Is that it?"

"I wanted to say I'm sorry I missed your graduation ceremony," he says. "We had to take down this alien cult that was using human sacrifices—it was a whole ordeal."

"I'm not sure I believe in aliens."

He scrunches his face, bewildered. "I watched a deity rip what was basically a cephalopod out of your chest cavity, but aliens make you skeptical?"

"We all have our boundaries, hunter boy."

Garhett Dulac, hunter and Knight of Lavant, actually chuckles. "I could show you proof. Peru's an extraterrestrial hot spot."

"And how would we get there?" I cock my head to the side and let my hair fall over my shoulders.

He licks his lip, and his dark eyes flick from my mouth to my scars. "I could steal one of our jets. Break protocol again."

I scrunch up my nose but smile all the same. "I think I should keep a low profile for now."

He leans forward, chest pressed right against the brick fence. The way he looks at me sends a jolt through my veins, something I haven't felt in so long.

"Maybe we could do something sinmagos do. Dinner?"

Say no. I inhale the scent of freshly cut grass and the new flowers in my grasp.

Say yes. He shoves a hand in his pocket and looks down at the ground.

I want him to stay.

I want him to go.

And I know that until I can pick one of those, I can't go anywhere with him.

"I can't," I say. "Not for a while."

"You know where to find me, if you change your mind." He flashes a smile that rattles me. "I'll check in on you guys another time. Make sure the new house isn't burned to the ground yet."

"Funny."

"Bye, Lula."

"Bye, Rhett."

I watch as he gets back in his car and drives off, and a feeling I haven't had in so long returns—possibility.

I return to my sisters and set our housewarming flowers beside me.

"What did Captain Scuba Pants really want?" Alex asks.

"It's dragon skin," I say. "And he wanted to make sure everything was okay with the house."

"You're the worst liar." Alex shakes her head. "And you know we could *hear* you, right?"

"Fifty bucks says he'll be back," Rose says. "With more flowers. Hopefully chocolates too."

Alex grins at me but keeps a wary eye on the road. "Be careful, Lula. That boy looks like trouble."

"Maybe he is." I sit back, a wicked smile on my lips, and sunlight kisses my face. "But so am I."

EPILOGUE

The Bastard King of Adas wanted it all.
His reign just and true,
his reign is my fall.

—THE KINGDOM OF ADAS

The canto to wake Dad's memory takes longer than we hoped. Nova searched for a seed from the realm where Dad was taken.

The seed is the size of a walnut and is smooth all around except at the top, where a ring of tiny spikes sprouted like horns.

"Do you remember this?" I ask Dad, but he only shakes his head.

We sit in a circle. The entire living room is lit with candles. Mom looks nervous. I think I can understand what she's feeling. Maybe it's better if we just keep going forward. Maybe it's better if he doesn't remember at all. We are happy now, and that's what matters.

But sometimes at night, I still hear Dad cry while he dreams. There are moments, even when he's telling old stories or singing his old song, when he'll freeze and space out. His eyes glaze over like a darkness is overpowering him, and in that instance, it's like we never got him back at all.

"I'm ready," Dad says, his hands jittery as he closes the Circle.

When we lock hands, I sit up straight. An image floods the inside of my mind—a place that glitters with gold, hidden behind a forest of white trees. When I see a woman walk through the forest, I know where we are. Her skin is dark tree bark and her ears end in fine points. Her dress is made of hundreds of flower petals, like they cling to her skin with nothing but magic. She's surrounded by dozens of humans and faeries alike, holding court right at the heart of the forest.

Then, a hideous face blocks our path. His face is like wrinkled leather, and when he smiles, a set of gold teeth shine back.

"I knew I'd find you," he tells my father. "No one—no one escapes the Kingdom of Adas."

AUTHOR'S NOTE

Welcome back. As I continue the stories of the Mortiz sisters, their magical Brooklyn keeps expanding. Alex, Lula, and Rose are three incredible girls with the power to do great things or terrible things—perhaps even both at the same time. *Bruja Born* is Lula's story. I'm often asked which of the sisters I identify with the most. Authors write bits of themselves into their worlds, and on many levels, that character for me is Lula Mortiz.

MORE BRUJAS

Labyrinth Lost introduced the world of the Brooklyn Brujas. *Bruja* is the Spanish word for witch. Brujeria is what their magic and practice is called. The brand of magic I've created in these pages is a combination of the popular culture I grew up consuming and what that structure would look like if the influenced came from Latin America instead of Europe. It's impossible to create a system of Latinx witches without considering where that magic comes from. Colonization, slavery, conquests, assimilation—it's all part of that history, and as the Mortiz sisters come into their powers, they get to explore what it means to be brujas in the world.

Lula and her sisters have grown up in a time where they keep their magic secret, but they didn't have to worry about the witch hunters their parents feared. Now that their world is changing and the magic of their generation is becoming stronger, they can feel that the magical New York of their childhood is going to undergo a shift.

THE THORNE HILL ALLIANCE
Established in 1987, the Thorne Hill Alliance is a supernatural organization responsible for keeping the peace between magical beings in the city. They take their name from the location where their treaty was signed, Thorne Hill, Brooklyn. The THA serves as allies first and foremost to the vampires, weres, faeries, and other creatures trying to find their way in the greater New York area. They first appeared in *The Vicious Deep* and are back to handle whatever threatens their city.

THE KNIGHTS OF LAVANT
Established in 1303, Gerona, Spain, the Knights of Lavant are an order of hunters sworn to protect humans from the threat of the supernatural. The New York chapter of the Knights of Lavant have worked side by side with the Thorne Hill Alliance since 1990.

WHY BLOOD?

Blood is important in many cultures. Catholics symbolically drink the blood of Christ. Pagan religions required blood sacrifice. In mythology, creatures drink blood to survive. Blood is vital to survival, and so in a magical ritual, it is the most valuable thing that can be offered to the gods.

Both Lula and Alex have offered their own blood to complete a canto or close a portal. In order to perform these rituals, both sisters had to harm themselves. Self-harm and the ideation of it should not be taken lightly, and if you need someone to talk to or are struggling with suicide, do not hesitate to reach out to someone you trust or a professional. National Suicide Prevention Lifeline offers twenty-four seven support that is free and confidential. Visit suicide preventionlifeline.org or call 1-800-273-8255.

ACKNOWLEDGMENTS

Writing can be a lonely endeavor, but creating a book isn't. *Bruja Born* wouldn't be possible without the constant support of Adrienne Rosado, agent and best friend all in one. I realized this long ago, but I don't tell you enough that one of the reasons I'm able to do this is because you believed in me from the start.

To the wonderful #TeamBrujas at Sourcebooks Fire for their constant magic: Alex Yeadon, Katy Lynch, Nicole Hower, Elizabeth Boyer, and my publisher Dominique Raccah. I'm especially grateful to my Alta Bruja and editor, Kate Prosswimmer, who understands these characters as well as I do, sometimes better.

Everyone who read this book in its early stages is my personal hero. An enormous thanks to C. B. Lee, Yamile Saied Méndez, Kristina Pérez, Diya Mishra, Anna Waggener, Anna Meriano, Angel D. Cruz, and Tehlor Kay Mejia.

To Cat Scully for another incredible map and my copy editor Gretchen Stelter.

To the librarians, booksellers, bloggers, and readers I've met the past five years. You keep books alive and in the hands of those who need them most. Thank you for your underappreciated and tireless work. Book nerds forever!

To my writing groups, FMC, Kidlit Authors of Color, and Yay YA! I wouldn't be able to get through this wild publishing ride without some of you and your wise counsel (and cocktails)—Dhonielle Clayton, Danielle Paige, Natalie Horbachevsky, Sarah Elizabeth Younger, and Gretchen McNeil, to name a few.

Finally, to my family and friends who always cheer me on. You know who you are.

ABOUT THE AUTHOR

Zoraida Córdova is the award-winning author of the Vicious Deep trilogy and the Brooklyn Brujas series. Her short fiction has appeared in the anthologies *Star Wars: From a Certain Point of View* and *Toil & Trouble: 16 Tales of Women & Witchcraft*. She is a New Yorker at heart and is currently working on her next novel. Send her a tweet @Zlikeinzorro.

Don't miss Book 1
in the Brooklyn Brujas series

LABYRINTH LOST

ALEX'S STORY

I was chosen by the Deos.
Even gods make mistakes.